A RUM WITH A VIEW

Follow Coleman and Endi in
their new treasure hunt.

Follow up to *Dirty Money*
hilarious money laundering

A JOHNNY WALKER INVESTIGATION
Book 4

JARVIS ENDICOTT WILLIAMS

Publishing Services provided by Paper Raven Books LLC

Printed in the United States of America

First Printing, 2022

Hardback ISBN: 978-1-7379167-7-2

Paperback ISBN:978-1-7379167-6-5

Visit www.jarviswrites.page for links to more books
by Jarvis Endicott Williams.
Or find them all on Amazon, Nook, etc.
More thriller/mystery/crime-fiction/suspense/humor
books, similar to *A Rum With a View*,
are being published soon.

Fiction books by the author:
Dirty Money

Non-fiction books by the author:
Feeding Your Dog and Cat, The Truth!
Prayer Lite

CAST OF CHARACTERS

Lieutenant Johnny Walker: Portland, Oregon, police department… drafted unwilling CIA agent…running guns to a desert island in the Bermuda Triangle.

Coleman: Retired Secret Service… inherited three acres and two houses on a nine-mile-long (golf carts only) island in the Bahamas. He gets out of bed to drink rum and nap in the hammock on his veranda. He subsists on conch fritters.

Endi: Coleman's best friend, retired Portland, Oregon cop…permanent-parasite-in-the-guesthouse-squatter… also devoting his life to rum, and… photographing his underwater-porn-star girlfriend. He started the whole thing by discovering that the big black blocks supporting Coleman's pier were silver ballast from the wrecked Spanish treasure ship *El Congrejo.*

April May June: Endi's gifted-body girlfriend…able to hold her breath underwater, or in bed, for two minutes… who rarely wears clothing…and is the cheerleader for the team's wealth-by-treasure free-for-all.

Amanda Albright: The only female Albright with a narrow waist, and a head not shaped like a watermelon…

the island's schoolteacher…nicknamed "Rainbow" (read on) …in horny-perma-heat… who stalks Coleman, seeking his non-Albright DNA.

Jack Slack, DDS: Islanders' smiles are all the same thanks to his laser cap making machine…who has gifted sedation skills… wanted in Germany…golf cart mechanic…ganga distributor…and found with a periosteal elevator deep in an ear.

Colonel Albright: Seceded from British rule…accused of committing suicide with a ball-peen hammer… into metallurgy and snakes…went on a Disney cruise, his stateroom, a freezer.

Albright Albright: Bad inbreeding poster child…mostly male… feet not matching…wears stolen bras as jock-straps… and terrorizes the Haitians.

Mano: Roid-raged, superbantumweight boxing champ from Hawaii out on bail for murder-wife-by-baseball-bat… sequestered by his lawyers on Conch Island so he can't make things worse for himself… but that isn't stopping him.

Luna Albright: Conch Island's Justice of the Peace, and developer of the island's gay-wedding industry… pear-shaped evangelical-celibate-prude…the colonel's right-hand man.

Detective Jergins Albright: Half Albright/half Haitian…got the worst of both gene pools…from the nearest law-enforcement the next island over…who escaped Conch Island…only to find herself back on the island to solve a string of murders…secretly delighted that they are killing themselves off.

CHAPTER 1

*Another beautiful day on a Bahama Island
paradise… sunny, warm, puffy white clouds,
light breeze… out of beer.*

Last beer in hand, Endi leaped into Coleman's outboard center-console 23-footer for a sprint to the liquor store on the next island. Forgetting to untie the boat, it rudely stopped at the end of its rope catapulting him over the bow. (He couldn't pass a breathalyzer test.) He recovered his hat, wallet, and sunglasses from the bottom of the crystal-clear, bathtub warm, shallow Bahamian water. He'd saved his beer. The big black rock caught his attention… again.

The boat practically steered itself to the liquor store island, having made the trip so many times, allowing him to ponder the mysterious big black rectangular blocks used for Coleman's dock foundation. Each was two feet long, a foot tall, and a foot wide. Really heavy looking and not made of sand, shells, concrete, palm trees, sea grapes, or dead coral, which make up the entire list of resources on Conch Island. These were something else… not of the island. The blocks were used for foundations, steps, retaining walls… they were everywhere. They all came from a long ago close-to-shore-reef wrecked Spanish galleon on the other side of the island.

There was barely anything of the wreck left now. It was a spot for divers… but picked clean. A pockmarked green brass cannon from it rested permanently on the island town's wharf with the ship's name barely discernible on a corroded green brass plaque: "El Congrejo."

Endi had done internet time (when it was working—another issue on the desert island with no liquor store) finding that most Spanish galleons, going to the Old World from the New World, were just freighters carrying stuff like lumber, spices, and slaves, which of course you couldn't salvage hundreds of years later. But many also carried partially refined boxes of rough silver coins called "cobs," which were a midway step in silver processing, but not the pure thing. These boxes of cobs doubled as ballast on the wooden ships. Not pieces-of-eight, or pure silver, but still…worth some bucks to a metallurgist with a smelting plant.

Endi also found out that the boxes of cobs, after years in the salt water, congealed together as the wooden box rotted away, leaving a big black block the shape of the box; two feet, by one foot, by one foot. He knew silver turned black in saltwater.

Endi was living on a cop's pension…couldn't help thinking about treasure. The big black blocks were all over town.

He'd also read that the Spanish kept meticulous records indicating that from 1500 to 1820 there were 17,000 voyages from the New World to Spain. The records revealed that the King taxed each one fifty percent. Ten percent of these ships were lost at sea, which would translate into two billion bucks, in today's bucks, in silver, on the ocean floor, according to their records. That's not counting pure silver bullion that was probably on the ship being smuggled home, that also fell victim to storms and shipwrecks. (People cheated on their taxes then too.)

Sinkings? Convoys got split up by storms and rough seas. Lost ships always seemed to find a reef to wreck on in the middle of nowhere. Ships following each other at night followed a lantern on the ship in front of them; there were clowns then too that would blow out the lantern to screw with the guy behind him. Or set the lantern on an empty grog barrel and watch Captain Looser behind them sail off to the edge of the world. It was also easy to "ping" the sextant; that's old time "nautical" for bouncing the delicate instrument on the gunnels when the navigator wasn't watching.

That night Endi asked Coleman, "You got a metal detector?"

"Yep."

"Does it detect silver, or just metal in general?"

Coleman mumbled with his mouth full of pepper conch jerky washed down with rum and Coke, "Who the hell wants to find iron? Of course, it detects gold and silver."

"Waterproof?"

"Not the big black rocks again?"

The next morning, catching his breath as a wave playfully squirted water up his cut-offs spritzing his balls, Endi adjusted his snorkel and mask and submerged.

He turned on the metal detector and waved it over a big black rock.

The metal detector went mad.

Back in Coleman's kitchen: "I wave the thing over one of those black rocks holding your dock up and it says *silver.* I swear to God…it says *silver.*"

"It probably just found a dime or a quarter, trust me," Coleman mumbled back. He grabbed the metal detector.

Endi said, "The thing says *silver* all over a black rock you got holding up the dock." Endi spiked his coffee from a nearly depleted bottle of Cuban rum. "We got another bottle of these?"

"We have most of a case left unless a Haitian has snuck in." Coleman impatiently waved the metal detector over a bowel with loose change in it, and it beeped *silver.*

Endi said, "That's what it did. It said *silver.* Does that thing tell you how *many* coins, or does it tell you there is just like *a* coin…like can it distinguish singular or plural? Like quantity, as well as quality? Like does it get all excited if there's a lot of coins, and start moaning or screaming?"

"Like May during nap time?"

That afternoon Endi took pictures of his girlfriend May underwater running the metal detector over the bottom and the black rocks. At one time May had been a model, and "soft" porn actress, specializing in underwater venues. She was very good at holding her breath. When the flat pancake foot of the detector passed over a big black rock, its face (now named *Lector-the-Detector* by May) read repeatedly, *Silver…silver…silver!* Lector also started making a "happy noise" (according to May) whenever its face showed *Silver… silver…silver!!* The happy noise was kind of an "ouu…weee!"

"Acting" under water, for the camera, May was trying to look earnest and industrious. She was cute doing earnest and industrious using her celebrated-pouty-earnest-industrious-look. Men waited on her hand and foot because of that pout.

Endi drug Coleman down to the dock who watched the photo shoot for a while, mostly because of May's pouty look and the bikini of course. Coleman's assessment of the whole detector thing was, "Lector must be screwed-up," where upon he headed back up to the house for the hammock and a refresher.

May and Endi explored the tool shed for something to break off a piece of big black rock so they could examine it closer out of the water.

The hammer and chisel they found didn't work under water. May insisted, "I told you so. I know hammering underwater. It's not all that satisfying. You can't get any speed up."

Endi tried to convince Coleman to come back and help but had to admit the blocks weren't going anywhere, and so the rest of another day in paradise was devoted to hammocks, dips on the ocean side, rum mixology, frying conch fritters, and toasting the sunset.

CHAPTER 2

The next day.

In the tool shed Endi and Coleman found a four-foot piece of re-enforcement bar that had been pounded into a chisel on one end. Endi wearing a diving mask, and holding his breath three feet under water, held the chisel end on the black block, while Coleman, using a large heavy hammer, beat on the exposed end while standing in an unsteady dingy.

Endi's thumb momentarily got between the re-bar and the rock as he was repositioning it, just as Coleman pounded on it. (This was the "first-blood" drawn on the salvage operation, but not the last.) The fight was short because Coleman ran faster than Endi since Endi was already winded from holding his breath underwater.

The second fight resulted from a mean-spirited-you-only-play-on-a-friend prank. A snorkel had been fashioned from a piece of garden hose. Coleman held the hose out of the water. Endi had tied a cinder block around his waist for ballast and breathed through the six-foot piece of garden hose clamped between his teeth. He was trying the chisel again pounding it with a rock instead of a hammer this time. It went well for almost five minutes until Coleman put his thumb over his end of the hose a couple of times enjoying watching Endi briefly thrash around on the bottom before he released his thumb. Bored with that, Coleman poured Kalik Extra Strength beer down the air hose. This was a colossal success. May and Coleman heard muffled bubbling coughing cursing through the air hose. The underwater action was hilarious, like a shark attack, complete with a small blood cloud; thumb started bleeding again. Second blood.

Endi, trying not to drown on beer, realized he should have had an emergency plan (a knife handy?) to separate himself speedily from 28 pounds of cinderblock he was tied to. Coleman was surprised to find out how fast a man could boil out of the ocean and chase him down the beach dragging a cinder block through the sand like a runaway horse and plow.

A cosmic payback—Coleman hit his forehead at a dead run on a Jacaranda tree limb—drawing the third blood. Endi hadn't gotten close to catching him with the cinderblock dragging behind him, and lungs full of beer.

Coleman stumbled to the house for a nap in the air-conditioning.

Coleman shouldn't have left Endi unsupervised.

"I've had it with sawing. I'm gonna go for the whole enchilada," Endi gravely and decisively vowed to May through clenched teeth.

"You go big guy. I'm with you," May vowed right back gravely. (She looked cute gravely vowing.)

Huffing alongside May (who wasn't actually helping—not wanting to damage her nails—which added another layer of pissed-off to his already dark mood), Endi drug the twenty-five-foot logging chain through the sand and mangrove tree roots. He breathlessly said to May, "This whole getting rich thing ain't gonna include that a-hole Coleman. It may be his dock but if I get that damn thing out, it's mine. All mine. Asshole trying to drown me… screw him. Salvage rights is what I'm talking about. I'm the genius who figured this out anyway. Damn thing's gonna be my big black rock. He can get his own."

"You tell 'em honey." May added, "I want a silver block too."

"I can get one out; I can get two out," Endi replied boldly.

"I'm gonna get my neck lifted," May announced brightly pointing her chin up and feathering her Adams apple with the back of her hand.

I'm gonna get us a sailboat. "Two masts, with a dinghy—a hundred-foot-long sucker with…" He was silent a moment and added, "and a helicopter landing pad. Or maybe just a big-ass cruiser, like with a crew and a chef. And a helicopter pad. I don't think they have helicopter pads on sailboats with the masts and all."

"You like my boobs? Maybe just a little more lift there too…?" She jiggled one. He involuntarily opened his mouth and flicked his tongue.

May held the garden hose swearing no tricks. Endi tied the cinderblock to his waist with rope again. He couldn't get enough air through the one-inch hose to match the exertion it took to muscle the chain, and drag the cinder block, combined. Besides the hose was old and had spent its life in sun and salt, so it liked to just fold itself randomly for no reason if May wasn't paying attention.

In a moment of folded-hose-anoxia-panic due to May negligence, he cut off the cinder block. (This time he carried a knife.) May was examining her nails when he boiled to the surface. She said distractedly, "What?!"

He finally got the chain around the block.

He found a jack in the tool shed and an assortment of scrap four-by-four pieces of wood. He planned to jack up the dock, pull the big black rock out by the chain with Coleman's golf cart, then put the cinder block and four-by-fours where the big black rock was, then un-jack the dock onto the new temporary footing.

The jacking up part of the engineering plan worked. Now to pull the big black rock out.

Endi quietly coasted Coleman's golf cart down the sloping noisy crushed coral driveway without turning it on knowing Coleman would not approve of this plan. He had peeked in on Coleman who was asleep under a ceiling fan next to a loud window air conditioner. The house was two hundred feet from the dock. He had to stifle a guffa seeing at the large purple goose egg on Coleman's forehead.

Coleman was very protective of his golf cart. They were as expensive as a car on the island (Bahamas Vat Tax). Plus, he'd removed the golf cart's speed governor which allowed it to cruise at twice the speed of the other golf carts all over the island. But since most of the one road system on the island was rough and covered with broken conch shells, you couldn't drive fast anyway, so it just mostly just burned more five dollar-a-liter gas. It did sound good though.

Endi figured it had power to spare—enough to pull out a big black rock.

Endi attached the logging chain to the back bumper of the golf cart, put it in gear, and eased on the gas.

The rock stayed put. The backward facing back seat, the footrest beneath it, and the hand hold, came off the golf cart, tearing rust and fiberglass like a hot knife through butter.

Endi said, "OK, a thou from my block of silver toward golf cart repair."

Undaunted he attached the chain to the back axle. This time he enlisted May's help as driver so he could supervise the operation. He told her, "OK, just ease on the gas until the slack is gone on the chain, then gradually give it more power while I watch under the rear end to make sure something else doesn't get torn off. I'll coach you."

He lay down behind the golf cart, head practically under it, and then gave one final tug to check that the chain was secured. He was surprised when he heard the reverse warning horn beeping. Panic consumed him as he heard the revving up engine above him and the realization that he was about to get his head crushed. Rolling out of the way just in time, he watched the golf cart, reverse warning horn screaming in terror, plunge stern first toward the ocean only two feet way.

If it wasn't for the logging chain bunching around the left rear wheel, effectively skidding the cart to a stop, the screaming-in-fear golf cart would have made it under water at least to the level of steering wheel that the bleeding girl was slumped over, her foot still pouring gas to the governor-free engine.

Endi managed to turn the cart off and held May's bleeding face. The cart reversing had caught the unsuspecting driver off guard for an opposite direction of travel than expected and had plastered her face on the steering wheel.

Holding May's lolling face in his palms Endi thought to himself *OK, couple thousand for dentistry and nose work.*

Gently shaking her head, and looking at her half-closed lids covering glassy eyes, tears pouring down her face, Endi said, "I figured you knew to go forward; not reverse for God's sake." He was getting a little pissed again. "What in the hell did you put it in reverse for?"

"I don nooo," she said nasally, "I tot u toad me dou."

(And that's how the *fourth* blood was shed. May's nose)

Endi put on the emergency brake, carefully set May on a towel in the sand out of the way.

The cart fired up, no problem. He unwound the logging chain from around the rear wheel by pulling the cart forward. Then he climbed into the cockpit double checking that it was in forward gear. He draped his right arm over the seat backrest and focused his eyes on where he imagined the block was under water. He mentally projected an image of the big black rock out of the water (thoughts in mind create like kind), adjusted his dark glasses, then fiercely gripped the steering wheel with his left hand, and still looking backwards while mouthing to himself, *this will work…this will work…*, he gently, and with cautious measured finesse, touched the accelerator softly with his flip-flopped toes. He perfectly eased the slack out of the logging chain. He gently applied a little more foot pressure.

The right rear wheel immediately spun slowly in the loose sand. Applying more pressure on the accelerator only made the tire dredge itself deeper into the sand. So of course, he floored-it. The engine screamed and the right rear tire sent sand blasting into May's face and mostly naked body, resulting in thrashing and rolling and screaming, "My face…my face…you…miserable…son…of…!"

The big black rock of course was just being a 250-pound object, and dutifully obeyed Newtonian physics, that is, objects at rest, stay at rest. In fact, it wedged itself in a little deeper having no desire to be messed with anymore.

With a waning adrenalin blood level, Endi found his confidence melting, and frustration gaining. This cascade of chemistry and emotion tilted Endi's cognitive teeter-totter to heavy on the poor judgment side, as anger took over all thought processes.

The cart beep-beep screamed, "I'm in reverse again; everybody run," warning sound as Endi backed out of the hole the right tire had made, releasing the slack on the logging chain. He almost backed into the water giving him a new, much needed, burst of adrenalin. Then in one athletically coordinated fluid motion, one hand on the wheel, one hand slamming the gear shift into forward gear again, two dilated eyes intensely focused on wealth, and all its freedoms, and with gritted teeth through stretched lips, and in a seething guttural throaty voice, he uttered those famous last words, "Watch this!" and he floored it.

This was just as Coleman made it at a jogtrot to the

scene, having been alerted by the multiple terrified screams that the golf cart had made in reverse.

He got there just in time to see the governor-less golf cart make its first drag race attempt at the quarter mile from a standing start. It was still moving when the back axle was ripped from its spine by the logging chain and the Newton's Law-abiding big black rock. The golf cart didn't make the full quarter mile, but it did go for a first down. It came to rest at its master's feet, its back-up warning horn mysteriously back on, but only emitting a faint squeaking now…like a death cackle through an old cavalry trumpet.

The still quivering back axle, wheels, shocks, and springs, and what appeared to be part of a transmission, slowly bled fluid onto the sand.

The two friends looked at each other. Endi, almost thrown through the plastic windshield, was somehow still behind the steering wheel. With one eyebrow up, the other down, and one corner of his mouth up and one down, making a bizarre wink, a broken lens hung for a split second, then dropped out of his dark glasses. A drop of blood dripped every second from one nostril. (Fifth bloodletting for those of you counting.)

He said nothing.

Over something whirring softly in the background from the fatally wounded golf cart Coleman said menacingly, "When is the ONLY time you're not drunk, Endi?"

Endi tried to think but nothing happened. Finally, his face brightened, and he blurted out like a kid in third grade with the answer, "Three o'clock in the morning."

"There's a front loader at the marina. You're gonna

steal it at three tonight, moron, and get this rock out of the ocean."

May stood up shakily. She was holding her nose with one hand and had the other hand over an eye. She tripped over the rear axle, her arms wind milling, and fell into the roots of a banyan tree. Endi didn't see it happen as his back was to her. The golf cart's Bimini top blocked Coleman's view, so neither went to her rescue, until her raging screams pierced the hot moist tropical air.

They thought they were going to have to get a saw to get her out of the roots. The thrashing was making it worse. Fortunately for the men, the many bracelets on both wrists, were caught in the tree roots and prevented May from clawing their eyes out.

After her arms were set free, the next setback was a caught hoop earring. Its extraction ripped the pierced earlobe some during the process. The surprised screaming girl, arms, and head now free, pummeled both men's faces, then chased them like a water moccasin as they backed away as fast as they could. Only her tripping herself saved the men from dentistry.

All three faces were bleeding, now including Coleman's. (Sixth or seventh bloodletting?)

CHAPTER 3

*Time for a little background about Conch Island,
where Coleman's house is, before we get on with this
epic tale.*

The Albrights have lived on this island in the Bahamas for centuries. In fact, since the year 1775. They were English sympathizers at that time and had to leave the colonies in a hurry. (Loyalists…Patriots…George the Third…Go, Red Coats…all that.) They went south instead of to Canada; the way the wind was blowing that day.

It's called *Conch Island*. It is also known to anthropologists as the *Island of the Big Heads*.

Conch Island doesn't have any water at all. It's your typical dead reef poking out of the ocean a few feet "desert island." But the Albrights that live there, and the ex-pats[1] that frequent the island, have a beach to watch the sun come up, and a hundred yards or so across the other side

---

1 Ex-pats is short for ex-patriots and refers to foreigners with excessive financial resources, mostly from the United States, that believe a dead reef in the middle of the Atlantic Bermuda Triangle, without water, that is subject to hurricanes from June until November, is heaven on earth.

of the island, they have another beach to watch the sun go down. Lots of them live in houses on a sloping palm tree covered mound right in the middle of the nine-mile-long island so they don't even have to go to either beach to see the sun do its thing.

Life grinds to a halt on the island. Time for naps. Rum all day long. Beach, sun, gentle breezes. Things happen so slow on the island that the first baby of the year was born in March.

Besides watching the sun go from one side of the island to the other, they have cleverly devised their roofs to collect rain in large cisterns under their houses. And since it rains almost every afternoon, they normally have plenty of water for everything. They don't use much. No Albright has ever admitted to being nude or taking a shower.[2] (With one exception—Albright Albright who never wears clothes.)

Unless it doesn't rain. Then they steal their neighbor's water while the neighbor is in Florida stocking up at Costco. (The Albright grocery doesn't have a large selection.) Or they steal from the rich American ex-pats' end of the island, as the ex-pats are rarely there because of the insane heat, and the hurricanes.

Social anthropologists have studied the Albrights on Conch Island since they were discovered in the early 1950's because they contain a genetic pool that has not been seen since the House of Hapsburg. (Except of course the entire country of Pakistan where everybody marries their cousin.) The last of the Spanish Hapsburgs, Charles II of Spain, who

---

2 They are very prudish and religious.

is the poster child for *genetic mal-purification*, was unable to chew his food properly as the result of six centuries of in-breading. This was because of his *Hapsburg-jaw*. (He did manage to get food down of course since lackeys smashed it up for him.) Instead of dying from starvation he actually died from a genetic pituitary hormone deficiency which led to distal renal tubular acidosis thus ending the line forever. Apparently besides being unable to chew his food he was a depressed emotional mess as well.

The Albrights are catching up with the Hapsburgs. It is believed that all the Albrights today descended from approximately one-hundred English colonies settlers. A certain few males of those original one-hundred were particularly promiscuous and no cousin was safe. (Mother's brother's daughter, for instance.)

Today, only another Albright will breed an Albright because of all the hair, big heads, cheesy crevices, and substantial hips. A big head in proportion to the rest of the body can be adorable in young animals and universally signals other troop members, and other species, that the young creature is harmless. But this ratio of head size to body on adult humans, that also have unibrows, thick legs and ankles, and six-inch hair in their armpits, does the opposite; the typical response by those who have never seen an Albright before is to want to attack them, or run.

Still, they breed each other like bunnies. If you have a big head, then someone of the opposite sex with a big head is sexy.

(A young Albright went to the mainland for eight months to find a wife. He searched and searched but, in the end, he just found another Albright whom he married, and brought back to the little island where the couple had more Albrights with big heads.)

The Albright women are built like pears (big end down) with a lemon (on its side) on top. Their heads, besides being huge are also rather watermelon shaped. One anthropologist wrote that they have hips of a wildebeest, so that large headed babies practically fall out on their own. In fact, it is not unusual for Albright females to not be sure that they are pregnant until another Albright falls out. (The newborn's overall hairiness becomes distributed similarly to other human groups by age three—top of the head, pubic area, axillary space, etc.)

The founder effect, and accelerated genetic drift, in the restricted Albright breeding pool has purified the tendency for hypertension, bipolar depression, gout, peptic ulcer, pulmonary atresia, non-fatal Tetralogy of Fallot, and osteoporosis (they all get shorter with age). On the good side, they all can see better than 20/20; there are no bald Albrights (women have moustaches and thinning hair later in life); they have excellent teeth, and no female has ever had breast cancer. (There have been undocumented reports of the occasional female Albright with three breasts. One author made a serious study of that with no similar finding's, although a third nipple was found on eight percent of the men.)

There is *one* Albright that stepped on the proverbial "genetic landmine." He is a mostly male offspring from an indiscrete dalliance by a female Albright with a Seminole Indian. He runs around the island in the jungle, mostly at night, and gets into ladies' underwear drawers and leaves presents (shells mostly) in exchange for bras. People leave food out for him. He lives in a "snore-box" (a portable one room building usually ten by ten feet) in the hibiscus and sea-grape jungle. He usually wears only a pith helmet and bra. (He wears bras as a jock strap. The range of colors provided by the American sector is quite festive the islanders report.)

The Albright Brothers Boatyard makes excellent outboard 23 footers out of fiberglass. The Albright Sail shop still makes the occasional sail, but there isn't a lot of call for sails anymore since China cornered the sail market, so mostly they make colorful (unfathomably expensive) canvas bags for the tourists. Occasionally, Albright carpenters build a hurricane proof house; they really can build stuff, which goes back to their boat building days.

There is: an Albright sandwich shop; Albright Harbor Store; Albright Lumber and Hardware; the First Albright Bank (which is only open on Wednesday from 11 p.m. to 1 p.m.); and the Albright Elementary, Middle, and High School in one building (21 kids total—most with big heads); the Albright Bakery; the Albright Gift Shop; and the Albright Dive and Salvage Shop. And there is the Albright Ferry Service to the neighboring islands. (There isn't an Albright liquor store, the absence of which plays heavily in this story.)

Additionally, there is the *Dr. Jack Slack Dental Clinic & Golf Cart Repair Shop*. Golf carts are the only means of transportation on the thin crescent shaped piece of coral called a Key or Cay. (There is no golf course on the island.) Everybody drives on the left by the way—the island was once a British subject, hence the driving on the wrong side of the road. Everybody thinks the name "Albright" is probably Welsh, where they have ponies with large heads and thick legs and lots of hair, like the Albrights.[3]

There is one rusty Toyota pick-up they use to haul trash to the dump and picnic area (which is combined and has an ocean view). It also delivers building supplies and the occasional appliance or mattress that comes by freighter from the States. The only road is made of crushed coral, stretches the whole length of the island, and is just wide enough to pass your cousins, aunts, uncles etc. in their golf carts. (It's called "The Queen's Highway—brass plaque and all.) It is nicely paved in the "settlement." There isn't really anywhere to go anyway. The citizens never walk anywhere, even if it is only thirty feet from their house to church (churches).

There are very few golf cart wrecks, and how bad can a wreck be anyway when you never get out of first gear? So, there isn't an Albright Insurance Agency. No one insures anything because there is no crime. (Stealing from, and lying to, a foreigner is not considered a crime.) There are no cops, judges, lawyers, accountants, financial advisors, politicians, salesmen, bankers, beauticians, personal fitness trainers, university professors, travel planners, gunsmiths, strippers, or whores. Everyone is an evangelist, however. There are three churches.

There are no skateboards, mountain bikes, or teens on the island either. Teens are shipped to boarding school

---

3 Anthropologists have discovered in Welsh tombs pictographs of men and women with large heads copulating with ponies. Medical experts can offer no confirmation that these unions ever produced offspring, but sociologists contend that these unions clearly produced offspring, otherwise why the hair and big heads.

during their terrible-teens years. Scooters and mopeds are banned by the Elders.

Everybody leaves their houses, garages and workshop doors unlocked, and the keys in the golf cart. Everybody has all they need of everything anyway. They rob each other's conch traps occasionally out of pure laziness, but conchs are like rats around Conch Key.

The only thing that ever causes any problems at all is the occasional hurricane. As already mentioned, the Albrights' cleverly collect thousands of gallons of rainwater under their houses and all that water acts like ballast during hurricanes. And since the roofs are shaped like an upside-down boat hull, the winds just go over them and on to the next island to try its luck there. The wind pushes the roofs down instead of lifting them up. After all the Albrights have ship building in their DNA.

Tropical storms and hurricanes help redistribute the wealth fairly. For instance, if a foreigner's dock is destroyed by high seas and winds, *right-of-salvage* kicks in and the lumber becomes property of whichever Albright wants it. The Albrights consider everything theirs anyway. Stealing from a foreigner is considered completely normal.

All this contentment, boat building, in-breeding, and canvas bag making would have gone on undisturbed if it hadn't been for two retired cops: John Coleman (Coleman) and his best friend since high school, Jim Endicott (Endi). Coleman inherited a house on Conch Key. Endi and his

girlfriend May have been visiting for a month with no
plans to leave.

And so back to our story.

CHAPTER 4

The night (actually Thursday morning) of the day of the totaled golf cart, around three in the morning.

"Wake up dill-weed," Coleman whispered, shaking a body that he thought was Endi's. He had hold of a May boob in the absolute darkness.

"Not now. Not now," May answered back. It came out an angry-hoarse-cavernous-tooth-clenched-swollen-bloody-nasal-blocked snarl, which sounded like it came from Endi.

"What you mean *not now!*" Coleman answered in a louder voice still thinking it was Endi and not being even remotely nice anymore. He was still fractious and ill-tempered from the eviscerated golf-cart disaster. Also, it was three o'clock in the morning, and he was hung over and headachy after drinking way too heavily, using mourning-for-the-lost-golf-cart as an excuse to drink excessively. (In fact, he was still drunk. It was the very testy back side of a drunk.)

He shook May's boob a little harder and finally poked her hard where he thought ribs might be.

May screamed, "I said not now ass-hole." She snorted twice and almost immediately sighed back into a short jerky snore and whistle. Coleman backed off like she was a coiled snake, realizing it was a boob he'd had in his hand. But it was kind of hard like he thought Endi's shoulder would be (they'd had some work—thus the hardness). But then women were confusing to him anyway. He liked them—he just never learned how to talk to them.

He impatiently shook the other body in the bed with no results whatsoever.

Tired of a zero response from his teammates, Coleman turned on the lights, but then instantly turned them back off again realizing neither of the sleepers in front of him had any clothes on. He muttered, "Screw the ass-holes," and turned the lights on again then banged sharply on Endi's skull four or five times with his knuckles, like knocking on a door.

May draped a forearm over her eyes, still on her back and didn't miss a snore. She'd taken three prescription strength pain pills for her swollen nose, torn ear, chipped teeth, and black eye.

Coleman couldn't help staring at her boobs, eyes squinting in the harsh light, the rise and fall of the C's temporarily mesmerizing. He wanted to touch them again.

Endi, lying on his stomach, moaned loudly, rolled over on his back and then eased out a long resonant fart, picking a leg up in the air six inches to facilitate its liberation. He giggled. He had a three-quarter hard on and he began rubbing it with one hand, eyes closed, licking his lips with a smirk.

Coleman grabbed a half full large glass next to the bed. About to throw it on Endi, he sniffed it first, then howled,

"Rum damn it. Endi, you got another drink after we said we were quitting. The mission asshole! Remember the mission?!" He turned out the lights again and threw the contents onto the two sleepers with destroyed-golf-cart-rage. Rum and warm Coke sprayed the sleepers. There was considerable cursing and flaying of arms and legs, May's nose taking a back hand. Endi yowled in rage as he hit the floor, May pushing him out of bed with her feet. There was another fart because of the effort. This time it was May's. Endi giggled again on his stomach on the floor.

When Coleman tried to turn the lights back on, they didn't come on. He went from room to room testing switches soon realizing that the island was in another power outage. He hit a door jamb sharply with the point of his shoulder, an open cupboard door with his head, and stubbed a toe in the dark, exponentially escalating his foul mood.

Endi had gone back to sleep on the floor while Coleman was trying light switches. Coleman kicked the dark shape next to the bed getting a satisfactory, "Jesus May, quit kicking me for Cris' sake." Coleman kicked him again, grinning savagely in the dark, his bare toes beginning to throb.

Thirty minutes later the three were stumbling the quarter mile toward town on the Queen's Highway, Coleman pointing the way with the only flashlight they could find, dimly yellowing the six-foot-wide sand, crushed reef, and shell road before them.

Endi had come up with another idea for the extraction of the big black rock, during his euphoric stage of inebriation earlier that night. Coleman admitted it was a better idea than "borrowing" the high loader. May had pointed out that even if they could get the high loader started, and even if it didn't wake some Big Head, (she was afraid of the Big Heads, both the males and the females), the thing wouldn't go down the golf cart sized Queen's highway.

They were surprised that May wanted to go, but with the power outage blackout, lurking Big Heads, (especially the mythical bra/jock strap Albright Albright), and curly-tail lizards, she insisted. (She refused to believe that the island wasn't crawling with snakes…which it wasn't.)

So, the three treasure hunters stumbled along the only road on the narrow island, quietly discussing things like, "Why would a smart guy like you Coleman have only one flashlight, and it with half dead batteries, on a desert island in the Caribbean, in a jungle, where they have power outages eighty-two times a month?" And other topics such as: "We could be in a golf cart with headlights," and, "I'll buy you ten damn golf carts after I get rich," and "You ain't taking' it out of my cut you ass-holes." And "If you weren't so cheap your piece of shit rusty bucket golf cart wouldn't have fallen apart."

They had to help May up from time to time. She was wobbly from the pain meds, booze still on board, and sleep deprivation. She'd had a couple more rum and coke nightcaps with Endi while they dreamed of spending unlimited spending money. They really hadn't expected

Coleman to wake them up. No one got up in the middle of the night on Conch Cay.

"OK, I think I know the sailboat we want. It's got a quadruple block and tackle," Coleman said in a low voice. They warily walked out the pitch-dark pier between sailboats and cruisers that were bobbing in the swells that softly slapped at their hulls.

"It's as black as inside a coal miner's ass," Endi offered. Coleman countered, "darker than a nun's nasty." Both snickered, amused as usual with each other.

Endi's new idea was to borrow a piece of rigging that all sail boats have…the block and tackle that connects the boom of the mainsail to the boat deck. Keeping the mainsail under control requires the pulling power that only a block and tackle can give to a hundred-square yard sail full of wind.

Endi reasoned that one or two sets should be able to pull the big black rock up the sandy bottom and onto shore. He also reasoned that the block and tackles on sail boats should be attached with quick release pins, so it should be easy to "borrow" one. All they would have to do was attach that powerful set of combined pulleys to a banyan tree and join the other end to the logging chain still around the big black rock and pull the thing out. Then return the block and tackle, no one the wiser.

Coleman was in the lead. He had picked the sailboat that was the farthest out the dock. No night watchman. The island didn't even have a cop.

A frivolous little breeze ominously strummed all the sailboats' rigging.

As May climbed on board, Coleman thought to himself, *I swear she doesn't have any clothes on.*

Using a pair of pliers, and with Endi holding the now even dimmer flashlight, Coleman easily got pins loose freeing the block and tackle.

Just as he pulled the final pin, a capricious ocean swell, just making it to them from Africa, rocked the boat. The boom, now freed from its bonds, "boomed" May in the face, and swept her off the boat's starboard side and into the black warm water. She made an eee-eee-eee sound. They heard a splash a second later. In the dark they both thought it must be one damn big fish that just jumped.

"Shit, what was that?" Endi whispered.

"Must be a dolphin. It was making an "eee-eee-eee" sound like a dolphin," Coleman answered.

With her weight gone, delicately changing the boat's balance, and as another frolicsome swell passed under them, the sailboat's deck tilted the other way, and Endi was swept off the other side by the loose boom coming back toward him. Coleman ducked it just in time being an old-time sailor.

Endi screamed like a little girl all the way into the water, scratching, clawing, and bicycle-pedaling at the thick moist tropical air wind milling arms and legs. He scrapped his back on the rough splintery planks of the pier as he ricocheted into the water.

After Endi's splash on the left, Coleman heard an extended, "Ohhh shhhhiiiiiiitttt, my teeth!" from the right side of the boat. And a lot more splashing. He thought *that's one talented talking dolphin down there! where's May?* Then he mouthed, "Oh shit."

Just then the marina's flood lights came on. Coleman had the block and tackle in his hands. He looked first over one side at May thrashing, and splashing, and cursing. Then he looked over the other side and saw Endi whipping the ocean around him into a froth. There was stereo, "Ohhhh…shhhhhhiiiiiiittttt."

Coleman looked up and down the deck of the sailboat, still not believing his friends weren't there. *Those people in the water must be someone else.* He looked back over the side. Now flood lit, he could see blood around both the thrashing screaming swimmers. He thought *SHARKS!*

Then he yelled, "SHARK!" He didn't know why. (It was the middle of the night, and his linear thinking process was short circuited.)

There was a lot more frothing and screaming on both sides of the sailboat.

The power went out again. The flashlight went out. The screams went up an octave, and many decibels. Even Coleman was screaming now too. He dropped the block and tackle overboard and it landed on May's up turned face. Her screams of fear turned to screams of rage, and fluent profanity—some in Italian. She didn't know what had hit her, but the water and churning was certainly invigorating, fatigue and sluggishness long gone. She figured whoever was still on the boat was the one responsible for her being in the water with sharks. Fear and anger were turning her superhuman.

The power came on again.

May came over the side like a monkey climbing a tree, grabbing rigging and railings and anything her fingers could get around, or dig into. Coleman swore he saw a prehensile tail. Up the side in a flash, she dug her fingernails into Coleman's flesh anywhere she could sink them as the momentum and fear kept her climbing. She had been a tumbler and stationary bar star in high school, and muscle memory jump-started itself using fear, rage, and adrenalin. Just to make sure she wasn't going back into the water she held on to Coleman with her chipped teeth too.

More blood. (Seventh? Eighth?)

Endi failed the first try to climb the ladder attached to the pier, as it was covered with moss and barnacles, resulting in him falling backwards into the water again. Still thinking there were sharks circling, he made it up the second time two rungs at a time and flopped on his stomach on the rough weathered dock's two by eight's, breathless. Salt was stinging his partly shredded back. With each exhaled breath he went through the alphabet of curse words one by one, alternating blasphemies with praise and thanksgiving for being alive.

The lights came back on again. Coleman peeled May off himself. Endi rolled over carefully and sat up groaning still muttering muted blasphemies. Coleman lugged May off the boat and parked the naked and bleeding woman next to Endi.

Coleman secured the still swinging boom with a rope, and then managed to get another block and tackle off the adjoining sailboat (securing the boom first).

The three made it back to the house with the block and tackle. They found May's clothes on the Queen's Highway on the way back which was mysterious to all three. They didn't make her put them back on. She hobbled on one flip-flop convinced the other had been eaten by a shark.

Coleman tried to comfort her repeatedly assuring her that there wouldn't have been any sharks as sharks and dolphins don't get along together. He still believed there had been dolphins. Probably May had fallen on the poor thing.

Power was on in the house again. May picked splinters out of Endi's back (enjoying his howls). Coleman found the Neosporin. May took a hot shower and more pain meds. They quietly had a drink.

At dawn, the red, orange, purple, and pink sun rose and shined amiably on the three buccaneers. The exhausted and wounded salvage operators were each enjoying an Extra Strength Kalik lager. They were in high spirits proudly sitting on two dripping big black rocks on the sand. They hadn't been to bed.

The dock was partially collapsed.

Endi said to no one counting fingers, "OK, another thousand, maybe two, for dock repairs."

CHAPTER 5

They easily chiseled off a chunk from a block now that it was out of the water. The chunk was on the bar between them. Coleman had fried some conch fritters for breakfast. They all had coffee and rum.

May's grins were crooked revealing two jagged broken front teeth. She looked like she'd been doing crack for ten years. Her hair was matted with small bits of seaweed and a lot of sand. Endi wore a "wife-beater" that was sticking to the newly formed scabs on his shredded back. Bags under their eyes. Twitching; coughing, raspy; a trailer-trash poster-couple. Coleman's goose egg on his forehead looked like he had been struck by lightning.

Coleman said, "I know exactly where the wreck is." He chuckled conspiringly, then added, "They been diving on it for years. It's picked clean. They think. Last time I dove it big black blocks were all over down there. Man, we're gonna be rich." Coleman was into salvage work full throttle now.

Endi said, "They're all over town. Like they are used as steps and retaining walls. I think the brass plaque that says Queen's Highway is mounted on one right in town. Right along the road!"

Coleman added, "They used them for foundations. You put them somewhere and they stay there. Hurricanes mean nothing to them."

Endi said, "We still don't know what they are. All we know is the metal detector says they aren't rock and are silver of some kind. They must be kina like concentrated ore. Heavy, and not pure silver."

May said, her nose swollen shut, so she sounded like she was talking into a bottle, "Couple of things heroes: one…how we gonna get them out of the ocean at the wreck site; two…how we gonna steal them from somebody's foundation; three…where we gonna sell them; four…I gotta go to the dentist."

Coleman went to the school to use the computer while Endi and May headed to the dentist.

Dr. Jack Slack, the dentist, was Haitian-French, born in Germany. He had black thick wavy hair and blue eyes, a square jaw on broad shoulders, narrow waist, and a dazzling fluorescent white smile, of course. His skin looked deeply tanned because of his mulatto roots. He was barefoot, in kakis shorts and wore a Hawaiian luau shirt, open. May sniffed a strong hit of Polo. Dr. Slack had splashed a handful under his arms and between his legs when he saw her coming up the walk. A thick gold chain with a cross on it snuggled in his thick salt and pepper chest hair.

He'd studied dentistry in Germany, where he also lost his license. Only he knew the reason, and no one cared anyway on the Big Heads' island because no one had a license to do anything anyway, including driving a golf cart, or for working on boats. "License" just wasn't in their big heads. He had quite a practice following from the neighboring islands and ex-pats used him too. He served rum drinks and marijuana gummy-bears during his patients' procedures.

Between dental appointments he repaired golf carts, and since the big heads had genetically purified their genes for great teeth, his dental work was keyed to the tourist industry, so was seasonal.

The third enterprise he pursued was the distribution of marijuana and other recreational drugs. The Albrights had good teeth, but they all suffered from depression—hence the brisk marijuana business.

He pretty much filled his day with tokes on the one-hit and eighteen-year-old Cuban rum and coke. He tried to limit the practice of dentistry to the mornings when he wasn't sloppy drunk/high yet.

He also owned the cemetery. The Albright Cemetery. He'd bought it after the last hurricane. The black sheep of the Albright family, Bertram "Bertie" Elizabeth II Albright, had inherited it. The Elders hoped that Bertie couldn't screw up a cemetery. But through no fault of his, there were now only seven left in the cemetery, after all the others floated away during the last hurricane. This had led to several lawsuits originated mostly from the liquor store island, as the Albright name is always associated with money. Bertie Albright had done a quick bankruptcy, under the tutelage of The Elders, then the First Albright Bank owned it again. Dr. Jack bought it from the bank. He'd assumed correctly that you didn't need a license to be an undertaker in Conch Key. He was re-selling the plots. Mostly back to the Albrights. Like most dentists, he was a pretty good salesman. He was the only game in town for dentistry, funerals, cemetery plots, golf cart repair, and Ganja. Entrepreneur of the year.

He decided that he was the coroner too since he was the only doctor on the island. He'd made up the coroner job—that way he'd know whenever someone died. He insisted there be a formal death certificate following every death on the island, including Haitians. Before his new rules The Elders just dumped dead Haitians in the blue hole. As a P.R. gesture of good will, Slack provided burials of unknowns at no charge in a corner of the cemetery which regularly was swept clean of graves during king tide tropical storms.

He was thinking about leasing an automated eyeglasses prescription and lens grinding machine. *Hey, a doctor is a doctor to these islanders. They're damn lucky to have a multitalented guy like me.* Except, as mentioned before, all the Albrights had perfect vision from diaper to diaper.

He drew the line at gynecology.

Since he had Bupivacaine (nerve block anesthesia), nitrous oxide gas (laughing gas), ether, and weed, even the occasional in-grown toenail came his way. And he did a The Elders ordered vasectomy on Bertie Albright, the previous owner of the cemetery. Albright Albright, with the pith helmet and bra jockstraps, never held still long enough for his castration, no matter what they gave him.

Dr. Slack was newly gay, having decided the first half of his life chasing women had been the cause of everything bad that happened to him so far, including losing his license in Germany, and they were.

But May walked in, and now all he could think of was reaching for one of her breasts. He had to confess, he did still like breasts a lot. (Breasts had a lot to do with the trouble in Germany). He'd only had one hit on his sneak-a-toke so far today, and one weak rum and orange juice for breakfast and so he was feeling quite up to some oral restoration work.

Dr. Jack Slack was a pretty good dentist. He had leased a computerized laser inlay, crown, and cap producing machine that made dental prosthetics on the spot in his office. This was good because the nearest dental lab was in Fort Lauderdale, and there was no Fed-Ex service to the island, and mail was iffy, and his credit score a minus-7.

In a couple of hours, he had May happily admiring herself in the mirror. She felt especially good after the valium, laughing gas, and ganja. The nose didn't hurt anymore, and she could smile. He had even sutured up her torn ear lobe.

He had taken laser "pictures" from every angle of the teeth he had prepped, and the machine did its thing, whirring, and zapping, and sculpturing little sugar cube shaped porcelain chunks into perfect caps which he mounted to her prepared tooth roots.

After Dr. Jack was done, and the three were enjoying a celebratory cocktail, Endi had an epiphany. *Dentists know about gold and silver.* He pulled the piece of the big black rock from his pocket.

Dr. Jack felt it in his palm and bounced it in the air a few times.

"I found it diving around an old wreck off of another island. Been carrying it around as a good-luck piece for a while."

Dr. Jack said, "I got a crucible in the lab. Come on."

In five minutes, they smelled the bitter almond smell of burned arsenic, and watched a red-orange molten glob of metal materialize from the grey black chunk of rock in the now cherry red crucible. Slack poured it out onto a piece of asbestos, and it cooled into a silver dollar sized piece of silver.

All three were stunned.

Excitedly Dr. Jack said, "Anymore where this came from? We gotta find a smelter. What'd this come off of anyway? You got a bunch of this stuff." His mind had jumped to sunken treasure in three heartbeats. He knew about the 17,000 voyages, 10% lost, two billion on the ocean floor…everyone on the islands had done the math and dreamed the dream at some point.

All her life, if a man had a "doctor" in front of his name, May trusted him unreservedly, wholly, utterly, unconditionally, and implicitly. Just the word *doctor* sometimes even made her wet. She brightly, but nasally, said, smiling her new smile, "Off a big black rock, and we know where a whole bunch more are."

Endi said to himself, *I guess we have a new partner.* "Can we borrow a golf cart? Ours died."

Dr. Jack didn't miss a beat and said, "Come on." He waved them to follow him. All three picked up their rum and Cokes and followed him. Dr. Jack had a yard full of golf carts.

Endi thought, *here we are, paradise, the view from his deck to die for, and what does this idiot look through to watch the sun go down over the Caribbean? A wrecking yard.*

Dr. Jack knew what Endi was thinking. "You live in Denver; you don't see the mountains. Come over here." He waved them toward a mini carport. "Look at this baby!"

It was the color candy apple red, and had gold flakes in it; and as Endi walked around it, it changed color from red to purple, to orange, to gold. It was trimmed in gold everywhere instead of aluminum. The top was smoky Plexiglas you could see through. The steering wheel had a padded leopard cover over it. The bench seat had been replaced with two eight-way white leather boat captain's chairs, complete with arms, and each with a five-point racing seatbelt. It had chromed roll bars. Between the seats on the floor was a console with built in radio, CD player, Sirius satellite radio, a VHF radio, and a GPS with satellite radar. Dr. Jack flipped the key on and pushed a button; a train horn sounded from speakers on the roll bar, almost as loud as the real thing.

May plopped on the passenger seat and bounced giggling like a little girl. (Laughing gas still on board.)

"I can make it sound like a piano, old car horn—it went *auugggaaa*—it'll play all kinds of songs like with a piano, harp, whatever, pipe-organ. You want a submarine…it'll make a sonar sound—pinging, maybe a bell tower, dog barking, siren? I can program it to sound like anything I want." He pulled out a remote from where you normally would keep golf tees and balls and fiddled with a button. The cart sounded like a motorcycle, then a drag racer. He hit another button and calypso music erupted from a dozen speakers. (XM, he said ginning.) He touched another button, and under the cart blue light softly spread all over the ground. Then changed colors.

"Piece de resistance." He punched more buttons, and the cart shook from side to side, then back to front, and finally hopped on its front tires. "Lift kit. What you think?"

"Has it got a bar?" Endi asked.

"Thought you'd never ask." Dr. Jack lifted the backward facing back seat and a complete bar and a compact refrigerator popped up. There were little bags of airline style peanuts and pretzels. A variety of plastic glasses and cocktail napkins. He grabbed a pint of Cuban rum and offered, "Can I top you off?" Endi reflexively offered his glass.

"Wait till you hear this." Dr. Jack climbed into the driver's side captain's chair and turned the key. Grinning at Endi and May, he started the engine and gunned it over and over. It roared like a sports car. He said over the noise, "Dual exhaust. Got a cam. Bored. High compression pistons. Supercharger. Computer ignition. Runs like a banshee. Of course, The Elders frown on it. But then I have the Mary-Jane and valium and they are all clinically depressed so at the end of the day I can do whatever I want."

Dr. Jack added with a twinkle in his eye, "Yours to use for the rest of your stay, my new friends."

They settled on a dually flatbed version more suited to salvage work.

Dr. Jack turned the machine off and touched another button. It made the sound of a cow bell being rung upside down, "kalik kalik." He added, "Just like the beer." He pulled a Kalik Extra Strength out of the little refrigerator handing it to Endi.

Endi gulped the last of his rum and Coke, and said, "Why not?" He tilted the long neck to his lips, and thought, *if you gotta have a partner you can't beat this one.*

CHAPTER 7

Thursday afternoon.

Coleman wasn't happy. "You told the damn dentist? You realize he's a convicted felon, you idiot?"

"We need him," Endi answered plaintively.

"And he's an addict. The only reason he can do anything is that million-dollar automatic computerized cap and crown-shitting machine. Talk to the postmistress. She says a bank in Germany is trying to figure out how to get here to repossess it. All kinds of creditors are after him. Registered, eyes only, letters every week to the asshole." (Mail only came once a week along with the once-a-week banker.) "The guy is everything bad you can think of. I doubt he is really a dentist."

Endi got defensive, shrugged, and said, "Do I look like I give a shit what you have to say?"

Coleman went on, "He never sent them one crapping Euro for the damn thing. But creditors don't just repo something in the islands, throw it in their car and drive off. That's the only reason he's still got it. No one can figure out how to repossess it without spending more than it's worth. Or which island out of 2000, Conch Island is. We are waiting for some TV reality repo-man show to build an episode around it. How much fun would that be?"

"But he pretty much gave us a golf cart," Endi answered brightly.

May added with confidence, "He's a doctor. He can get the silver out of the big black blocks. He knows all about metal. Here." She handed Coleman the small pancake sized piece of silver that Slack had melted from the chunk of black rock.

"He's coming over now." Endi said, holding up his hand for silence. They heard the high-performance dual pipes of the red golf cart on the Queen's Highway getting louder and louder the closer it got to Coleman's house. It was playing Wagner. The vibration was causing coconuts to fall off trees.

"He's coming over? Like we're having an island meeting, you ignorant dick?" Coleman glared at Endi irritably. "God, who else have you told? And May…love the teeth by the way…but I bet he doesn't know squat about industrial smelting like we gonna have to figure out how to do."

Dr. Jack had drug a couple of compressed-gas tanks on a two-wheeled cart, one yellow and one green. The yellow tank said *Methylacetylene Propaliene Stabalized*, and the green one said *Oxygen*. He had a pair of dark welder's glasses around his neck, and a canvas bag with tools. He put a porcelain crucible, about six inches across, on the bar and ordered a rum and Coke.

"Let's get a little spending money," he said to the three.

They chipped chunks from the big black rock. Dr. Jack set up a work area in a secluded cleared part of the thick vegetation around Coleman's house where Coleman burned leaves and palm fronds. Jack ran the torch until he ran out of gas, melting big black rock chunks into pure silver. He imprinted small ingot shapes in the sand and poured the molten silver into those impressions and when the silver cooled the little blocks looked just like a silver ingot. They were about five or six inches long, two inches wide and an inch thick. Coleman weighed each one with a fish scale and marked the weight with a Magic Marker on each one. They ended up with eleven.

Meanwhile Coleman went to town to use the internet at the school. His was still down.

School was out. Amanda Albright, the school mistress, was at her desk. She'd had her eye on Coleman's non-Albright genes. She had a small waist unlike most Albright women. Her head wasn't shaped like a watermelon either; a pair of C's; she shaved thoroughly; but she had the wildebeest hips. Her Albright depression made her endearingly vulnerable looking, and needy looking on the outside, but she was pure conniving female through and through on the inside.

"You find anything out about the wreck?" Endi asked Coleman when Endi got back.

Coleman answered, "Yea, it has had the hell researched out of it. I think we can screw around the wreck site all we want without attracting much interest. If we can figure out how to get the blocks up, and then just put them in the water under my pier like we're using them as a foundation, we'll be OK."

He picked up an ingot. "Internet said the price of silver is down. Like a record low of $20 an ounce, but it's predicted to go up soon… maybe forty percent by the end of the year. At twenty bucks an ounce, a three-pounder is worth $1,000."

The four whooped and hollered and danced and kissed and hugged and passed a bottle of rum around.

Amanda sat down at the school computer as soon as Coleman left hoping to see what he had been so interested in. She just Googled every letter in the alphabet and saw what came up in "history," and when she got to "s" up popped "silver prices."

Amanda Albright had gone to the U.S. to college. She had graduated eight years ago with a master's degree, and here she was. Thirty-two. She couldn't believe she'd ended up back on the island teaching. She couldn't find a job teaching in the States. She'd tried Canada too. Green cards, work permits, and on and on.

She was terrified of growing a pear-shaped body with

diabetes like the rest of her family. She was still pretty. Blond long hair, not fat at all with a nice figure. Everything was in the right pretty-girl proportions—even though she was a little "big-boned," and hippy.

She had a short, nice dress on that day. A little make up. *That was lucky,* she thought.

Coleman was at least twenty years older than her she figgured, but fresh genetic pools were hard to come by on the island, and even though he was bald, he wasn't bad looking at all. Kind of rugged, weathered, sea-captain-ish. (Albright women had a genetic predisposition for sailors.) He'd been a Secret Service agent, the thought of which, made her hyperventilate and fan her face with her hand. He was lean and hard and tall. Self-confident. She was sick of fat, hairy, short, and depressed.

Besides there were no cousins left that she hadn't rejected.

Moreover, being an Albright, she was genetically programmed to want to breed like a rabbit, which she hadn't done in a good long while. She was horny. She craved a good Florida singles bar.

She looked at some of the other stuff Endi had Googled: *Spanish galleons, trade routes, wrecks in the Caribbean.* Then she read: The *El Cangrejo.* She thought *that's the wreck off Albright Reef!*

"Holy shit, did he find himself some silver sunken treasure? Would that be hysterical? Right under our Albright noses all these years."

CHAPTER 8

Still Thursday afternoon.

Amanda Albright called her brother, Andy Albright, at the Albright Dive and Salvage Shop. "Is there anything new about the *El Cangrejo* going around? Is it even still there?"

Andy was depressingly polishing conch shells for the next wave of tourists. The season started in November, and this was still September. He hadn't made a dive trip for a while. He lived above the dive shop and had a small three-room hostel for divers. Any divers lucky enough to find Andy, were in for excellent shallow, clear water, reef diving. Andy knew where all the good wrecks were because the Albrights originally made their living claiming and salvaging wrecks, and The Elders loved to talk about the good old days. He knew where *new* wrecks were too… insurance scams.

Lobster season was coming up for divers. He was booked solid. The Elders looked the other way when it came to his refrigerators full of beer if there were money spending tourists. In four or five months, he made all the money he needed for the year. Dr. Slack helped him supply the divers with recreational drugs.

He was like most Albrights; no desire for things to change even though he was depressed about the way things were. In fact, he'd found change to be depressing. He could never even imagine wanting to leave the island, like his sister. Besides, like all the depressed Albrights, he didn't know he was depressed.

He made extra money doing salvage with his sometimes partner Chance, the all-around dock worker, and gas pump attendant. Chance always seemed to know right where recently sunken boats were (because he had sunk them?). The island had no crime against persons. That was not tolerated. But there was rampant thievery and larceny. It was in their hearts, and their DNA.

"Who wants to know about that stupid wreck?" Andy answered his sister with surprise in his voice. She normally took no interest in the island, much less his dive business at all until the season, at which time it was just to check out the visiting male genetic pool. "And I'm fine. You? Thanks for asking," Andy added cheerlessly.

"There's nothing on the *El Cangrejo* anymore is there? No silver or anything. Any men coming diving soon?"

Andy sighed dismally, "Amanda, there never was. It was a freighter. Never had any treasure. They think it was carrying teak and other hardwoods to Europe. And silk from the Far East that was transferred in Mexico. Dry goods. Tobacco and sugar from Cuba. Maybe a few slaves. The found some porcelain China way back when. All its cargo was salvaged the day after it wrecked. Then it was stripped clean by your great, great, great-to-the-fourteenth-power Albright cousins two million years ago. I ought to know what's down there; I've dived it ten to-the-fourteenth-power times personally."

Amanda thought to herself, *God Andy, take a pill.*

Andy sighed cheerlessly, and continued, "Nothing but ballast left. And whatever those ballast rocks are they're too damn heavy to screw with much, although they're all around the island holding stuff up, or even being used as steps, I think. I got a couple of the things here at the shop my compressor sits on. I don't know who brought them up, when or how. Uncle somebody."

"Any new men around, Andy?"

"You already asked that. I don't have any divers booked until November. Put your panties back on," he said bleakly.

Amanda said, "Brother-unit, you are tedious."

Andy said back, "I embrace tedium—it prevents me from having to think of something to do—or feeling guilty about not doing something. There is so little left of the wreck I'm thinking about buying a piece-of-shit boat and sinking it there just to have something for the tourists to dive. Hey, they've done it in Florida."

"Good-by Andy."

Amanda hung up. She forgot about wrecks and silver and switched back to Coleman. How could she work on Coleman a little? Get his attention. She knew he wouldn't dream of asking her out because of the age difference if nothing else. Besides, she thought, there's no place to "go out" to on the island anyway. About all you can do on a date here is meet on the beach for a conch fry. She couldn't think of any way she could ask him out. They weren't having their school bake sale and silent auction benefit until November. The only time she ever saw Coleman was when he wanted to use the computer.

God, I hate this island. Half the couples have only one set of grandparents. Hi, this is my uncle-grandpa.

Fantasizing: *Could I ever use a night in West Palm with Coleman! I'd teach him a thing or two about how appreciative plain girls can be in the dark. And something besides rum and Kalik beer to drink. Nice wine…and I'd visit that lingerie shop…Oh God, I need a Taco Bell! A bucket of chicken!*

Acting on an impulse Amanda decided to print off the pages of what Coleman had been looking at, put them in a manila folder, and take them out to his place, neighborly like, and say he must have hit the "print" button, but it didn't print until later, like probably out of paper, and "here are your copies." She thought to herself, *anything to get the balls rolling* (she smiled at her little play on words). That included lies, fabrication, subterfuge, and deception…all part of her female toolbox.

Coleman didn't know he was being stalked. If he knew a woman was interested in him, he would have rolled over and told her, "Happy New Year; hop on!" There were no women on the island that didn't look like an upside-down pear, except Amanda. He missed a good singles bar too. Hell, he missed bars.

She prepped for war: makeup tarty; frilly short pink skirt over an almost fluorescent hot-pink thong (she thought about going "commando"); dangly ear rings and matching jingly jewelry; perfume slathered on, and between; double applied anti-perspirant (it was hot as hell); pink high-heeled sandals, pink painted nails (all twenty), pink lipstick; a close shave everywhere; a nipples-not-concealed sheer sleeveless pink blouse; and finally… hair fluffy, roots dyed, and free of sand.

She headed up the Queen's Highway in her golf cart, Coleman's papers carefully tucked under one thigh.

Amanda rang the ship's bell at the bottom of Coleman's forty-foot driveway that wound up a slight hill through thick vegetation that isolated the house from view from the Queens Highway. As she turned into his driveway, she couldn't help wondering about the glimpse she got of his partially caved in pier and the damaged golf cart with its rear axle off and parts sticking out of the water (it was low tide again). Also, she thought, *why is a black rock, with a huge chain around it, attached to a block and tackle that's attached to a banyan tree. And it looks like someone has been chipping* pieces *of it off too.* She saw the hammer and chisel lying next to it.

With that image filed in her tidy organized master-de-gree-in-mathematics-brain, she parked behind Dr. Jack's candy-apple-red golf cart, and frowning, whispered to herself, "disgusting pervert." She had quit going to him as her nipples and breasts always hurt after her dental visit, and she once found a new cap in her mouth that she didn't know she'd needed. Of course, she had stalked him, and started it all. And she did like his sedation, even if she couldn't remember much after a visit. She slid out of the golf cart, liking the way the skirt rode up her thighs.

Coleman, at the front door, got a glimpse of the backside of a hot-pink thong as Amanda bent over the cart's seat to retrieve the file that had slid off onto the floor. As she bent over even further, her blouse drooped revealing a free swinging, no-bra, breast…and he saw nipple!

She straightened up, turned around, and coyly pulled the blouse and skirt down and flashed him a cheeky smile. He leered wolfishly, genetically programmed to stare at women's breasts. Nipples were clearly outlined through the thin silk blouse. They had been aroused by the soft rubbing of the blouse on the bumpy road.

He felt a spasm between his legs. That muscle group's tremble, having for so long been somnolent, but now stirring, caused him to jump an inch, and catch his breath.

God, I just gave the schoolteacher an old man-lascivious-letch stare! He stood there like a narcoleptic who had just fallen asleep on his feet, the vision etched on his retinas.

"Are you in pain or something Coleman? Why is Dr. Jack here? Death in the family?" She knew why Coleman was temporarily paralyzed and deadpanned it. She cocked a hip, arms akimbo, as if to say, *"You see something you like big boy?"*

She was feeling possessive toward him, and instinctively unsheathed jealous claws when she heard a female laugh come from inside the house.

Amanda said, "Coleman, after you left the school, the printer printed this stuff you were working on from storage after I turned it on. I thought you might want them and so I'm dropping them by." She offered him the manila folder. "What the hell happened to your forehead?" She couldn't help noticing the goose egg on his forehead, now mostly purple with black streaks.

"Don't ask," Coleman answered rubbing it. "Tree limb."

She was craving a rum and Coke. She was sweating between her legs. She was thinking about asking to use his bathroom and just taking the thong off. Coleman asked, "How about a rum and Coke?"

"In fact, I am dying for something. Got a little lime?" She was starting to sweat between her breasts. She made a mental note to herself; *put anti-perspirant between legs and boobs.*

She recognized May and re-sheathed the claws. *Jeeze, she doesn't look right. I wonder if they're into sadomasochism?* A flash of May dressed in stockings and boots with a riding crop flashed by. May's gloomy face was still showing golf cart and sailboat-rigging damage.

Amanda saw the little silver ingots just before Jack covered them with a bar towel. She remembered one of the web pages Coleman was browsing that reported the price of silver. It was something like seventeen to twenty dollars an ounce, and rising, her organized mathematical brain recalled.

She said hello to Endi and May, nodded coldly toward Dr. Jack, and hopped on a bar stool pointing her knees purposely toward Coleman. She thought maybe she was laying it on a little thick but crossed her legs lasciviously anyway. Besides, there was no way she could keep that skirt under control.

Drink in hand, she took a long sip and said, "What's

with the silver bullion guys? You found a wreck? If you did, it probably belongs to an Albright and has belonged to an Albright for over two hundred years. Better put it back. Or can I be of any assistance? I happen to be an Albright."

The four salvage operators stole looks at each other and stonewalled.

Amanda smiled sweetly. She examined a fingernail, waiting for a response. Flirting female, had been superseded by conniving female.

Not getting any reaction, she said, "Hey, maybe it's mine by inheritance already." She picked up the towel covering the bricks of silver, picked an ingot up and read the weight, counted on her fingers, looked at the other bars of silver, and did the math in her head. "Over ten grand here, huh? I think you need an Albright for a partner." Looking in the air and thinking, she said into space, "Let me guess, that big black rock that is being chipped at down by the pier is really silver, eh? Dr. Sleaze here, is melting it into ingots. Are any of you residents of the Bahamas? No? Then you are pirates. Which do you want? You want to be hung by a yard arm, or walk the plank off into the deep Blue Hole? I gotta hand it to you, none of us Albrights figured it out."

They were speechless.

She continued smiling her sweetest smile, "I have a master's degree in mathematics. You also need someone with brains, like me." She frowned at May for a split second, then smiled a satisfied smile, seeing by their furtive looks that she was at least mostly right about her analysis.

Coleman spoke first, "We didn't find it on a wreck. It was under my pier all the time. Since my father's days.

Finders-keepers. What'd you mean someone 'with brains,' as in none of us have brains?" He was trying to add a little levity to the situation recognizing murderous looks in May's eyes.

Ignoring Coleman, Amanda took her drink, slid off the bar stool, skirt riding up, oblivious to Coleman's eyes glazing again, and said, "Let's have a look at that big black rock." She slipped off her high-heel sandals and marched for the pier in her bare feet. They all followed drinks in hand.

When Amanda got to the beach, she kneeled next to the big black rock and said, "Holy shit, I got two of these. I'm using them as steps into the back door of my house! I have no idea how they got there or where they came from." She drank the rest of her drink in two gulps. "How many of these little silver ingot thingies can you get out of one of those rocks?" Her mind instantly projected itself into beatific future in West Palm Beach, and off the "Island of the Big Heads" forever.

Dr. Jack said, "By the look of it, maybe thirty, forty of these things." He had picked up a three-pound ingot and pocketed it in the kitchen. He pulled it out holding it up.

Endi answered, "At least. Maybe even more. Why did you bring that down here Jack?" pointing to the ingot. "We split them up already?"

Jack answered belligerently, "How can you insinuate…"

Amanda interrupted doing the math as she talked, "At thirty of these things in one block, we're looking at $25,000 per big black rock. At forty ingots per big black rock…let's see, we're looking at $34,000. I got two big black rocks. I'm looking at fifty to sixty to seventy thousand I been cleaning the sand off my flip-flops on. We gotta find out who these rocks belong to by law and fast, people. And if they don't belong to us, we gotta get them out of the islands before yesterday. Hey, wait a minute…where the wreck is. The ballast. Those big black rocks are all over the bottom there. Hooooly shit! Coleman, weren't you looking up the *El Cangrejo*? I know everybody thinks those things are just ballast rocks. You think they are silver?"

Coleman said, "Who knows? Maybe they are just rocks, and we got the only one. Maybe the original salvage dudes left just one or two, who knows? Maybe my dad knew and hid the good ones under his dock."

Amanda's eyes grew wide, like a light bulb over her head had just snapped on. She shouted, "Holy Jesus, Mother Mary, Son of God, and Holy Ghost, they're all over town too! The damn rocks are all over the damn town." She sat down on the sand with a plop, lay back on her back and raised her arms and legs straight up in the air, skirt around her hips, and started flaying arms and kicking her feet like a baby, hot-pink thong in-view-for-the-world be damned. "We're rich…we're rich…we're rich…" she said over and over, a maniacal grin on her face, eyes squinting, and head thrashing left and right, sand sticking to sweat and hair.

Watching the girl writhing around in the sand, Endi muttered from the corner of his mouth, "Well, she gets a trophy for being the most enthusiastic partner."

May said, "Emphasis on 'partner' I'm afraid."

Coleman said quietly, "I think her head's gonna turn around."

Dr. Jack said, "Man, she sure can count fast."

Amanda put her legs and arms down and lay flat on the sand staring up into space grinning, breasts heaving up and down as she panted.

Coleman said, in a business-like tone, even though most of his brain was supporting his eyes busy with the hot-pink thong and nipples, "I guess there's enough to go around."

They all nodded in agreement to each other, except Amanda, who was still on her back now dancing the twist.

Coleman offered Amanda a hand and she stood up, sheepishly shaking sand out of her hair, and brushing it off her clothes, and said, "Wow, you know what this means to me guys? I might be able to get off this piece-of-shit island, once and for all."

Endi said, "You know what this means to me Amanda? I might be able to get on this piece-of-shit island, once and for all."

CHAPTER 9

Later, Thursday afternoon.

The daring party of five, Coleman, Endi, May, Dr. Jack, and now Amanda, stumbled back up the short hill to the house. Amanda had never been in Coleman's house before. Coleman took her on a quick tour. Floors scrubbed pine. Two bedrooms, two baths, a large living room, large kitchen and breakfast area. A few rag-rugs. Windows and doors everywhere, so there was very little wall space, so, just a few watercolors of ocean scenes were hung here and there, but there were books in every nook. The ceilings were high and peaked, with ceiling fans whirring.

She thought the best feature of the house was the veranda; ten feet wide going all the way around the house. There was always a breeze, and shade, somewhere. The roof extended three feet past the veranda and was completely outlined with a rain gutter, which collected and led rainwater to the down spouts, and into the cistern under the house.

(The cistern held ten thousand gallons which when full, doubled as ballast during hurricanes; the house and cistern were held together by hundreds of mutually shared re-enforcement bars. A simple electric demand pump delivered the soft pure rainwater to sinks, tubs, showers, dishwasher, and even the icemaker in the refrigerator.)

They all refilled their drinks and headed to a sitting area on the veranda, furnished with thick pillowed wrought iron patio furniture. Coleman picked up a legal pad and pen. He had pulled a quart of conch dip from the refrigerator, a brick of island cheese (English style Cheddar), assorted olives, napkins, a knife, some Ritz crackers, and set it all on the coffee table within everyone's reach. They dug in hungrily and one by one found themselves returning to the bar for drink refills.

Talk was animated and energized.

"We gotta make a pact. This has got to be an all-for-one, one-for-all, deal here," Coleman said to the group.

Amanda eagerly agreed, "Yea, we got to promise. We all have things we can add to this project, but I gotta suggest adding one more person to the team. I think we need my brother. He runs the dive shop and has a lot of equipment left over from his dad's, and granddad's, days when they ran salvage operations. His forty-foot dive boat has a four-inch pipe welded vertically to its afterdeck and roof that a crane fits in. It's an electric driven crank crane that swivels out, picks up whatever, then swivels back, so you can lower whatever you pulled up on to the deck."

Endi agreed, "A crane would be good."

She went on, "He still does some salvage work. For insurance companies. Sunken boats." She didn't bring up the fact that she suspected that Andy and his buddy Chance did the sinking as well.

Dr. Jack said, "His dive boat is enclosed pretty well too, as I remember. We can stay kind of clandestine. And get good protection from the sun. Plus, he could probably haul the blocks off the island in that boat, to a freighter that would take it to a smelter on the mainland."

Amanda continued, keyed up, talking fast, "Not only do we need my brother for salvage, but he's an Albright, and that lets him get away with a lot; no one is going to say anything if he is hanging around the wreck. He takes divers out there all the time anyway."

Coleman asked the group, "What you all think?"

Endi said, "We need him. He's worth his weight in silver. We would have to find someone anyway, or buy a boat, and winch, and all that."

Amanda added, "It's easy to get in trouble out there. He knows the tides, channels, all that nautical stuff. He has depth finders, radar, GPS…he knows weather."

Dr. Jack said, "But can we trust him to keep this close to the chest. Under his hat?"

Amanda said, "He can be all business when he needs to be. He'll keep it quiet."

Coleman said, "If not him, someone like him. Might as well be him."

May jumped in, "What about the big black rocks in town? Anybody got any idea how many there are?"

Coleman answered, "People have been pulling these things up and finding uses for them for generations. We're using them for our dock. Probably others are to."

"If there's a house sitting on a foundation of them, we

take money from the pot and buy the house, then tear it down," Amanda answered.

"We gotta somehow check out the whole island, without anyone knowing what we're doing," Coleman said. "Each of us do sections in town, make a note then reconvene, and draw a map."

May clapped and enthusiastically said, "Oh goodie! A treasure map!" Amanda gave her an icy stare. Being both breeding age females, they pretty much hated each other.

Coleman asked Amanda, "How do you want to get your brother on board?"

Amanda answered, "Coleman-Sugar, you and I are gonna head to the dive shop first thing in the morning."

Coleman said with consternation, "I just got it. So, this is how you tracked us down." He picked up the papers Amanda had printed off, took them out of the manila envelope and smiled, "I didn't hit the print command, did I?"

Amanda, shaking her head with a smile, said to the group, "Lesson learned people. If I can figure out what you are up to, someone else can figure out what we six are up to. Loose lips, sink ships."

Endi said, "What do we do with these silver bars we just made?"

Coleman answered, "The cistern under the house."

They threw the eleven bars of silver through the two and a half square foot trapdoor in the laundry room that acted as access to the cistern under the house. They glittered briefly as they quickly sank to the bottom—back in dark water again.

After Coleman and Amanda left, Dr. Jack left too. He said he was going to order more oxyacetylene. It would probably take a week to get it, at least. He also said he was going to research silver smelting.

But Slack went into his own smelting business that night. There was a big black rock in the empty lot next to his house. It had been there forever. He chipped off chunks.

He modified his process of silver smelting by tapping into his house's five-hundred-gallon propane tank and converting a small water heater he'd torched in half, into a crucible, placing multiple burners under it. He'd "borrowed" four, five-foot-tall, green oxygen bottles from the marina used for their cutting torches. Once the first big black rock pieces melted, he found he could chunk in more in a rhythm and they would melt almost instantaneously in the red molten metal. He worked until dawn.

CHAPTER 10

Thursday afternoon.

Mano listened from the edge of the jungle. He was only twenty feet from Coleman's deck where the gang was eating, drinking, and planning. He could see and hear them through the leaves. He knew they couldn't see him. There were many places on the island he could hide and hear people talk in their houses. No one closed their doors or windows; a perfect target-rich environment for a window-peeper. He was sweating profusely in the airless thick vegetation.

So, they found silver. He smiled to himself. *Well, well, well.*

He'd been in over half of the buildings and houses on the island, including Coleman's, Amanda's, and Slack's. He rarely took anything. Sometimes he moved things. He went through drawers, closets, and looked under beds. He picked up throw rugs and knew where trap doors were. He knew where they had cash hidden. He knew who had sex toys. He knew people's clothes sizes. He knew the drinkers, the druggies, the pedophiles. The cheaters. The abusers, thieves, porn addicts, and palm tree stealers. He wasn't surprised at the mix of perverts, drunks, and thieves; it was the same everywhere.

He'd been a window-peeper since he was eight years old in Hawaii. He had taken up the sport again.

He had watched Endi and May fall in the water the night before when they were stealing the block and tackle off the old sailboat with Coleman. He was barely able to keep from laughing out loud.

He ghosted around the island on narrow footpaths he'd discovered in the jungle's dense banyan groves, sea-grape thickets, and sharp leafed thick clusters of grasses. He encountered a cat marking the path with urine once; he'd done the same. It was not like the jungle in Hawaii where he was from, which was a rainforest, where tall overhanging trees made a canopy that stopped rain and sun from getting to the forest floor, stunting, or preventing the growth of ground growing vegetation. On this island, there was just a few tall evergreen pine trees, planted by sailors long ago, so they could spot the island from long distances, but no canopy. The underbrush thrived and was so thick a machete had to be used to clear a path. The roots of all the trees and bushes were vast, as the vegetation had adapted to gripping each other's roots to withstand hurricanes.

The people on Coleman's porch were laughing now. He heard one of the women say, "Loose lips, sinks ships." *That must be the schoolteacher,* he thought to himself. She was a favorite because she often walked around naked in her house.

Then he heard, "In the cistern under the house."

Mano noiselessly slipped back into the sea grape, thatch palms, and Lignum Vita trees, having heard all he needed to know for now.

CHAPTER 11

Friday morning.

Coleman left to pick up Amanda and go see her brother Andy.

Endi and May were down by the water with the two big rocks on the sand.

Endi hit the second block with a hammer and a chunk fell off easily. He realized it was made of actual coins that had corroded and stuck together.

He polished one using an electric grinder in the shop that he'd changed into a polisher by swapping heads.

Carefully turning it over in his hand under a light, he said, "This one looks like it has two candle sticks, or columns on one side," He and May's backs were to the door.

"Those are probably the Pillars of Hercules at Gibraltar," Colonel Albright shouted as he walked through the shed's door. He spoke in a deep bilious voice with an English accent. "I saw the damaged dock, and I wanted see if I could lend a hand."

Endi and May jumped at his voice. It was the next-door neighbor, Colonel Albright, who lived on three acres adjoining Coleman's four acres. The two properties were separated by dense jungle affording each privacy from the other.

He glowered at the two from his pallid oversized head. He displayed a scornful mouth under a long moustache that attached to pork chop sideburns. He wore a white Cuban guayabera shirt worn outside his shorts, long black socks, and combat boots. The pith helmet made him look like he was from another century. He had fought in WWII, and multiple English engagements including Grenada. He was Artillery Corps and consequently hearing-impaired so that he felt he had to shout every word thinking no one else could hear either.

He introduced himself, gave a slight bow, then he put out his hand for the coin, which Endi reflexively put into his palm (a man-who-must-be-obeyed). The colonel shouted, "By Jove, this is a silver piece-of-eight young man. I haven't seen any of those since the three kilos of them we found when we were repairing and cleaning out the grandfather's cistern. He must have hidden them there last century. I gave them to the museum, of course. They're not worth much. Trinkets really."

Endi thought, *he must be in his nineties.* He shouted back at the colonel, "We just found these in the workshop. Must have been Coleman's dad who had them. How about that? Thought we'd polish a few up and see what they were."

Colonel Albright coughed, and then shouted, "I gave them to the island museum right off. Not ours any way you look at it. Spanish government's if nobody else's. Or maybe Portugal. Even the English had them. English stole them from the French. The French stole them from the

Spanish. I wouldn't allow the Spanish bastards to even lay eyes on the damn things if I had my way. We had to fight Franco in Europe, as if Hitler and Mussolini weren't enough. Artillery you know. Italy, and then Vichy France. The big one. WW Two. Gallant Cross personally awarded at Windsor. We have to give any of these little silver beauties we find to the English government."

Endi was horrified. *Give them up? You miserable old bastard, if you think…* May gasped.

Endi shouted, "The Bahamas hasn't been English since…"

Ignoring Endi, the colonel blathered on. "Still a Great Brittan protectorate in my book, young man. The sun never sets on the British Empire. Don't care what anybody says. England has long ago laid claim on any cargo salvaged in the Bahamas for time immemorial. It's the law. Anything found in the Bahamas that was there before the liberation of the Bahamas Islands, still belongs to the Queen." He stamped his cane for emphasis. "Don't worry. They usually let the local museums have the trinkets. We'll be able to keep them on the island. Don't you worry about that. I'll see to it."

May saw a hole in the conversation. She injected quickly, "Well there are only a few. Probably not worth much even melted down, these days, price of silver being down and all." May had a large heavy ball-peen hammer behind her back. She eased over to Endi and poked him in the back with it. Like he was supposed to take it from her.

He thought, *she wants me to knock him on the head with it!?*

The Colonel put on a pair of ancient looking wire rimmed glasses, then turned his body toward the sun streaming in the open shed door. He held the coin in the direct sun, scrutinizing it intensely. He shouted, "OK, yes, these are the Pillars of Hercules, Gibraltar on the north, and then its sister mountain on the south side of the Strait of Gibraltar marking the gateway to the seas that connected Europe to all the continents. This is a four-reales piece made probably in Mexico City during the reign of Charles the Fifth. The pillars are Emperor Charles' emblem. It also says Plus Ultra which means, More Beyond. His mother, Juana, who was kept in seclusion because she was mad, was technically his co-ruler, and her name appears here as well. See… there is the coat of arms of Castile…her coat of arms."

He pocketed the coin and sneered, "If you need anything I'm always around. Watching that is. I am the island magistrate, the only law so to speak on the island. Always check with me before you ponder anything I might find roguish."

Both bid him farewell as he tottered off down the Queen's Highway toward his house. Endi said, "Shit, another partner."

"You should have hit him on the head with the hammer, is what you shudda done."

Mano listened to the conversation between the Colonel and Endi and May. He could hear everything from his dense cover. He thought, *right on about the hammer.*

He followed the colonel using a parallel to the Queen's Highway trail in the jungle. The Colonel spooked and turned around to see if anybody was following him. He thought he saw a face peering at him through the dense underbrush. He straightened up and picked up the pace, showing no lameness or feebleness whatsoever. It was a face he hadn't expected. He thought it must be Albright Albright. But it wasn't. He didn't recognize it. Then he shook his head and discounted the thought. He blamed his eyes.

"Shit. I think the old bastard saw me." Mano spun off deep into the jungle, and hastily headed to his compound.

Another face, the one that the colonel expected to see, kept pace with both the colonel, and Mano, on a trail that paralleled the Queen's Highway, but on the opposite side from the trail Mano was using. Albright Albright had been watching Mano, as Mano spied on Endi, May, and the colonel. He was also wearing a pith helmet, like the colonel's. That, and a black lace bra, one cup over his genitals, and the other over his butt crack.

He followed the colonel and Mano a short way, then doubled back, and hid again outside the workshop-boat-house eavesdropping on Endi and May, who were back at polishing silver coins. Hoping that they would stay busy for a while, he worked his way across the Queen's Highway, and up the low hill that Coleman's main house was situated on. He listened for signs of life in the main house from a tiny clearing five feet deep in the thick underbrush bordering Coleman's sandy back yard. It was only fifteen feet from the veranda. He didn't hear anything. He knew the house should be empty.

He rose slowly and felt his right kneecap shift out of its groove. He put it back. His kneecaps didn't match either... like his feet.

He snuck into Coleman's house. He had been there before plenty of times over the years and knew it well. He'd even lived in it sometimes when Coleman was away. He'd chased Haitians out of it. Haitians feared him.

He went straight to the access area to the cistern under the house. He flipped a light switch on. He opened the trap door. He saw the silver bullion bars shimmering back at him in the black rainwater.

They were pretty so he took off his hat and bra and jumped in, grabbed one, then hoisted himself out. He figured he'd drill a hole in it and hang around his neck.

He closed the access hole, put on his bra and hat, and carefully tip-toed back out onto the veranda, down the four steps, then retraced his steps through the sand toward the thick vegetation. As he retraced his steps, he dragged a palm leaf behind him to cover his footprints. He vanished into the jungle. His wet footprints in the house evaporated almost instantly in the heat.

CHAPTER 12

The next day; Saturday…noonish.

Endi was doing yoga with May. She was on the floor. He was sitting on a bar stool next to Coleman. Endi had a glass in one hand and was moving it into various positions mimicking May's movements. Occasionally he stretched a leg. He held a partly frozen wash cloth on his forehead with his other hand, the water dripping down his face. It was over ninety in the shade, and he had a hangover.

Coleman watched May stretch and fold, and thought, *she's got a good engine, but her hands aren't on the wheel.* He nibbled a bologna sandwich in one hand, and sipped rum and orange juice with the other.

Endi said, "My goal in yoga is to be able to lick myself."

May grunted, "Perv."

Last night the two friends decided treasure hunting was not for them. They had their retirement. In a few years, Social Security would kick in. They could live on the island for nothing, and wear rags the rest of their lives. Eat conch. Drink cheap smuggled tax-free Cuban and Barbados rum. No cars. No insurance. No taxes. No colds. No crime. No guns. No watch. No cable. No water bills. No cell phones. No internet. Less is more.

They had decided that getting the heavy blocks out of the ocean, processing them, selling the silver, dodging all the Albrights, especially the colonel, and maybe the Spanish, Portuguese, and English, not to mention crooks and the Mafia…well… it just wasn't what retirement was supposed to be like. They just didn't feel like "doing battle" anymore.

They decided they didn't even have enough time left in their life to do it anyhow. Besides, why do anything? Drink, eat, sleep, and screw. Legal, cheap, easy, fun. They'd paid their dues. Done their work. Had all they needed. Who the hell wants to be rich, and go to Monte Carlo?

Of course, May had other plans. Women always do. There is, until the end of time, stuff to spend money on if you're a girl. She was the one who had brought up Monte Carlo.

The bell rang from down the path on the Queen's Highway announcing that someone was at the foot of Coleman's driveway. Coleman jumped at the sound. He was kind of fractious, his hangover brittle. He swore to himself that bottles of bootleg rum were different as far as alcohol content, and even toxin content, when it came to Cuban rum.

Thirty seconds later a golf cart wound down at the front door, and fifteen seconds after that Amanda walked in. This time she wore a pink "skort" (shorts that have a flap in front that looked like a skirt), with a pink spaghetti strap top, pink flip-flops, and pink sunglasses. Everything pink had a yellow sunflower on it, including the dark glasses. Coleman idly wondered if there was a pink thong with a yellow sunflower too. He got a soft-on now whenever he saw her.

"You're drinking already?" Amanda asked no one, with a disgusted tone and a wrinkled nose.

"We never quit," Endi answered honestly.

Coleman, studying the pink vision, and hoarsely verbalized a thought. "You know in Vegas when everybody is walking around at seven in the morning with coffee? Well, me and Endi, we're the ones with drinks still in our hands at seven in the morning, that everybody stares at with disdain." He posed a serious question to Endi. "Are we still up, or did we pass out and now we're up again?" He scratched the week's growth of hair on his chin. He was thinking about a ponytail to keep the hair off his sweaty neck.

Amanda bent down to have a closer look at Coleman's goose egg. Coleman tried to focus on her face. His eyes crossed and stayed that way as she backed up.

Amanda was thinking, *if this is what he looks like at noon, do I want to know what he looks like at midnight?* Trying to recover her mood Amanda added brightly, "I've never been to Vegas, so I wouldn't know. Now, everyone, we're all going for a nice boat ride. Doesn't that sound marvelous? Look at some pretty black rocks. My brother wants to visit the *El Cangrejo*." She couldn't help sounding like the elementary school teacher she was.

No one reacted. Coleman and Endi took sips, blank stares on. May still in her yoga trance, did a squatting dying swan to the left, then to the right. Amanda stomped her foot and said with frustration, "Come on you guys."

May stood up, shook her hair out, and joined Amanda looking at the two guys with distain. She said with authority in her voice, "Endi will take his underwater camera. Coleman can just sit there on the boat and watch for Albright-big-heads. I frankly can't see him doing much else. I'll swim down and look around the wreck with Lector the Detector and the camera. I can hold my breath underwater forever."

She punched Endi causing him to spill a little of his drink onto his bare stomach. He scowled, then smiled remembering what May could do underwater holding her breath. Then he scowled again thinking he had no use for authority, even if it was from a C-cup underwater porn star. Especially if it was from a C-cup underwater porn star. His little wave of anger left with the next breath, anger not being worth the trouble.

Coleman thought absently, *I swear May has not talked to Amanda, but she just took up where Amanda left off. They're scary things.* Then he said out loud, "We decided last night that salvage work is too much trouble. You girls go knock yourself out, and just as soon as you get rich, we'll marry you. We'll have a double wedding. In Vegas."

Both girls felt shudders of glowing harmony deep in their wombs at the word "marriage." The fleeting feminine reflex feeling left just as fast.

Endi's eyes were trying to see through the skort. They were still a little crossed. They were fixating on an imaginary yellow daisy on an imaginary pink thong. He hated skorts; "deal killers" he called them.

Endi caught Amanda up on the colonel episode, and how the colonel managed to show up right when they had polished a silver coin.

Amanda said she didn't like the colonel. She said, "He's a sneaky, gossipy, arrogant, condescending, hateful-to-women, bigoted, screw-anything-he-can… even-screw-the-hair-on-the-barber-shop-floor, type of guy…a first-class letch-asshole."

With a deadpan expression, Coleman asked Amanda, "How do you really feel about the guy?"

She glowered. "Watch him, he has the only gun on the island, and has more buried, because he organized a revolution forty or fifty years ago, declaring that Conch Key was succeeding from the Bahamas. Hail to the queen and all that crap."

Colman said, "Old story. The Bahamian armed forces never showed up. That's when he declared himself the magistrate. His guns are rusty paper weights and door stops by now."

May said, "I tried to get Endi to hit him with a ball-peen hammer."

An hour later, with a cooler of Kalik Extra Strength beer, Coke, limes, and a liter of Bacardi, cheese and crackers, conch jerky, Lector-the-Detector, and an underwater camera, the foursome found themselves holding on for dear life as Andy raced his twin outboard, center console Albright Brothers 23-footer, out to the wreck of the *El Cangrejo*.

Coleman did see a pink thong with a daisy. Amanda made sure of it.

CHAPTER 13

The year 1733 C.E.

The *El Cangrejo's* real name was *Nuestra Senora de Cansancio del Carmen San Antonio de Vacilar y Borracho.* (Who knows what it meant in Spanish back then, but today's translation comes out: *Our Lady of Weariness from Carmen San Antonio of Vacillation and Hangover.*) She came to be known as the *El Cangrejo* (Crab in Spanish). One of her captains, sardonically, christened her "Crab" because of her crooked laid keel. He swore the ship must have been laid by blind drunken sangria saturated boat builders in Genoa where she was built. The Spanish used up ships so fast in those days that the shipyards would hire practically anyone.

The misshaped keel made her crab to the right, always sailing in a side slip. The captain had to point her fifteen degrees to port (the left) to follow a straight line. As for ever making a left turn, forget it.

King Philip V in 1733 sent the already tired (she was only nine years old) *El Cangrejo* with the fleet to Veracruz. The *El Cangrejo,* like the other ships in the 1733 Nueva Espana Fleet, anchored off Veracruz and took on silver that had been transported by mule trains from Mexico City. The Spanish scribes carefully recorded the cargo put aboard the king's ship. Included in the recorded inventory was, Chinese porcelain wares, exotic hardwoods, local carved furniture, cochineal dye, cacao, vanilla, leather (sheep, goat, cow) hides, AND 76 boxes of silver coins, with 3,000 coins to the box, for a total value of 228,000 pesos. What the scribes didn't mention, because they didn't know about it, was that half her ballast was silver in some not-completely refined form or another. Only the captain and ship owners knew about it. Just like today, lots of well-to-do citizens were into tax-evasion. The scribes decided they were boxes of rocks (they took bribes).

In records still maintained in Spain to this day, three hundred years later, the notation in the *El Cangrejo's* ship's log during the fatal storm reads in part: *The ship is now opening up between decks, further filling the hold with water…at noon the wind changed to the south with as much, if not more, violence than before, the blows of the seas always continuing to add to our torment. If it were not for the double hull we would be lost. Of course, the outer hull is eaten though in many places by the hateful teredo worms. We continuously work the pumps. Our pilot fears there are reefs south of us. Woe is ours were it true.*

Built in 1724, The *El Cangrejo* was a lightly armed galleon with only six cannons, eighty-feet long, thirty-feet wide and displaced 200 tons. It was sailing with the fleet from Havana and was on its way back to Spain the day of its death. She had mostly been used until then in the Caribbean to transport mercury that was essential for refining silver. Mercury from Mexico was a commodity the crown carefully monitored and monopolized. It was another level of control over silver production. You couldn't smelt silver without mercury. Half the crew couldn't see, hear, or talk, thanks to mercury poisoning. The other half lacked full coordination for the same reason…the fortunate ones fell overboard for a merciful drowning.

The ships log went on: *At 8:00 p.m. the ship struck bottom and continued to do so taking horrendous blows. Some of the crew have already fallen overboard due to their vision and balance issues. The deck finally separated from the hull and rafted toward the beach. At daybreak, the weather was clear and we could see land past the reef. It of course appeared diserted, as no natives were gathering. Our pilot assumed it was another God forsaken waterless desert island. Rafts were made to take passengers and crew ashore as the survivors now saw that other ships in the convoy were grounded on reefs nearby. Salvage is already underway. The bucco (diving) commences this day and continues with good results. The other ships will be pulled free from the reefs and will be able to sail to Spain with minor repairs. Postscript: We lost all the slaves somewhere during the storm. But God has been bountiful. We have plenty of conchs to eat. No water has been found. We managed to salvage many of our freshwater barrels.*

The log continued three days later: *We received notice that all the silver had been taken off the* Cangrejo *and taken ashore. The divers of the* El Congrejo *stated this day that they were finished and having salvaged 70 boxes of silver coins, lacking just six from concluding the registry. Also recovered was a lead water pump, the lead-sheathed rudder, five of six cannons, silver dinnerware bearing an English maker's marks, and many personal items such as ivory-handle razors, combs, as well as ceramic crucibles used for smelting bullion, and also various weapons, including swords, knives, muskets, as well as corn meal and other goods. Satisfied with the work, the Spanish salvors burned the ship to recover fastenings and to clear the coast so unwanted looters could not benefit from the spoils. Some of the blindest and more unbalanced crew decided to remain, desert island or not, swearing that the* El Cangrejo *soured them to the seafaring life forever and vowing never to set foot on a galleon again. God speed them and their offspring.*

Not reported in the log was that amongst the fifty-foot by thirty-foot ballast pile (that was supposed to be made only of large river rocks, and flat red ladrillo bricks), that was smeared over the outer and inner reef, there were also many, too numerous to count, big black oblong wooden boxes supposedly filled with rocks for ballast. A "connected family" in Spain turned homicidal when they found out about the loss of their concentrated silver ore hidden in those boxes in the ballast hold. That was another reason some of the crew opted for staying on the desert island thinking that preferable to dealing with "The Family" back home.[4] They also wanted to stay with the boxes, hoping

---

4 This period was the beginnings of the Galician Mafia. Galicia was a poor fishing region in Spain whose inhabitants supported themselves with the smuggling of tobacco, whores, and whatever else they could get away with. (Now they specialize in drug smuggling with primary contacts in the British Isles—competing with the Charlin Clan with whom they are currently in a feud with.) One particular ruthless family, the Castineira Clan, got its beginning during that time and achieved fabulous wealth from the

that they might be able to salvage them somehow after the fleet moved on.

(One of the very youngest cabin boys shipwrecked on the island outlasted his mild mercury poisoning and was able to contribute some Spanish DNA to the newly arriving Albrights that arrived in early 1777, and that is why Amanda Albright, in college, was often drawn to dance a hand clapping, heel stomping, Flamenco, on the bar.)

Also not reported in the carefully scribed log was the jig performed by the captain as he watched the *El Cangrejo* burn, cursing loudly that if he could have just been able to make a left turn, he'd have missed the reef altogether and would have been on his way to Spain, and pitchers of sangria, and a radiant Flamenco-dancing prostitute he paid well.

---

smuggling of silver in different forms from the Americas. Interestingly they now are said to own and spend their days drinking sangria on several undisclosed desert islands in the Bahamas where they manage a global multimillion-dollar empire of fine prostitutes. Some things never change.

CHAPTER 14

Friday afternoon after Andy's dive boat trip
to the wreck.

The colonel's golf cart was parked next to Coleman's tool shed. They found him face down in a pool of blood on the dirt floor, with the round end of a ball peen hammer embedded deep in the back of his big hairy head.

Coleman felt the colonel's neck for a pulse. "Dead. Still warm." He felt a shiver go up his spine. "This didn't happen too long ago."

Endi said, "This is about the goddam silver, isn't it? This is the worst-case-scenario I predicted, murder over treasure. I knew we should have put the shit back under the dock and forgotten the whole thing." He pointed to where the block of coins was. "The block of coins is gone." There were still a few chunks of the big block laying where it had been.

The two friends stared at each other glumly. Coleman said, "There was a little two wheeled hand truck in here. It's gone too."

Endi asked staring at the body, "Who do you call? You said there isn't any law enforcement on this island. The Bahamas must have an FBI, or something?"

Coleman said, "The colonel was the so-called magistrate, the closest thing to an authority we have on the island… had. Someone is a Justice of the Peace; does the gay weddings. Slack is the coroner, which is a made-up job. I don't know if there has ever been a murder on this stupid island. Maybe a Haitian, nobody missed, but no Albright, or property owner. At least that I've heard of."

Endi said, "We may be the primary suspects. It's on your property. I was the last to see him. May even had the hammer in her hand," he added miserably. "Fingerprints! Our fingerprints are on the weapon; May's, and mine."

Coleman verbalized his thoughts as they rose. "Why was the colonel even here? Don't worry, my prints are on absolutely everything, too. Why here in my shed? If someone wanted to kill him…why here, and not at his house, or take him out in a boat and drown him and sink him in the Blue Hole? Or at least drag him into the jungle."

Endi said, "We may have interrupted the killer. He got the coins stashed and was coming back for the body. We may be being watched right now. Like we interrupted the killer. Like if we leave, maybe the colonel will disappear!"

Endi grabbed a two-foot piece of pipe, and Coleman a monkey-wrench.

Coleman, straight-faced, said, "Maybe we should walk away and let the killer take care of business?" He guffawed dolefully. "We should look for tracks. The hand truck, or footprints."

Endi said, "You gonna head off into the jungle hoping to find the killer? Then what if you find him? He'll kill you from behind too."

Coleman squatted over the colonel. Their backs were to the door.

May screamed behind them, "Oh my God, you killed him!" Then both May and Amanda screamed at the same time. Startled, Coleman lost his balance, and sat on the colonel. The colonel farted like an automatic rifle.

They turned around. Amanda had one hand clamped between her knees, and the other hand balled in a fist in her mouth, muffling her continuous screams. May was stomping her feet and howling into both her hands that covered her mouth, eyes bugging out.

Amanda took her fist out of her mouth and shouted, "Is that the colonel? Is he dead? What's that sticking out of his head? It looks like a tomahawk. Like he got clubbed by an Indian?" She made a few tentative steps toward the body then froze as if she was expecting the colonel to spring up and yell surprise!

"Why did you kill him? You shouldn't have killed him."

"Is he dead. Really dead?"

Endi went to the girls, put a hand on each girls' shoulder and answered, "It's Colonel Albright, and he's quite dead. No, we didn't kill him."

May wailed in his face, "Endi! I was just kidding when I told you we should have killed him with that hammer. Holy shit!"

Endi, glowering, said, "Had to happen while we were on the boat looking at the wreck. Or while we were headed back."

The terrified girls looked around with wide eyes. He added, "Get real, May. Neither of us killed him. We were with you the whole time. We just got here one minute before you."

Amanda, bug eyed, said, "He just took a breath, I swear." The colonel belched. Being sat on stirred some things up. A faint foul smell suddenly permeated the shed.

Coleman said to Endi, "You and May were the last to see him. What'd he say? Was he nervous, looking around, spooked?" They both said no.

Endi said, "He did instantly piss me off with his pompous attitude. He was going to take the silver; get in the middle of this mess somehow. Like it belonged to England. I told you all last night we should abandon this silver shit. Now I know I don't want to play anymore." He made the shaking, sobbing, girls sit on a bench.

Endi said, "Whoever killed him may be listening."

Coleman said, "Maybe it was suicide? Killed himself with a hammer." Only he and Endi cheerlessly laughed at his cop-dark-humor.

Coleman tried his cell phone. "No service. I got to go up by the road a little; be right back."

Endi still had his camera. He took pictures of the body from different angles. He photographed the doorway. He found blood spatter on the walls and ceiling, so knew the colonel had been hit at least twice; the first strike caused blood to flow and coat the hammer, which then, when lifted rapidly in a back swing, splatters blood in a predictable arc. He looked for a second hole in the thick haired scalp and found one full of blood, but not as deep as the one the hammer was still in.

Coleman came back and said, "I got hold of someone at customs at the airport at Marsh Harbor where we fly into. I guess they are going to try to pass it up the line. Whoever answered the phone panicked; I couldn't get much out of her. The police didn't answer. We don't have a 911 system. I also left a message on Slack's voice mail—he's the self-proclaimed coroner." He added, "I think I saw fresh blood going into the edge of the jungle. And what looks like a cart tire track."

Endi said, "The murderer has to have blood on him. There is splatter. And whoever it was, tracked blood in the dirt floor in here. Maybe the colonel put up a fight and the killer is hurt? At least there should be blood on his shoes that he will track. Never thought I'd be happy to see a cop."

May said snarling, "You are a cop! Do something, Endi!"

Amanda asked Endi, "What was the colonel doing back here? He had to know we weren't here. He was snooping."

Endi answered, "He was. And he paid for his curiosity. Somebody else was around too and wanted him out of the picture. Someone on this island. Still on this island. By the look of the position of the murder weapon, it looks like whoever killed him caught the old man unawares. From behind. I don't think the colonel knew what hit him."

Coleman said, "The colonel knew when to come back to nose around…that we were gone. Someone else also knew we were gone and knew about the silver."

Endi said, "The store; someone at the store, when we were buying ice for the cooler for the Andy's boat. The killer knows about the silver. I very much doubt this was a planned murder; like what we cops call organized. Or premeditated. I think it was an opportunity crime, not preplanned. Maybe they confronted each other, and the colonel made threats. Turned his back and the killer lost it…raged."

Coleman said, "Maybe it was two or three people, and the colonel was screaming and had to be silenced. Whatever happened, whoever it was, wanted the silver coins now, as opposed to waiting. Maybe the colonel was about to break the block of coins apart and haul them off himself. Send them to the queen. Maybe the colonel did his arrogant rant about the silver belonging to England, and the killer lost it."

Endi said, "The coins don't need to be refined. Someone knows his silver treasure. It's probably just one person, and that person wanted the coins so bad he didn't care about leaving behind a dead body. And he wanted them now, as in believing this was his only opportunity. Hide the money, and then, maybe, get rid of the body."

Coleman said, "Or get on his boat and disappear with a bag full of treasure."

May said, "I am *really* scared, Endi."

"You ought to be scared my little *Ipo* (Darling in Hawaiian)," Mano whispered to himself, remembering May under Endi, having sex, when he watched them through their window one afternoon. He imagined her struggling and screaming through a gag with him on her. He imagined tying her up. Hurting her. Biting her. "Mano will teach you little *Alamea* (Ripe, Precious)." He could clearly hear them talking from the edge of the jungle that completely hid him. The girl's screams had luckily halted him in his tracks before he entered the shed again to deal with the body.

He'd come back to drag the colonel into the jungle and cover his tracks from dragging the silver on the hand truck.

He'd easily broken the block of coins into large chunks. He'd used empty boxes and the hand truck to haul the coins off, and buried the pieces shallowly, then covered them with palm bows. He'd hidden the hand truck too. He had planned to take it back and use it to move the colonel. *It all took too long,* he thought.

If I'd had twenty more minutes, I would have had the body hidden in the jungle and no one would have missed him. Then floated him out to sea in the middle of the night. Shit. I am an idiot. I should have dragged the colonel out first. What was I thinking? The silver wasn't going anywhere. Better yet, I should have made the Colonel walk into the jungle on his own power, and then killed the pompous ass-hole. Gonna give it to the queen of England? You gotta be kidding me.

Mano decided he wasn't that worried. One thing he didn't lack was confidence. He knew he had the upper hand since no one on the island even knew he existed; no one had ever seen him. The only one that had ever gotten a glimpse of him was now dead with a hammer in his skull.

The two couples locked the shed and went up to the house to look for more things Endi and Coleman could use to at least preserve the scene. They couldn't imagine the perp or perps returning to the scene now. Endi wanted to get some baggies to cover the Colonel's hands with. Anything else they did at the scene of the crime would just muddy the results that a pro CSI tech might find.

Mano, still hiding in the edge of the jungle, said softly to himself: "Burn the shed, Mano." He heard them coming back and headed back to his compound.

He dragged a palm branch behind him to obliterate his footprints. He was moving too fast to do a good job. He wasn't worried about his footprints anyway. He was wearing a pair of sandals that had been made from an old tire tread. He figured there were maybe a billion pairs of tire-tread sandals in the world.

Endi found Mano's faint tire-sandal prints. They weren't really clear. He photographed them. He saw they seemed to head toward the jungle. He snapped close-ups of the few deeper treaded prints. They ended as soon as they entered a trail in the jungle, obviously having been swept over to hopefully cover them up. He had nothing to follow.

Mano had murdered his wife. The cops were relentless. Hawaii 5-O. They knew he had done it. A celebrity murder. She had been beaten to death, asleep in her bed at three in the morning. With a blunt object. He'd wanted to beat her to a pulp with his bare fists, but he'd used a baseball bat to save his hands—his "fish-stunner" from the boat. They never found the murder weapon. Wired to a rock, it was on the floor of the Pacific dropped over the side of his fifty-foot yacht. His girlfriend was in the stateroom, drugged and unconscious. She was his alibi. He had taken the dinghy to the beach and snuck into his own house to do the deed and then back to the boat. The girlfriend vouched for him that he had been on the boat the whole time.

He spent time in jail, but his lawyers got him out fast. It had scared him deeply. Prisoners taunted him. Told him they knew how to take care of him. They were jealous of his success and anxious to be the one to take down the great Mano. He knew fighting under the rules of the ring was one thing, but in prison, he would be killed. His lawyer moved him to the other side of the world, to a desert island in the Bahamas. Conch Island.

He had money. Money was freedom. But he couldn't get to it. Thirty million completely out of reach. Everything had been seized; house, boat, cars, everything. All assets frozen. The lawyers paid themselves well out of the seized money. And they brought him everything they could think of. But he could go nowhere. He couldn't even go to the store for a six-pack of beer. He was helpless. Trapped and alone. Time was dragging. He was feeling his life fading away. He missed the glory. The adoration. The thrill of winning. The thrill of beating a stranger to a pulp in front of thousands, maybe millions, watching pay-for-view. His fans.

He was out of shape now. No trainers, no sparring

partners, no gym, no steroid stacks, stuck in this Conch Island prison. The nagging fear of being back where he started from, broke and on the streets, was eating on him. The teasing, the taunting, and the beatings he suffered as a child never left his psyche, keeping him perpetually volatile and mean. He called it his "mojo." His mojo was fading.

The girls they brought for him to the island were too scared; too timid. They didn't perform well. Even for the huge amount of money they were paid. It was hard to find pretty, very young, *real* kinky girls. He could find them. Or they found him. They were out there. Plenty of them. But his lawyer couldn't find them.

He needed a new source of money to escape and start again. His own money, not his money that was everyone else's money too. The trainers, agents, lawyers…all the leeches riding his fists. This silver could get him a new life. He could disappear where even his lawyers and the cops wouldn't find him. The silver could be his ticket to freedom. South America probably. Africa. New Zealand. If the lawyers showed their fat, greedy, soft faces he would kill them. *First, you kill the lawyers.*

Mano Kamea was a talented, disciplined, and ferocious welterweight boxer. Beating other men into submission his size was what he did, and well. But between the cauliflower ears and thick scarred eyebrows, his brain had taken a beating. He had become even more simple with each blow. Like a mean little child with a bizarre talent to hurt and maim.

He was born *Ipo Alamea Hokulani.* In Hawaiian that meant *Darling, Precious, Star of Heaven.* When he went pro, he changed his name to *Mano Kamea…Shark/Passionate*

Lover, the One and Only. His fans called him *Kalama…
Flaming torch.*

His mother was white, his father Hawaiian. He had always been a small kid. He got teased. He came home bloody. He never grew like the other big Hawaiian boys. They called him a Haole, their insult toward his whiteness. No better than a white tourist. No better than the whites who had taken their island. Not belonging there. His father shamed him for his size. But his grandfather taught him to fight and fight dirty…and to take blows.

Ipo caught the eye of a trainer. He had begun to win fights in high school. He had won the featherweight championship for the state of Hawaii sophomore year in college. He quit college, or was kicked out, and eventually bulked up to 145 pounds, and had the same success in the welterweight division. He was a lefty. His opponents didn't know what to do when that left hook barreled at them like a howitzer round.

The Olympics might have saved him, but they had just happened, and weren't coming around for another couple of years. He couldn't wait for the next Olympics, so he went pro.

He was sixteen when he started fighting and weighed just 105 pounds—a Light Flyweight. He fought in local venues at first, shown on *Round by Round,* an evening televised boxing show. In his debut fight he won by decision because his young opponent was near death. The referee stopped the fight just in time. He became an instant star of the program. He gained weight, but had not made weight for his twelfth bout, so was forced to use heavier gloves, putting him at a disadvantage. That was the only fight he ever lost.

His record: won 45; lost 1; draws 2; wins by KO 35.

He grew to 122 pounds and went into the Superbantumweight Division. He defended that title five times.

He fought at the Staples Center in Los Angeles; the Thomas and Mack Center in Las Vegas; the Araneta Coliseum in Quezon City, Philippines; San Antonio, Texas; The Mandalay Bay in Las Vegas; the MGM Grand in Las Vegas, and a host of other venues. He split purses of millions, while raking in pay-for-view dollars, signed endorsements for detergents, medicines, foods, garments, shoes, telecommunications, and even political ads. There were pictures in *Time* magazine, movie offers. He was named in *Ring Magazine,* as Fighter-of-the-Year, and Number-1-Pound-For-Pound; *Sports Illustrated,* Boxer-of-the-Year; *Yahoo Sports,* Fighter-of-the-Year; *BoxingScene.com,* Fighter-of-the-Decade; *ESPN Stars,* Champion-of-Champions; and *World Boxing Organization,* Boxer-of-the-Year.

Three combatants were permanently brain damaged, and one was dead, thanks to him. His speed was sensational, and his strength like an ape, his arms long, legs short and powerful, and his soul that of a homicidal-maniac-with-no-regrets. No matter who the opponent was, Mano could get under him, and break jaws, noses, teeth, chins, temples, and tear ears, eyebrows, lips, and cheeks. And beat men to unconsciousness.

And he did it with style. He played with his opponents, like a cat with a mouse. That's why the crowd loved him. Because he was a showman. He knew what they wanted, and he gave it to them. He loved to play his victim, dragging the beatings out until just before the referee called the fight, or the opponent was about to throw in the towel…then the knockout. He gave his fans as many rounds as he could. He gave millions of fans their money's worth, at $45 a ticket for pay-for-view.

He'd walked on a lot of red carpets. He'd flown all over the world in his own jet. He'd had a lot of women. He had a room full of belts and trophies. He'd partied with movie stars. Now he lived on a desert island with the big heads. Alone. He didn't weigh 145 anymore. Now, one-sixty-five. His fighting days were gone forever. He wanted that silver. If he had to kill the whole island to get it, he would kill the whole island, if that's what it took.

CHAPTER 15

Friday afternoon.

Dr. Jack Slack gagged, and left the tool shed to vomit. He sat on the sand next to the water and refused to come back in.

Coleman asked him with irritation, "What about at least pronouncing the colonel dead?"

Jack whined, "OK, I hereby pronounce the colonel dead. Jesus, I'm a dentist. I make porcelain crowns. I can't go back in there. I use Haitians to bury bodies. I can't even touch something dead. Or even old."

Coleman and Endi looked at each other darkly. Coleman said under his breath, "So much for him taking charge."

Amanda had become a deaf mute with a thousand-yard stare. No help whatsoever. Zombie. Sitting in the sand under a palm tree staring out at the ocean, humming to herself.

May was hovering over Jack, trying to comfort him. He gagged and she recoiled, but nothing came out.

Jack loaded a sneak-a-toke and took a deep hit. They watched a little color return to his face.

Endi asked Jack, "You know how to get a hold of the Justice of the Peace? Come on Jack, we need help here.

You're all we got. We don't even live on this island. We're foreigners. Who is the law around here? Who do we call?"

Jack mumbled something unintelligible at the sand. He was holding his head in his hands and rocking back and forth, sitting cross legged. He looked up glassily, and looking through Coleman, said with a cracking voice, "Colonel Albright was the magistrate. If anything happened on the island at all, we all went to him. He, and The Elders, whoever the hell they are; no one seems to know. All we ever had to decide on was stuff like do we allow the only gay Albright to open a café. Like, was the island going to get AIDs from his conch dip if he didn't wash his hands? Or do we allow kids to have mopeds again? It was 'yea' on the gay restaurant, and 'nay' on the mopeds, by the way. I think The Elders don't even allow kids past a certain age. When they turn thirteen, they put them in a fifty-five-gallon drum and feed them through the hole in the side." No one laughed.

Coleman explained to Endi, "The only gay Albright-in-the-clan is named Neal; he has the restaurant. The only way I can remember his name is imagining him kneeling to give a blow job."

Endi laughed out loud. Coleman couldn't help laughing back. Jack scowled, eyes dark, then he said, "Can't you two clowns give it a rest?" He gagged again.

Coleman held his hand over his mouth and coughed unsuccessfully trying to hide another laugh, "I hate it when I get the giggles at a crime scene."

Endi tried with Jack again. "Jack, come on, who do we call about a murder?"

Jack standing up, with the help of May said, "I really don't know. After the revolution, the colonel just took over, mostly sighing documents and things, and the Justice of the Peace, well she's pretty busy licensing and taxing all the golf carts. And she has the gay marriage thing going… that really takes a lot of her time."

May asked, "Revolution? Gay marriages?"

Jack went on, "Whenever the colonel, I mean the magistrate, had an issue that required muscle, he just called Chance, and Chance rounded up a couple of dock workers, like when the Albright seventy year old twins fight over whose conch traps are whose, Chance and his buddies would hold them apart until they promised to quit fighting and all the colonel ever had to deal with was physical." Jack hiccupped deep a couple of times.

Coleman sighed deeply, and added, "I've never been anywhere in my life where there wasn't a damn cop… except this island." He shouted at Amanda, "Wake up! Add to this conversation!" She continued to look out at the ocean saying nothing.

Jack went on, "So after the revolution the colonel decided he was the magistrate and appointed Luna Albright Justice of the Peace. During the season, she can't keep up with the same-sex marriage racket she's so busy. Otherwise, she pretty much does nothing. Well, the golf cart racket. I think the golf cart licenses pay for the garbage barge."

May asked again, "Revolution?"

Coleman explained. "Help me out here Amanda! OK, fifteen or twenty years ago this island, and the ones to the north and south of us, seceded from the Bahamas. They had a revolution. They had one gun. No one came. The Bahamas doesn't really recognize this island anyway since there aren't any cars to license, roads to maintain, government owned buildings to staff with bureaucrats, or crime to police, or court rooms to prosecute in. Not even a liquor store to license and tax, not to mention income tax to collect because the Albrights never paid any anyway, some kind of grandfather clause. The school isn't even on the tax dole. It's private. No snow removal, or roads to repair, or sewers to maintain, or public transportation, or an airport. Not even a fire department. Everybody has a pump in their cistern, and a back-up generator. But generally, the Albrights just let whatever catches on fire burn to the ground."

Jack Slack added, "There are seven hundred other islands, and twenty-five hundred keys, or kays, in the Bahamas. The Bahamas government doesn't give a crap about most of them. So, the colonel decided to revert back to English law on Conch Island, with a magistrate, and a Justice of the Peace. Come on Amanda…you're better at this than anyone."

Amanda stood up and walked over to them. She said sullenly, "This island doesn't really exist for the Bahamas. There are less than two-thousand people living on these three islands. That's not counting the Americans. We never even have used Bahamian currency. We just use the U.S. dollar. Ever since the first Albrights left the colonies during the War of Independence, no one has bothered us. There was even some debate during the so called "revolution" (air-quotes) in the newspapers as to whether this island had ever even been part of the Bahamas in the first place. The reporter reasoned that there can't be a revolution from the "tyranny" (more air-quotes) of the Bahamas government if you aren't even part of the Bahamas anyway. Nobody even votes here. England cut the Bahamas loose in 1973, but the Albrights never got the word."

Coleman said, "There was some legal thing that actually caused the revolution. Some lawyer from Marsh Harbor took issue with The Elders doing judgment of guilt, or whatever crime, and doling out their own justice. Really, essentially, he wanted to become the island lawyer; create a position called Summary Judge. In other words, he would be the law. He saw an opportunity for gainful employment. He tried to take over the justice system here saying we were in violation of due process by allowing a non-lawyer to preside over criminal trials. Plus, a defendant needed legal representation before sentencing. Of course, there is no jail. Mostly The Elders just make you walk the plank over the blue hole." He snorted a laugh.

Amanda went on, "So this lawyer comes over here all ready to become the law of the land, and the boys at the marina head him off before he even got off the Albright Ferry. Chance and his friends captured him and held him hostage until the Bahamas backed him off. Well, that is they never came to the lawyer's rescue is more like it, so the boys let the lawyer go after a few days. He was lucky he didn't end up in the Blue Hole. Well, that's not for sure. He might have ended up shark bait. But, anyway, he did leave some of his law books. They're at the school, if anybody wants to use them. Nobody uses them. We just download legal forms from the internet. The colonel signs them."

Coleman said, "So the end result is anybody can pretty much do whatever they want on Conch Island. Until they piss off The Elders, whoever they are. And they use the Blue Hole for everything."

Jack said, "I hereby put a first lien on Colonel Albright's estate for funerary expense. If you cops are finished with the scene, I guess I'll ask you for a couple of big ass trash bags, and let's get him loaded and to town. I think I can handle it now."

Endi couldn't help digging Jack Slack a little and said, "You're gonna have to do some kind of autopsy, Doctor Jack. Like what if the victim was poisoned, and then hammered?"

Coleman said, "I'll call Marsh Harbor and try the cops again. Maybe I can convince them that a murderer loose on Conch Island could turn into a murderer loose in Marsh Harbor."

Amanda said, "You know if it wasn't for you two clowns none of this would have happened. You're the ones who started this whole thing."

Endi said to Coleman, "See, I told you; let's forget this stupid silver shit."

Coleman said, "And the spoon made Rosie O'Donnell fat. You're the one that wants to get off the island."

Everybody glared at everybody for a while.

Endi finally broke the staring match and said, "OK you all, I've processed this scene as well as I can. Got pictures. Made the sketch. We need to check out the perimeter some more, see if we can pick up a trail through the jungle that silver on a hand truck would make. Maybe the silver is still around here like we disturbed the thief and he just had to drop it."

Coleman said, "Or thieves."

Endi said, "Or Chance and his Haitians."

Coleman said, "We need to check the colonel's house too."

Jack said, "How are we going prevent the whole world from knowing about the silver angle and the colonel?"

Amanda said, "They don't have to know. We just say we discovered the colonel dead, and a retired cop, and a retired Secret Service agent, are trying to find some authority to turn the death over to. He was in his 90's for crissake. He was supposed to be dead anyway."

Coleman said, "That's withholding evidence. The cat is out of the bag. Silver is gone and the colonel probably got in the way of who ever wanted it, although I can't figure out how anyone knew about the damn stuff in the first place. I say we keep a lid on the silver thing for as long as we can because few care about an old man, but many care about old silver. It will keep getting uglier and more complicated."

Jack Slack said, "I haven't spilled the beans."

Endi said, "I haven't, and I know Coleman and May haven't."

Amanda said, "I certainly didn't."

May said, "What about your brother?"

Amanda shook her head. "He was with us! This happened while we were out of the way, on the boat. Someone found out we were going to be gone who already knew about the silver we had found. Some sneaky lurking islanders. Or they have always known about it and decided to thin the competition."

Endi added, "Or the colonel blabbed. Served him right if he did."

They all glared at each other again.

Coleman finally said, "Someone on this island is a killer. And we have zero ideas who."

Endi asked, "Can we turn this over to The Elders?"

Amanda answered, "It's probably The Elders that killed him."

Coleman came back in ten minutes with trash bags, baggies, markers, tape, and a six-pack of Kalik, in a little cooler.

"You are not going to believe this; I got through to the police on Marsh. Some sergeant answered at the police station in Marsh Harbor said it would be tomorrow, or possibly the next day, before someone could come over to the island. The only detective they have went to Fort Lauderdale for a couple of days; the usual once a month run to Costco and Walmart. Besides the sergeant said he was sure it was just an accident and recommended that we do something with the body in the meantime; he wanted me to make sure I knew that there is no such thing as murder in the Bahamas. He actually said get ahold of Colonel Albright. I had just told him it was Colonel Albright who was dead, and that he had a ball peen hammer two inches into the top of his head. He said it clearly had to be a case of mistaken identification on my part; he had just talked to the colonel last week."

Jack Slack said, "Let's sink the colonel in the Blue Hole and be done with this. That's what the colonel would do."

Coleman added, "Whoever I was talking to finally told me to call his pastor, then hung up on me."

Endi couldn't think of anything to say. Amanda said something about getting off the island. May took off all her clothes and walked into the water until her head was under and didn't surface for several minutes, and then popped up to breathe and dunked back down again.

Endi said, "Don't worry about May. She can do this all day. Hey, this dead body is already bloating in this heat. Guess we better find a cooler." Looking at the dead colonel lying in a pool of blood he said, "Never worked a murder without EMT's, and firemen, or the body-snatchers we called them, to haul off the damn body."

Coleman said, "I think I know where we can take the colonel. Let's get this over with. It ain't gonna get easier. I hear gurgling. It'll explode if we don't get the damn thing out of this heat, and fast."

Albright Albright, watching from the jungle, was getting a hard-on, which wasn't anything new. He got one about every thirty minutes anyway. He was watching May stand up out of the water, take deep breaths, with breasts heaving.

Mano "The Shark" Kamea narrowly missed being spotted again. He had lost audio when the scene shifted to loading the colonel onto Jack's golf cart. He tried to move around to hear better but fell over a vine, knocking the wind out of him and perfectly nailing a broken rib from early in his career that every opponent knew about, and now a goddam tree apparently knew about it too, he thought to himself, through clenched teeth.

Holding his side and sweating profusely, Mano gingerly worked his way back to his compound. He discovered that he'd missed a call from his lawyer via satellite phone. He listened to his voice mail. "You stupid Hawaiian imbecile, call me pronto. What, you too busy to answer the phone? I know you're there. You better be there you fucking pineapple head."

His Italian mob lawyer didn't have much respect for the featherweight Hawaiian boxer. ("When I go to fight, I bring a gun. What good your fists do against a gun? Bring fists to a gun fight? You one stupid Hawaiian. Besides you're a little shit. We got boys three times your size… make you antipasto.")

Mano spit bitterly on the hand painted tile floor and shouted to no one, "I pay you dickheads a hundred dollars every ten minutes. That insult cost me three hundred dollars due to your goddam thirty-minute minimum."

He stripped, depositing his bloody clothes in the washing machine, and took a shower. He took Tylenol for the rib. Every breath hurt.

CHAPTER 16

Still Friday afternoon.

Coleman carefully pulled the ball peen hammer out of the colonel's skull. It made a sucking noise. That was it for Amanda. She turned creamy-grey and stumbled out. Coleman had his hands covered with baggies; no exam gloves being available of course. He put the hammer into a paper bag instead of a plastic bag so moisture would breathe out. He sealed it up with masking tape. Endi put the colonel's hands in plastic bags and used masking tape to secure the bags on the wrists; forensics might want to look under the nails. They looked for froth in his mouth, suggestive of drowning, and for evidence of choke. They put a small trash bag over his head and secured that with tape and rolled him over.

They went through his pockets. They took his shoes off to see if there was damage to his feet, like him being dragged, or from running from an assailant. His blood had begun to pool due to gravity into the lower half of his body which was turning blue, while the upper part was getting paler. They looked in his wallet for numbers, notes, anything. They concluded there was no sign of a struggle. There was nothing on his person suggestive of a clue as to why he was killed, like incriminating evidence against someone, or a title, or deed, he may have been working on. No notebook full of enemies.

Next stop his house.

They bagged him in a mattress cover from one of Coleman's beds. They managed to get him into the front seat of Jack Slack's golf cart propped between Jack and Endi, with Amanda driving her golf cart behind them. May wouldn't get out of the water. Coleman stayed at the house to do more detective work and provide at least some security and keep an eye on May.

Of course, the colonel didn't cooperate. He did a lot of flopping around, plus he was passing gas and fluid. The mattress cover wasn't a good alternative to a body bag. Fluid and fumes were escaping with every bump.

The Queen's Highway to town, or "settlement" as the natives called it, wasn't paved. Trying to drive with a dead body propped next to him, Jack Slack, having had a two more quick hits of weed for the nausea, and an extra-strength Kalik beer, was having driving issues. As the bagged colonel swayed side to side, he and Endi would push back at the body hurling curses over the golf cart's rumbling glass-packs. Endi finally pushed a little too hard, and the colonel wedged himself (probably not on purpose as he was dead) between Jack and the steering wheel, obstructing steering, and caused the jamming of Jack's foot on the accelerator.

Gaining speed, they left the Queen's Highway, rocketing over a conch shell decorative border, and a Haitian gardener. A rake, and a large palm frond, blinded Jack as the golf cart went head-to-head with a life-sized bronze alligator sculpture. The alligator ripped a front tire off the golf cart. On impact the cart's surround sound system switched on, blaring Jimmy Buffet singing, "Somewhere there's a woman to blame…"

Endi and Amanda transferred the colonel to Amanda's golf cart. They tied him on to the backward facing back seat, with a spider web of duct tape. Lots of chemistry was going on inside the now torn mattress cover. The smell could be tasted. They had to squint against the sting of its fumes. Movement of the package to Amanda's cart just stirred the stew. Amanda said she'd walk.

"What the hell we gonna do with him in town?" Endi choked, nose held closed by one hand, as he drove with the other. Jack couldn't drive because the Haitian he'd run over, once free from being pinned between the golf cart and the alligator statue, sat on Jack slapping him over and over with a flip-flop. Endi bribed the bleeding Haitian to get off Jack with a fifty. Other Haitians appeared out of nowhere ready to start a race riot. Endi found weed and pills in Jack's pocket and threw them like rice at a wedding.

The late colonel was quite a bit bigger than the original colonel by the time they got him to town. Slack was having a pity-party…lamenting, complaining, crying, and trying to hold one swollen eye open… and trying to stop the nose-bleed. Besides the concussion from the beating-by-Haitian, he was smoking part of a fatty he'd stashed in the glove box for just such an emergency.

Endi said nothing the rest of the drive; less breathing that way. He had learned not to talk when on a "suspicious odor" call. He wished he had some chewing tobacco, and Vick's Vapo Rub, to spread under his nose. The marijuana fumes were making him cough.

They stopped at the ice cream shop which had closed some time ago. Amanda hoped they could get the freezer running. (The ice cream shop had done well for a while, but the Albright who ran the Albright Ice Cream and Conch Chowder Parlor, wasn't overly fastidious. Yeasty-conchy ice cream didn't go over with tourists, although the Albrights never stopped eating it.)

Endi, Jack, and Amanda stuffed the colonel in a twenty-four-cubic-foot chest freezer, which sounds plenty big, but it actually only measured two feet front to back, four feet long, and three feet deep. It required taking him out of the mattress cover, and a lot of cramming and jamming. A large quantity of gas, solids, and liquids were released. Mercifully the freezer had started up.

Endi knew he was going to smell and taste dead-colonel for days. Besides he hadn't had this much physical activity since the academy forty years ago. He threw himself face down on the grass next to the ice cream shop. He rubbed his face in the green cool grass. He didn't quit panting for five minutes. (He had not taken a full breath for over a half an hour.) At the end of each pant, he gave a little whimper. He thought about stripping right there and burning his clothes.

Still dazed from the beating and cart wreck, Jack Slack sat on the steps of the defunct Tasty-Freeze hyperventilating and gagging, still trying to stem his nose bleed. He stood up slowly and walked to the boat ramp next to the ice cream store, and just kept walking down the ramp until he was completely under water. He had all his clothes on. Endi watched the dentist's head disappear. He saw bubbles and dimly wondered if the man was committing suicide. He dozed off.

Amanda got in her cart without saying a word, and drove to her pink bungalow, hosed off the cart, took her clothes off in front of God and everybody, threw them in the trash, went inside, grabbed a gallon of bleach, came back out and poured the whole gallon over her clothes in the trash can and the back seat of the golf cart. She emptied the hot water heater over herself in the shower. She sprayed every crack, fold, and crevice, with lilac after shower mist, and covered herself in a cloud of lilac baby powder. She sat in the kitchen completely naked and drank two Cuba-Libra's in the time it took her to smoke two Marlborough Reds. Finally, she could open her eyes the rest of the way.

Among a cacophony of hundreds of random thoughts streaming in her brain, she wondered how she was going to be able to skip out on the colonel's funeral, being "family." She thought to herself, *if you like long funerals, die on Conch Island…four hours, with 4 ministers thundering Jeeee…ZZUUUS a million times…and having to endure heat stroke and dehydration, to the point of desiccation, at the same time as having your bladder burst…and that's just the part in the church before the graveside service.*

After the internment personnel (Slack, Amanda, and Endi) had left with the colonel to the ice cream shop,

Coleman continued his investigation of the crime scene. May, had finally come out of the water and changed clothes.

He found blood on a Lignum Vitae tree. Then he found more on a Thatch Palm. He found more tire-tread tracks and determined that they were from sandals made from tire treads. He found hand truck tracks, and the hand truck. May discovered a large piece of the rock of coins buried in a shallow sand. They found most of the rest of it nearby, shallowly buried too.

They put the coins back in the tool shed. They jumped in the ocean to cool down. Then they nailed boards over the door and windows of the shed, after locking the door again.

May, after a shower, lay asleep on her back in bed with her legs spread under the ceiling fan, with Albright Albright, window-peeping on her. His question-mark-shaped penis was getting hard again. He figured what the hell; it wasn't like he had a meeting or something.

CHAPTER 17

Later Friday afternoon.

Endi tried 911. Nothing happened like Coleman said. He tried information. None. He tried the airport. Customs and immigration had gone home. Bahamas Air gave him the police department's number, no answer.

He called the U.S. Embassy in Nassau. The only law enforcement they had was a security detail for the embassy itself. "Are you calling in an official capacity? …It's a Bahamas problem. …No, I cannot put you through to the CIA. Make an appointment in person. …We can do nothing over the phone." Endi got whiney, then surly; they hung up on him.

Endi called his friend and colleague, in Portland, Oregon, Jud Justice, who was the FBI Bureau Chief for the region. It was four hours earlier there. While working as a detective with the Portland Police Bureau, Endi had rubbed shoulders with the FBI on numerous cases.

He explained the murder—who, what, why, where, when, and how—and that there was no police presence at all on the island, that the police on a neighboring island weren't doing anything because they believed that the victim couldn't be dead because there was no such thing as murder on the islands, and that they may send an officer someday, if they were sure the Colonel was dead, and not just asleep.

He explained to Jud that he, and his ex-Secret Service friend, partly in self-defense, since the colonel was found dead in Coleman's shed, and partly because there was no one else to do it, would be looking for the killer, or killers, without police resources or protection, if for no other reason than personal safety. He asked if Jud could get ahold of someone in the CIA that covered the Bahamas to protect two endangered U.S. citizens.

Jud Justice said, "One word; leave."

Endi said, "It's complicated. There are women involved. Which reminds me, can you find me a lawyer familiar with sunken treasure ownership in the Bahamas?"

"Jesus, Endi!"

Endi said, "We need arms, ammunition, communication gear, maybe some land mines." He asked, "Can you at least run a search to see if there are any known crime organizations, or known dangerous criminals, on the island, or the neighboring islands, and any criminal activity involving the Albright clan, specifically Colonel Reginald-Henry-the-eight-Albright-the-Third?"

Jud answered, "Seriously? That's his name?" Endi said yep. Jud answered, "OK, I guess, after all, England has been our enemy before. Congratulations: you are hereby deputized as a CIA deputy field agent. Agent-in-Charge, Endi of… what's the name of the island? I'll order a name-badge."

Endi said, "That's bull shit."

Jud answered, "How do you think we recruit all our double and triple agents? Craig's list? We are reaction-oriented here at the agency. Opportunists. Now the United States has got a man in the Bahamas. You. That simple. No need for an application. We'll just give you a trial run; see how you do."

"But you're FBI?"

"No problem. It's, me casa; su casa, between all us agencies since 911."

"Jesus you're in Portland, Oregon, not Portland, Maine. Aren't I just a little out of your jurisdiction?"

"OK, fine, you're an FBI agent then. A badge is in the mail. Hey, you remember Johnny Walker? I just remembered he is in Key West. Maybe I can get him to run some tackle over the Bermuda Triangle to you." Justice knew Endi and Johnny Walker had worked together for the Portland Police Department before Endi retired.

Jud continued, "You can't believe the mess he just got himself out of this time…hostages, arson, murder, torture, international jewel thieves…almost sunk a drug cartel's sailboat and got himself drowned… ended up working for the CIA, the FBI, and the Key West police. Oh, and the Sherriff of whatever county Key West is in. I'll give you our Florida Keys CIA man's private cell number. The guy's name is Jim Rand. Got a pencil?" He gave him Rand's cell phone number. He also gave him his own e-mail. "I'll see what I can find on the colonel. E-mail me, and then I'll have your email, and if I find anything, I'll send it to you… Special Agent Endi."

Endi said nothing.

Jud added, "Listen, the Bahama police ain't gonna do shit for you. Your best bet is to call Rand, talk to Johnny Walker, and beg him to sail the druggie sailboat that we gave him for just such an event, over to the Bahamas, for a nice little vacation. Get him to run guns and communications equipment. Just tell him I told you to call and that you need a satellite phone and all that. I'll back you up. In fact, I'll call him right now. I'll call Langley too and tell them we got problems in paradise. That's the best I can do."

Endi said, "Add smuggling to my resume. And don't forget about the maritime salvage lawyer. And thanks."

A half-hour later Endi called Jim Rand, the CIA's man in the Keys. Rand answered second ring. Endi introduced himself and asked if he knew where Johnny Walker was. Rand said, "All three of us are here."

Endi asked, "Who? Three?"

Rand said, "Johnny Walker is on my couch under my alligator right now. Me, him, and the alligator. You wanna talk to him?"

Endi said to himself, *he's drunk.* "Yea, let me talk to him." Endi and Johnny Walker talked a quick catch up and the highlights of Johnny's last case and why he was in Key West. Endi told Johnny he needed some supplies and that Jud Justice had suggested Johnny. He also told Johnny a little about the murder. And the absence of Police. He left out the silver.

And that's how Detective Lieutenant Johnny Walker of the Portland, Oregon, PPD (Portland Police Bureau) found himself, the next morning, sailing a drug runner's confiscated sail boat, called the *Drama Queen,* from Key West, across part of the Bermuda Triangle, to a desert island, being propelled by the same southerly winds, and the three miles per hour northerly gulf stream current that the conquistadores used centuries before to help speed the hauling of treasure from the New World to the Old. Johnny's sailboat also had treasure. It carried CIA confiscated guns and high-tech communication equipment taken from drug runners. And a lot of booze. He was happy about it. He thought that he was beating the system by not having to go back to work in rainy Portland, Oregon.

In high spirits, he kidded Rand just before he left Key West that he felt like a pirate.

Rand said, "You're a captain if you're employed by King and country. You're a pirate if you're not."

Walker answered a little stilled, "And you're not going to bail me out if something happens, are you, as in you'll deny that I am employed by you?"

"Yep."

"So, I'm a pirate?"

Rand said, "Aye matey. Thanks for volunteering to run guns and alcohol to a sovereign foreign nation. Hope the Bahama authorities don't catch you. They don't have a navy and their coast guard only has one boat and it's been run aground so many times I doubt it even works. You'll be fine."

CHAPTER 18

*Still Friday afternoon, only a little later.
(A lot happened today, didn't it? We're just getting
started. TGIF!)*

Ten minutes after the colonel had been packed in the freezer, Justice of the Peace Luna Nausea Henry VIII Albright, waddled down to the dock in her yellow with white-lilies-pattern Mumu to greet the LET'S GET MARRIED ferry. The dock was fifty feet from the derelict ice cream shop.

She poked Coleman still laying on the grass with a flip-flopped foot. She made a face and said loudly, "Shit, what died?" Coleman rolled over and said hello, then rolled back over putting his face back in the cool shaded crabgrass. She thought that was strange behavior, but figured he was probably just drunk. *Damn Americans!*

A fresh load of clientele was scheduled. Her two-hundred-pound pear-shaped body with wildebeest hips, narrow shoulders, and a watermelon shaped head, didn't stop her five-foot-three, Albright body, from jumping two feet in the air when Jack Slack's head popped out of the water right in front of her. She threw her short arms in the air, and screamed with an English accent, "Shit—piss—cocksucker—whore!!!"

Just then they heard music, singing, and shouting, as the Albright LET'S GET MARRIED ferry rounded the corner of the island and entered the small harbor. Bongo drums, a trumpet, and guitar, could be heard above the singing and merry making. The old ferry was covered with faded fake flowers in every shade of pastel, and a huge sign across her bow that said, LET'S GET MARRIED.

Hearing the commotion Coleman got up on all fours, finally stood, and walked toward the dock. Jack had come out of the water the rest of the way and stood facing Luna, who was wagging a finger inch in his face. He had taken his pants and shirt off in the water and had left them in there. He stood there with no expression on his face, taking the verbal whipping from Luna in Albright Pigeon-English. He was wearing just a yellow thong. You could see his man-brains, and pubes. Coleman assumed Luna was taking issue with Slack's public indecency (especially with a wedding party docking). Coleman thought this is a hell of a time to have to tell her that her boss is dead via ball peen hammer.

The wedding party was from Key West. They had flown to the liquor store island where the ferry picked them up. Luna and the colonel had created a profitable niche for themselves by performing gay matrimony ceremonies. The colonel handled the paperwork including license, permit, and so forth, and Luna, Justice of the Peace, did the marriage service, right out of the Anglican Book of Common Prayer.

Thinking Luna should know about the dead colonel before the wedding party set foot on the island, Coleman told her. Luna promptly fainted. Coleman tried to stop her fall but was exhausted from the colonel's lifeless-body's hauling, and instead, steered her toward Jack, who didn't pick up the baton, and instead, fell back into the water with her on top of him. She was a natural floater with all the fat tissue. Jack hung onto her, rolling her like a log, as he grappled for something to grip onto, which was finally her large breasts, one of which had floated out of her thin loose Mumu.

She was wide awake within seconds from the full immersion baptism and the breast grappling and ended up straddling Jack's neck with thighs the size of whole hams, and both hands wound in his hair. She was screaming the shit-piss-cocksucker-whore thing again. Luna was afraid of water (most Albrights can't swim and only wade and sit in the shallows on hot days) so switched her grappling thighs and hands from Jack to Coleman as he waded in to help. All three went down.

As the ferry reversed its engine for docking, Coleman, Jack, and Luna were sitting shoulder to shoulder, on the slanted concrete boat ramp, in water up to their waist, like the proverbial three monkeys. Coleman was wiggling fingers in both ears trying to extract sea water, Jack Slack was rubbing his eyes, and Luna covered her mouth with her hands, embarrassed at having just screamed another outburst of potty words.

The captain of the Albright Ferry hooted the horn at the three, shut his engine down, and men in brightly colored Speedo's, began jumping gaily off the sides of the boat into the shallow water, all holding bottles of beer. Soon there were ten people sitting shoulder to shoulder with Coleman, Jack, and Luna, with the bottom halves of their bodies in the warm, clear, water, laughing and playfully splashing each other, thinking this is apparently what one does in the Bahamas. A beer cooler magically materialized, and Jack and Coleman, knowing they deserved a chilled Kalik Extra Strength, helped themselves. Luna had never had a drink in her life but was considering it.

Jack Slack, the quintessential opportunistic entrepreneur, rallied, and assumed command, broadcasting to all that he was Minister of Health and Welfare, and introduced himself as the one who would be signing the legal paperwork, as the colonel was indisposed. He also offered 20% off any dentistry that any of the wedding party might need prior to the wedding to make their smiles better for the wedding pictures. The office was open.

Coleman stayed in the water with a cold long neck in each hand.

Jack Slack, newly gay as he blamed women for everything, decided this group was an excellent way to test his new orientation, a veritable smorgasbord. One of the "hors d'oeuvres" had already made eye contact with Jack, after perching his rose-colored lens, gilded-and-sequined, dark glasses on his thick bleached and streaked honey colored hair, revealing very blue eyes thanks to colored contact lenses. He introduced himself as "Touch Me Not." Touch squeezed his own balls twice and said, "I make exceptions. If you whisper in my ear something singular, I will let you touch something special." Slack was having second thoughts.

When the marriage party found out that Luna Albright was the Justice of the Peace, they made a human chair and carried her up the short hill to her house so she could change clothes. She could barely stand up, still shocked by the news of the colonel's demise.

After changing her dress, blow drying her cropped hair, combing her unibrow, parting it in the middle, shaving her moustache, and dousing herself with Old Spice, Luna went back to the wedding party and took them to their accommodations. Luna and the colonel had an old paddlewheel ferry boat shipped from the mainland and turned it into a permanently moored party barge and sleeping accommodations for their same-sex wedding enterprise. Neal, the only gay Albright, did the catering. He had already provided the revelers with canapés and fresh fruit.

Coleman had a couple more beers and finally pulled himself out of the water realizing he was on an island with a murderer and had to somehow get back to his house without getting killed. He grabbed one more Kalik and headed down the Queen's Highway.

That evening, Conch Key transformed itself from drama to comedy, the way most Caribbean islands do around cocktail hour (don't worry…be happy). The sunset was turning the color of a well-built tequila sunrise. Coleman poured purple Crème de Cassis carefully down one side of a tall glass of ice with tequila and orange juice, then poured red grenadine syrup down the other side—the swirling concoction looking like a sunrise—a "Tequila Sunrise."

Coleman and Endi were on their second, sitting with backs against a shared post on Coleman's veranda facing west, watching the sun go down. May had taken a Demerol (a la Dr. Jack Slack) and wheezed naked in the rope hammock next to them.

Albright Albright polished hooked erections from his vantage point hidden in the sea grapes. He didn't often have girls from the mainland accommodate him with near constant nudity. He aimed to take advantage of the windfall. He had his bar of silver strung around his neck and his pith helmet on. Nothing else.

They could hear the gayety (pun intended) in town.

Mano, alone in his compound, also heard the party, and was trying to enjoy his vodka, and pineapple juice, but he was too angry about everything to enjoy anything.

The colonel was assuming freezer temperature.

CHAPTER 19

*Flashback to Friday afternoon, and how
the colonel got killed.*

The *ONE*, Mano Kamea, (Shark/Passionate Lover/The
One and Only) tried to relax as the Demerol interceded
between the brain and the pain receptors surrounding
his damaged rib. The fall over the big root in the jungle
had been like being stabbed. "Everybody knows about
my fucking broken rib; even the roots in the jungle." If it
was another fighter that had purposely jabbed him there,
he at least he could beat the shit out of him. He had to
admit it would be senseless to beat the shit out of a tree.
Still, he was considering going back into the jungle, and
see if trees could be made to shit.

Mano had been addicted to pain meds since his teens.
Boxing causes pain. TBP—Total-Body-Pain. Pain killers
were not the only drugs. His trainers were believers in
stacks—*stacks* of anabolic steroids. The Asian Stack and
the Australian Stack. It involved the use of more than one
type of anabolic steroid at the same time. Mano didn't
know what he was taking, he just took them. Whatever

his trainer gave him. He remembered some of the names: Anadrol, Anadur, Anavar, Aratest…and those were just the A's. They went all the way to the W's…Winstrol. Those were the anabolic steroids. There was another alphabet ending in Xanax. He was coming off all of them now in his forced isolation. He was like the addicts coming down off drugs in the New Orleans' coliseum during Katrina, their stashes swept away by God's giant toilet flushing. Alcohol was pretty much his only drug now. And Demerol.

Of course, the brilliant wizardry of that early trainer was part of the reason Mano could beat the shit out of his opponents. Without that edge, he would have drowned in the shallow end of the fighter pool, with all the rest of the dancing, fist waving, and mat stomping, wannabe ring fighters.

His lawyers assured him that he had a chance in court of beating the murder wrap if he could somehow transpose his obvious guilt into an insanity plea… caused by "roid-rage," thus blaming his behavior on a side effect of anabolic steroids. And, that it wasn't even his fault that he took the growth hormones and steroids—it was his trainers' fault because they made him take them. So, his wife's death wasn't his fault because he was insane. The game plan was to turn his trainer, doctors, and suppliers, who had forced the performance and body building drugs on him, into the criminals. Little poor Mano, the "pawn." Besides it was *justifiable homicide* Mano reminded his lawyers; she was a bitch. And the lawyers would counter with we told you not to marry a plasticized drug riddled red-headed alcoholic hooker named Tiffany. (He had learned the hard way what all males learn eventually; to be wary of red heads. And women named Tiffany.)

He was diagnosed by a friendly psychiatrist, and prospective expert witness, as being left by these evil manipulators with extreme uncontrollable aggression, or "hypomania." The "expert" shrink blamed the anabolic steroids for causing Mano's mania, and overexcitement, part of a bipolar manic-depressive cycle. The psychiatrist explained that "poor little Mano" was just a cork on the storm-torn ocean of testosterone and roids that caused his aggressiveness and increased sexual desire, resulting in violence spilling over outside the gym and ring. The confusion and sleep disorders required yet more drugs, which also took their toll. Pathological anxiety, paranoia, and the hallucinations required even others. Poor little Mano. He was not responsible for his actions. It certainly wasn't even premeditated. He was simply "out of his mind," all of which was true. That is if he did it, as he continued to swear he was on his boat with his girlfriend, his alibi.

Now Mano was in drug withdrawal. His handlers knew it wasn't going to be pretty—another reason for parking him in a walled asylum on a desert island. They figured he could just bang off the walls all he wanted there during detox and not bother anybody. They didn't know he was window peeping all over the island and thinning the population by killing colonels. He was not like Richard Nixon (he behaved) whose handlers had squirreled him away for a short time in the very same compound Mano was in in the 70's during Watergate.

A doctor "managing" Mano's detox program came to the island twice a month. Mano was the poster child of depression, idealization of suicide, drastic mood changes, and the suffering of acute psychosis. He also was sure his testicles had shrunk due to the steroids. And he was damn unhappy about it. The doctor refused to come to the island, no matter what the fee, without a bodyguard.

In reality Mano was handling his own addiction recovery program, and it wasn't going well. His concept of the workings of a body was rudimentary. He imagined that there was a revolving star right in the middle; food went down one hole and made muscle and shit; booze went down a second hole to take away brain feelings; and pills went down another hole and fixed what needed fixing pretty much based on the size, color, and quantities of the pills. He didn't think it really mattered what he took as long as he took plenty of everything; the body would sort it out.

He was also struggling with acne and seborrhea all over his back, a side effect of steroid use. He was furious about his hair loss. His full head of black hair that had hung halfway down his back, had been one of his hallmark features in the ring. Now he was bald in the front half, and he couldn't keep the comb-over in place on this sweaty island without hairspray and hair gel which his thoughtless handlers never seemed to remember to bring. The doctor established that the skin disease and hair loss was caused by the roids. Mano so wanted to beat his trainers' bowels open. But they had taken their percent of the Mano-money-machine when they knew the run was finished and scattered like roaches when the light comes on.

Mano felt a sort of euphoria and pain relief flooding through his body as the narcotic trickled and seeped into his remains.

He'd returned his lawyer's call on the satellite phone. The lawyer told him the doctor was coming today, flying from Ft. Lauderdale to Marsh Harbor, then taking a private boat, with the bodyguard and a new prostitute, and supplies. The lawyer said the boat would come back for them the next day. The lawyer added scornfully, "Mano, you little prick, you better not do to this woman what you did to the last one. This will be the last one I send if you do that shit again. You understand? God, I never thought I'd be running an escort service."

(The lawyer should have vetted the Arian-perfect-human-specimen-blond-male-Adonis—the Greek god of beauty and desire—and found that this "Adonis" bodyguard was, of course, gay, and therefore would be distracted by thirty gay guys, at a gay wedding, but then the attorney, half-way around the world in Hawaii, didn't know about the gay wedding, did he?)

Mano bristled at the lawyer's demands. But he knew he had to control himself. He admitted he shouldn't have squeezed the carotids so long on the last whore. He said, "You just get me out of here before I cut you off the gravy train. I will fire you if you don't do right by me. Or worse. Don't think I won't."

"Mano, you think you can pull strings from where you are? You think you scare me? You are completely at my mercy you pineapple rat. One call and you are back here in jail, and you and I can visit through glass. I'm doing you the biggest favor of your life trying to get you off this murder wrap. Everyone knows you killed your wife. I don't care. Your trial is coming, and you better be all done with your damn roid-rage, and whatever else drives you homicidal, by then. I am going to be in contempt of court if I don't produce you soon. I am fighting for a change in venue. The great stall—the first thing they teach you in law school—is all I'm doing. You cannot get a fair trial anywhere in Hawaii. We both know that. Buying time, that's all I'm doing. Time that you would be in jail, not screwing whores in paradise. You would be cold turkey too in jail; not having anyone to hold your hand and say, there-there little Mano. The longer you are out of the news, the more time sentiment against you will ameliorate. Everybody in Hawaii is looking forward to another O.J. media-circus trial, but with time the mood is waning. So, you watch yourself, keep your head low, a low profile, no one must see you, and don't hurt the bitch I'm sending you, and you might come out of this without the death sentence. I'm paying her for discretion, not disfigurement."

Mano grunted into the phone angrily. "Go to hell." He didn't know what the words ameliorate or waning meant, but he didn't like them.

The attorney answered, "Hell would be a nice reprieve from dealing with your sorry ass. The best thing I could do for myself right now is walk away from your case before I get in trouble myself. You do one thing to piss me off, and I'm gone. I'll throw your ass to the hyenas." Mano heard a click. The lawyer had disconnected.

Mano mumbled, "First thing you do is kill all the lawyers." He didn't know he had just quoted Shakespeare.

Deep in his arrogant psyche, Mano just knew he was going to survive, and in style. Mano always lands-on-his-feet! This time he would land his feet somewhere in South America where he could live like he was entitled to. After taking beatings his whole life, he had earned the good life in retirement. And he had been given the way to do it. Pirate treasure! Silver!

He had been spying on the colonel and was convinced that the old man had a pile of silver somewhere on his property. He also knew that the colonel had a silver purifying process in a shed on his property. It was locked and he didn't want to risk breaking the door in making a ruckus. When the time came, he would just burn it down if he had to. (Silver doesn't burn? Does it?)

The colonel, when talking to the guy named Endi, and his hot girlfriend, in Coleman's shed, made it sound like there was silver all over the island. And that there was a big hunk of silver coins in the shed just ready for the taking. And in a museum somewhere too.

Mano, full of drug and alcohol induced courage and bravado, decided to slip out of his compound and head to Coleman's shed where silver coins were just waiting for him to grab up. Get them while the getting was good. (Hold my beer.)

The colonel happened to be in the way. Rage. Dead colonel. Took the coins first, instead of the getting rid of the dead colonel first. (Dammit. I'm an idiot.)

He forgot to ask the colonel where he kept the silver

before he killed him. That was typical Mano he thought; kill the guy, and then ask him questions. (I should of hit myself with the hammer.)

Never one for long self-flagellation, he quickly decided that all would be fine because Endi and Coleman, and the girls, were on the scent of all the silver on the island, so they would find the colonel's stash, and all the rest of the silver all over the island, and then he would steal a boat, and sail away. They were even going to bring up the silver from the shipwreck.

When the time came, everyone would get out of his way, one way or another. He'd burn the whole island down if he had to. The island uses silver blocks everywhere! I'm gonna be rich! (Hello Argentina!)

CHAPTER 20

Late Friday afternoon, after putting the colonel in the freezer.

Coleman and Endi headed for the colonel's house from Coleman's house, walking down the Queen's Highway. The "highway" was only about eight feet wide. Coleman hadn't been to the colonel's house for years. Hedges and jungle made it impossible to see many of the houses along the road. In many places, the road was covered by overhanging trees giving it a tunnel feel.

Endi asked, "How you want to work this? You been there."

Coleman answered, "His house is configured in the usual island set up. Sliding door on the ocean side; a Dutch door on the road side, veranda all the way around. You come from the ocean side through the sliding door; I'll come from the road side. Everything is probably unlocked. The colonel I assume planned on returning home, and not getting killed. I think there is a path you can take to the ocean side here somewhere soon. We got all the usual stuff to worry about. Maybe disturb an intruder; maybe get ambushed—like maybe somebody's waiting for us.

Whoever killed the colonel probably wouldn't hesitate to kill us too. Let's clear the house first, and then search it thoroughly after that."

Endi said, "Ring the doorbell, and yell 'police,' then kick the door in…or stealth around?"

Coleman answered, "Stealth around. If the perp is there, maybe we can sneak up on him, and with the element of surprise might have a chance to catch him, or her, or them. Let's watch for a few minutes and see if there is any activity in the house before we go in. There shouldn't be, he lived alone."

Endi said, "I hope it's not 'them' as in…multiples perps. We need a password, so I don't shoot you. Ideas?"

Coleman answered, "Colon; Cleansing."

Endi said grinning, "OK." That was the last they talked. They knew how to conduct a search as a team silently until the structure, whatever it was…house, apartment, business, warehouse…was clear. They came to the trail off the Queen's Highway to the ocean side and Endi wordlessly disappeared into the overgrowth.

Coleman had forgotten about the colonel's shed halfway up the slight hill between the main house and the Queen's Highway. He had to check it out, and fast, or Endi would be in the main house before him… alone. The path to the shed off the main path was almost overgrown.

As he approached the shed, he smelled a metallic burned sulfur odor. The building measured about twenty-by-twenty feet. All the windows were shuttered and secured with locks on them. He noticed a stainless-steel chimney going up the side a good ten feet above the pyramidal roof and struck him as very unusual. The door to the structure was locked in two places. Also, unusual for the island.

It didn't take long for him to find the keys; they were hanging on a rusty nail in a palm tree he easily spotted.

Coleman slid the key into lock one and it turned. He got the same results with the second lock and slowly swung the door open. He assumed no one was locked in there, only locked out, so he wasn't worried about being surprised by someone inside. He took three steps in.

He was noiselessly knocked unconscious and faceplanted on the floor by a black bowling ball suspended by a sail rigging cable that swung into the back of his head. He had tripped a booby trap. He lay motionless, bleeding from his mouth and nose due to face-plant. He hadn't made a sound, other than the thump like a bag of cement, or a watermelon, makes when dropped from six feet.

Minutes later Endi entered the ocean side of the house. It was unlocked as expected. He slowly swung the door open into the house. There was very little light. The storm shutters were closed. Just cracks of light filtered through them. And the light from behind him was blocked by his silhouette, or he might have seen it coming. He felt a little tug that wasn't supposed to be there on his bare shin. A trip wire he thought? A one-pound coffee can filled with cement suspended by an eye bolt embedded in it, and attached to a thin rope, swung from the ceiling, and struck him right between the eyes. Stars, white lights, a single bleat like a separated sheep, then blackness.

They regained consciousness at about the same time, neither knowing the other had been similarly hurt or how much time had passed.

Coleman tasted blood in his mouth and ran his tongue over his teeth to check if they were there. He rolled over on his back not being able to stifle a cry. He thought he must have been clubbed. He saw the bowling ball dangling above his head. It took him a few minutes to focus and think.

"That looks like a bowling ball," he whispered to himself incredulously. His next thought was *I'm right under it.* His addled brain processed the fact that that was what had hit him on the back of the head. He watched it fascinated. It was spinning a little, first to the left, then the right. It was pink. He'd never seen a bowling ball hanging from the ceiling. He thought he should move in case it dropped but the command to move was ignored by his body.

He felt the back of his head. Another goose egg. A matched set; front and back. He giggled.

He rolled his head to the left and saw something that woke him up another notch. Then he looked right. He smiled. He got it. He knew the whole story then. He slid his body over a foot from where he was, so he wasn't under the bowling ball anymore, and then passed out again, his rattled brain hoping to re-boot. This wasn't its first rodeo.

Endi, lying on the floor of the big house, felt the aromatic supple ocean breeze from the open-door drift over his body. He was laying spread eagle in the entry area on his back. He felt at utter peace, torpidly aware that all around him was colored differently than it should be for some reason. The colorful shooting stars whirling around his peripheral vision shouldn't be there, but they were fun. He wiggled his toes in his flip flops. He wiggled his fingers. He was pleased they worked. He was confused about everything, but it was kind of funny. Suddenly his head screamed in agony as if the pain-door had been abruptly opened. He remembered the blow to the forehead. He focused on the still swinging coffee can above him and put two and two together. He wondered how long he had been out. He wondered about Coleman.

He sat up slowly, the peace gone. He felt like he better get ready to fight, maybe for his life. He patted his side and felt the revolver. It was still there. He pulled the gun. He checked it. It was still loaded. He listened. All he heard was the ocean. It began to sink in that he had been cold cocked by a booby trap, not assailed by an attacker. He put the gun back in the holster.

Endi wondered what the reason was the colonel had for this booby trap? What's he got to protect?

He heard from outside the house "COLON." He answered, "CLOGGING!" They exchanged stories quickly.

Clearing the house, they discovered another booby trap over the other entry door on the road side of the main house. And others at two other doors; one into the master bedroom, and another into a laundry area both having doors to the outside.

Coleman led Indy to the shed and said, "Looks like the guy beat us to the punch. He's been processing the big black blocks."

There were brown ceramic crucibles that were round on the bottom like a drinking glass, but on top, their openings were triangular. There were different sizes. Some had small crustaceans on them. They looked like they had been in the ocean…maybe had come from the wreck. The colonel had propped the two biggest ones, that were about the size of a two-pound coffee cans, on stands that looked like they came from a chemistry lab, each with a burner under it. There were maybe a dozen large tanks of acetylene and oxygen chained to the walls. And a bank of ten microwaves.

There were firebricks lining the bottom of each microwave. There was heavy electrical wiring leading from the microwaves through the wall of the back of the shed. They discovered a big diesel generator behind the building. Power for all the microwaves they assumed.

Indy said, "The colonel has a smelter going here. That's what the smell is. I don't know how all this works, but the guy was processing the big black rocks. Look…" he said, stooping down to the floor with a grunt. He pointed toward a big black rock that had been chipped on and was half gone. The large chips were obviously being further processed as there was a small hammer mill with a pile of what he assumed was granulated big black rock. "Looks like the colonel pounds them into almost a powder and then cooks them in these things that look like some kind of crucible, or somehow uses the microwaves."

Coleman spotted a notebook and flipped through it. He said, "Listen to this." He read in the colonel's perfect handwriting: *"Found another way to process the rock today. I found that a silicon carbide sharpening stone is a microwave susceptor. It absorbs microwaves and turns them into heat just like food, but the silicon carbide can withstand much higher temperatures than my fish sandwich. I found if I put pulverized black rock, the same size as I had been melting in the crucibles, almost a powder, in a stainless-steel measuring cup, and that measuring cup in a microwave-safe covered casserole dish, and put the whole thing on the silicon carbide sharpening stone, the carbide turns red hot in the microwave and the pulverized rock melts. It even works better if I fit bricks around the casserole dish. After the silver melts, I pour it into a cast iron fritter mold for cooking fritters and cornbread. Each silver fritter weighs about a pound.*

Endi exhaled, "Wow. The colonel has known about the big black rocks all along. He must have freaked out when he saw us hauling them out of the water."

Coleman said, "He couldn't stay away. He had to see what we were up to. He must have peed down both legs when he saw you polishing those coins. Where is the silver he has processed already? It's got to be here somewhere. Holy shit, who knows how much he's got? Did he just get started, or has he been doing it for years? Or does he unload it as fast as he makes it."

Coleman asked, "And who killed him, and is the silver why he got killed, and does the killer have all of his silver now?"

Endi said, "If the colonel has a large stockpile of these silver bars, I doubt they have been moved. They are somewhere close probably, but well hidden."

Coleman answered, "If we don't find the colonel's silver, and word of this gets out, the whole island is going to be torn up and burned down by all manner of folks looking for his treasure trove, and big black rocks. And not necessarily by Albrights either. By treasure hunters."

Endi answered, "Like us?"

"Right." Coleman started reading out loud again. "*The makeup of the black ballast rocks varies considerably. Some can be melted back into a relatively pure form of silver.*

Others apparently are composed of coins that have already been struck, but have congealed during their centuries long saltwater bath. Those can also be simply melted, and the oxides burned off. But the real puzzle is the ones that are some sort of partially processed ore. They are problematic. They also comprise the largest number on the island, and at the wreck.

These must be smelted. The process I have devised uses a cupellation furnace, one of which I have made with rocks and concrete and is deep in the jungle. It is covered by brush and tree trimmings, which I burn, the smoke being a diversion, whenever I run the furnace. I always run it after midnight and before dawn."

Coleman injected, "It's almost as if the colonel wanted us to read this. Like this is his legacy, this notebook."

Endi went on reading: "*My process works well but is time consuming. If one could eventually build a decent sized version for large scale smelting, he would be rich. However, the industrialization of the island cannot be allowed, as it would most probably lead to denuding the island for fuel, its total decimation by treasure hunters, and finally the eventual abandoning of the processing plant after all the ballast is processed, with the resulting being that the value of all property would be deeply depressed, if not valueless. Not to mention the inevitable fight concerning ownership of the silver in the first place. It would be Armageddon.*"

"*Certainly, our succession from the Bahamas was paramount as a beginning. We undoubtedly don't want government getting wind of this. We shall see what we shall see about that.*"

Coleman looked at Endi and said, "Maybe that's what the revolution was really all about? Keeping government from confiscating it all. And not just the Bahamian government."

Coleman kept reading, giving Endi the highlights as he went: *My process is this:*

- *The furnace's firing chamber is lined with a layer of fine ash from burned vegetation. It is made into a paste with vinegar and water and tamped down with a mortar to produce a smooth concave surface. Pieces of lead from salvaged marine batteries are arranged on the floor of the furnace. The lead is then heated with oxygen and acetylene until it is a molten bath.*

- *After the lead is molten, large spoonsful of ground silver ore from the big blocks (the pieces should be no larger than sand. I have acquired a hammer mill for the purpose), are then added on top of the lead bath. When all the lead has either evaporated, or been absorbed by the ash lining, the puddle of resulting pure silver that remains can be lifted out with a hook and plunged into water. Lead is added and the process repeated.*

- *Acetylene so far is the preferred fuel and is delivered as needed although a hotter energy source would be welcomed. So far, my acetylene usage has not raised eyebrows as I have secured a source delivered directly from the U.S. that asks no questions in return for pure silver.*

Coleman continued reading silently, scanning the document quickly. "Apparently, that is for one kind of ore. There are others. Each one has its own process. The big black rocks are concentrated ores of different types." He read: *Silver bearing ore is crushed and ground. All contain sulfides and are amenable to flotation separation resulting in a 30-40% increase in minerals in the form of lead, copper, and zinc concentrates. These "concentrates" are what many of the big black rocks consist of.*

He scanned and then read on: *From copper concentrates; a copper sulfide" blister" contains 97 to 99 percent silver. Some of our blocks that made up the wreck's ballast are the slime from the electrolytic refining of copper and contain only 20 percent silver and must be smelted in a furnace to oxidize all metals except silver, gold, and platinum of which silver is more than 95 percent of what is left. Processing of this kind, on this island, is impossible as the only known reasonable approach to that business would be electro refining...*

Endi made the football "time-out" signal with both hands. He said, "OK, I get it. Only some of the blocks have even a remote chance of us being able to process. If it was so easy, someone would have figured it out years ago. Most of those blocks are worthless. Someone did figure it out years ago"

Coleman said, "Yea, but a lot aren't. A lot of blocks are almost all silver. And then there are the congealed coins blocks that are all silver. All we have to do is melt those. Or do some kind of electrolysis cleaning in acid or something. The colonel's been doing it."

Endi said, "Think of the work to even figure out which blocks are which? Maybe he's found them all that melt easy. He probably knew about the ones under your dock. They're all over the island—maybe other islands too. I bet he has, OK *had,* cataloged every one of them, and maybe even knows which type each are."

Coleman said, "And the colonel got killed for all this. And we are hot on the trail like a couple of idiots. We're lucky we haven't gotten our throats cut. I can't believe he was doing this under everybody's noses for probably years. If someone had discovered it the island would have become a strip mine."

Endi answered, "I still say we get the hell out of here. Sell out Coleman, let's find another desert island. You ought to see the back of your head. You look like something is ready to hatch out of it."

Coleman quoted, "Those as hunts treasure have to leave a little blood behind them." He added, "Come on Endi. Too soon to quit. By the way, you're getting twin black eyes."

Endi answered with a quote, "Nor has any civilization sustained beauty without returning it to the earth. Put the silver back in the ground."

"Shh…what's that?" Coleman asked, holding a finger to his lips, looking around, suddenly at the alert.

"What you mean, 'what's that?'" Endi answered whispering too, looking around alarmed.

"You don't hear that?" Coleman said again.

"Hear what?"

"It sounds like drums. Like drums, and horns. Like musical instruments maybe." Coleman headed toward the path to the road. His hand on his gun.

"Wha…the…fu… It sounds like it's coming this way." Endi said, following Coleman.

They walked down the colonel's driveway to the Queen's Highway. They heard whatever it was getting nearer and nearer, and then they saw the first wave of what was known later as the "First Anal Gay Parade and Magistrate Inauguration" on Conch Island.

CHAPTER 21

Coleman and Endi just stood there, mouths open and not sure they should be even be watching. They recognized the wedding party from the ferry.

The music cut through their respective head injuries. Each drum roll echoed around in their brittle skulls. Each screech, a dull saw across their frontal lobes. Each trumpet note a car crash between the eyes. Coleman said, "Who the hell is that being carried in a chair?"

The ones not blowing horns were shouting, "Long live the magistrate…The magistrate is dead."

"Is that Jack Slack in the chair?" Endi answered.

Leading the parade was a man in a fluorescent lime-green Speedo and sunglasses to match and a lot of piercings; jewelry, rivets, hoops, chains, studs, bells, bones…and of course tattoos. He pranced toward Endi and Coleman like a drum major. His hair was green as were the pubes peeking out above the Speedo that joined a swath of green hair going clear up his large belly and chest.

Endi muttered, "That is the nastiest thing I have ever seen in my life."

Green Speedo pirouetted, salsa danced, and shimmied toward Endi and Coleman grabbing Coleman's hand trying to drag him along. "Hey handsome; my name is Loddie… Loddie-Da." He kissed Coleman on the cheek with a loud smack, right below the ear. It sounded like a dropped chandelier to Coleman's inflamed brain. When Loddie was that close, and Coleman looked down, he couldn't see the Speedo's anymore for the pot belly hanging in the way.

Coleman recoiled instinctively snatching his hand away. Loddie pouted a lower lip betrayed by eyes filled with conviviality and then a wink, and yelled over the drums and horns, "I'm not done with you, *gorgeous*," and then high stepped away, pumping a pink parasol up and down like a baton. He looked over his shoulder and blew a lascivious kiss at Coleman.

Coleman was thinking *alcohol hand sanitizer*.

Endi said, "I think when a gay guy is eighteen, they must issue him one Speedo. That is the only one he gets for life."

Coleman said, "He can't see it anyway for the gut hanging over it."

Behind Loddie, in the middle of the long line of prancing and laughing noisemakers, was Dr. Jack Slack perched on an aluminum lawn chair resting on four boat oars. Eight men in Speedos were carrying him. He was beaming. He had a feathered tiara on, and flashed Endi and Coleman his perfect-teeth smile. He shouted at the two of them, "The Justice of the Peace said we had to have a Magistrate, so she anointed me. Just got sworn in." He leaned over too far, and the throne bearers almost lost him. Recovering, he completed an expansive wave, and looked majestically into the jungle from side to side, as if he were greeting adoring subjects lining the streets. "You coming to the wedding?" he yelled and was gone, blowing kisses to his imaginary subjects, and doing Queen Elizabeth parade waves.

A man in a red sequined evening dress drove a decorated golf-cart filled with coolers. Endi darted at it and extracted two Kalik beers with speed that even surprised him, considering the head injury. He handed one to Coleman. He drank almost half of his then turned and yelled toward the parade, "Anyone got any Tylenol?" No one broke ranks.

Endi said, "Just where do you think they would be carrying Tylenol?"

Coleman watched another cross-dressed male strut by in a red, white, and blue sequined cocktail dress split up the side to the hips, wearing high heels, a Marylyn Monroe wig, and inch long eyelashes. Coleman murmured to himself, "Queen on the Queen's Highway." The man shouted, "We're headed to the end of the island for a party at the picnic beach there. Join the parade. Come on."

The parade left Coleman and Endi sitting on a big black rock paralyzed in the silence. They finished their beers and found aspirin in the colonel's house.

The parade passed the compound where Mano was hiding. He peered at the procession through a crack in the wall. He whispered to himself as he saw Slack pass, "I gotta get off this fucking island."

At the island's little bayside park, there was dancing, skinny dipping, massage therapy, yoga lessons, and a Twister game. The only gay Albright, Neal, had sent a boat to the picnic area with conch fritters, conch dip, and an assortment of other freshly made dips, an extensive collection of cheeses, crackers, pita, fresh fruit, and sliced vegetables. He also delivered another huge cooler with a great selection of cold alcoholic beverages.

At dusk, Jack Slack, in his lawn chair (this time with twelve completely shit-faced bearers stumbling under his weight) slowly went by Mano's compound on the way back to the wharf. Slack could see over the compound's six-foot concrete block wall and hedge. He thought he saw somebody by the pool—getting a blow job. He thought to himself, *the place is supposed to be empty. Mr. Jefferson died.* Then he thought, *as Magistrate, I must drop by and introduce myself, and offer my services to the new residents. Maybe they need something signed. Maybe I need to chase them out of there.* He forgot all about the vision as he was tossed into the jungle by the throne bearers several seconds later. His bearers had given up. It took him a while to find his Tierra and he had to hustle to catch up. (He hadn't spilled his long neck.)

Every non-Albright, including Chance and his whole dockworker gang, got wasted that night along with the wedding party. Mano's doctor and his bodyguard were not surprised when their boat driver told them that the boat wouldn't start.

The doctor worked the crowd diagnosing venereal diseases (they all had Molluscum contagiosum), and a few insect infestations (crabs—they had mange shampoo at the Albright Grocery), various rashes, anal tears, etc. He handed out all the erectile enhancement drugs that he had brought for Mano and in return ended up with three bottles of Cuban rum, a twenty-four pack of Coke, a bag of ice, and a ham. And enough money to rent a snore box that was on the furthest southern tip of the island. He drank rum and Coke and medicated himself with Mano's narcotics into a near vegetative state through Friday night, all day Saturday, and into Sunday. It was the best seventy-two hours he'd had since he started college eleven years ago. He vowed to do it every six or eight months thereafter.

The doctor's Adonis bodyguard had gone "over the wall" and joined the gay parade.

The colonel was almost frozen solid when they got him out of the ice cream freezer for the speeches during the Friday night wedding rehearsal dinner. He ended up falling into the bay when no one was looking and went out with the tide. No one missed him. He ended up having quite a little adventure. More on that later.

The Albrights shut themselves in their homes praying for a serious smiting from the Lord. The Elders declared that the gay and lesbian marriages had gotten out of hand, not to mention they were blasphemies, however lucrative they were to the economy, and that they had to stop. That was typical of The Elders; even though the entire economy of the island was derived from foreigners and tourists, they did their best to obstruct anything that made that industry robust (including the absence of liquor stores).[5]

So much for Friday. Whew!

---

5 A popular country music star landed on Conch Island who was following everybody's dream of finding an undiscovered island in the Caribbean. He was ready to buy the entire north end. He decided after a conch salad and Albright pigeon peas and rice served by mustached large headed woman shaped like a pear, that his sexy love songs that had made him famous, would be hard enough to sing even now, after just one night on the island with the Albright women, much less if he lived there. No developer by the way has ever made a go of it on Conch Island. That's why the country music star was there. The whole north end had been developed, but without a casino, or at least a disco, much less a liquor store and bar, so no one came, so the property was being offered at a fire sale liquidation price. The country music singer never returned.

CHAPTER 22

Saturday night after the wedding.

Mano heard the music and laughter from the settlement's dock area from his compound. The island wrapped partway around the bay, so his sanctuary was only three or four hundred yards across the shallow bay from the festivities. He loved a good party. He was pissed that he was missing it. He couldn't sleep. He'd been careful with the whore, so wasn't very satisfied. The doctor went to the party and left him sleeping pills, but he didn't want to take them. He wanted to go to the damn party. He was restless. He was lonely. He wanted to flirt and dance, and pick up a tall skinny mean black nasty woman. The whore wanted to go too.

About one-thirty in the morning he couldn't take it any longer and snuck through the jungle to town. He watched for a while and was about to leave, realizing it was a weirdo-gay wedding, but the schoolteacher (Amanda) entered from stage-left riding a golf cart driven by some guy grinning a mouth full of incredibly white teen wearing nothing but a feathered tiara. The golf cart had a built-in light show, and was blaring Billy Idol's *White Wedding* from its heavily amped up sound system. The schoolteacher was wearing a pink Little Bo-Peep dress, and turquoise cowboy boots. Mano was thinking he'd give a gold-plated championship belt to see what she was wearing under it. He didn't have to.

The customized golf cart's sound system switched to Bolero. She danced the Flamenco on the picnic table and was down to thong, thigh-highs, cowboy boots, and starfish pasties. Those fell off quickly due to the heel stomping dance.

Mano went back to the compound for a quickie with the whore.

He tied the whore up a little too tight. She was pissed and fought him. That turned him on. She complained she needed more money, as she was getting sore and didn't sign on for a gang bang. *How many times can this fucker fuck?* Mano said call his lawyer. Then he said he'd use a hole he hadn't used much yet.

CHAPTER 23

Saturday, the day of the wedding. Somewhere in the Bermuda Triangle.

Johnny Walker made a fish sandwich with sliced avocado and tomato on bread that he had baked in the sailboat's tiny galley. He'd made a spread of mayonnaise mixed with lime juice, salt, and pepper. With beer from his battery powered refrigerator, he never remembered being so happy.

He was thrilled that he didn't have to go back to rainy Oregon yet. Besides the guns and communications equipment hidden on board, he had four cases of beer and a case of Cuban rum. He'd heard his destination, Conch Kay, was dry. He didn't want there to be any chance of cocktail-gap. And… so-what about the murder? Some colonel? He didn't have a dog in the fight. He was just a supply ship. He probably wouldn't even spend the night. Even if women dripped from the trees. He was sick of women.

He'd trolled a line behind the sailboat Friday until he caught a nice sized Mahi Mahi that he'd filleted, cooked on his little propane grill, and what was left over he'd just made the sandwich with. The passage from Florida had been uneventful so far and he was almost to his destination, Conch Island. He'd had a strong steady wind behind him from the south-west. He let the GPS tell the autopilot where to go.

The sun was thinking about setting. Colors were changing with every swallow of beer. He switched from beer to rum. He loved being alone on a sailboat in the shallow seas of the Bahamas. He could see the bottom at twenty feet as clear as if it was at two feet. He could see starfish, conch, and even the occasional lobster.

Johnny anchored in a quiet natural cove for the night. He didn't want to enter Conch Key until tomorrow. Endi told him about the gay wedding festivities. He wanted no part of that. He would have an easy morning sail to the island tomorrow morning, drop off the supplies and then wander the Abaco's, just he and the *Drama Queen,* for a week or two. Or three. Piece of cake. He congratulated himself again on his luck. *In fact,* he thought to himself *it just doesn't get any better than this.*

After a long swim, naked, in the 90-degree water, and a rinse off with fresh water, he munched on a little cheese, apple, and grapes, while sipping straight rum. He fell asleep in the deck hammock blissed out.

At first light the next morning (Sunday) there was a body on the beech thirty yards away.

Johnny launched the dinghy thinking that whoever it was, maybe was still alive, although the birds working the scene looked intense. The body was very dead, and Johnny nearly lost it even though he had seen plenty of dead bodies over the last twenty years as a homicide detective for the Portland Police. The body didn't have eyes, lips, or a tongue. Those birds.

There was a hole on top of the head. He positioned the head with a stick, so the sun beamed into the hole. He startled a crab that exited out of the skull, side stepping with blurred little feet and sprinting to the surf. The skull was empty.

The detective asked himself the detective-axiomatic-question, *time of death?* He knew it had washed up during the night. He wondered why there were baggies on the hands. He had a suspicion.

Johnny knew very little about the situation on Conch Kay. From the urgent phone call two days ago from his old friend Endi, he knew that there had been a murder and there was no "law" on the island. Endi, and his buddy Coleman, were taking things into their own hands, but lacked even basic communication equipment and reliable weapons, and didn't even have handcuffs. He thought that if this was the body from that murder, they had gotten damn casual about keeping track of evidence since retirement, or if it wasn't that victim, then there was a war in progress somewhere, probably a drug war. *But this dude is old!*

He correctly concluded he should head right back to the States thinking, *isn't this the Bermuda Triangle?* Against his better judgement he headed to Conch Island.

Johnny dropped sails and motored into the Conch Island harbor Sunday morning. There were bodies everywhere. One appeared to be in a wedding dress covered with blood that was lying spread eagled on the bow of an Albright Ferry. There was another body lying on the dock next to the ferry. Johnny slowed the *Drama Queen* down to a crawl, and raced below, grabbed his shoulder holster with the '38 Special, and a shot gun. As he guided the boat in close to the bodies, he heard a groan from the one on the dock. He could swear it was wearing a coat of tails and a bow tie and a Speedo. The seemingly mortally wounded man rolled over on his side groaning and urinated into the bay.

The wedding dress victim sat up, looked at the man urinating and said, "That's crass honey," and then lay back down with a grunt and a fart. The wedding dress voice was baritone.

Johnny glided the sailboat into a slip next to the ferry. There were bodies draped over golf carts, picnic tables, benches, fish cleaning tables, and boats. There were bodies in the grass, on boat ramps, in the street. They were everywhere.

Johnny saw his old friend Endi limping toward him down the dock walkway. Endi helped Johnny tie up the *Drama Queen.* Endi had a bottle in his hand and two shot glasses.

"Welcome to the Island of the Big Heads, Lieutenant Johnny Walker," Endi said beaming. "You missed one hell of a party." He poured two short drinks and handed one to Johnny. He said, "Twenty-years old. Like I like my women."

They took a sip. Johnny said, "Not your 'daily-drinker' is it?" He sighed and sipped it again. Endi pulled a cigar out of his shirt pocket and offered one to Johnny. "Cuban; hand-rolled on the inner thigh of a sweaty Cuban virgin," he said grinning behind his Ray-Bans. Goes well with the Cuban rum."

Church bells pealed from three churches simultaneously. Johnny almost hit the deck. Golf carts zoomed by from seemingly nowhere, filled with dressed up Albrights heading to church. Organs started playing simultaneously with the bells. Endi grabbed his head, trying to hold his forehead and cover his ears at the same time.

Johnny shook his head smiling and said, "What's with the dead people everywhere? And blood."

Endi answered, "Wedding. Gay wedding. That's not blood on the guy's wedding dress. It's mango/pomegranate tequila sangria they used for communion and endless toasting. Boy, these guys know how to party. Absolutely shameless. Had a parade. A fashion show. Strippers. They're more like women than women, I swear. The local school-teacher, who is ALL REAL GIRL, let me tell you, was the best-of-show. I'm gonna get a brass pole installed on my buddy's veranda. Wait till you meet her."

Johnny said, "Schoolteacher?"

Endi continued, "She's Coleman's girlfriend sort of. And you ought to see my girlfriend too. She's an underwater porn star."

Johnny said, "What happened to a quiet retirement. You got anymore dead bodies besides the one washed up on an island south of here?"

"What? The only dead body we got I know of is the colonel. And he's over at the ice cream parlor in the freezer."

Johnny said, "Well there's a body curled up on a beach on an island close to here feeding the gulls. He's got baggies on his hands."

Endi belched and hiccupped. He waved Johnny to get off the boat. The two headed for the ice cream shop. The "bodies" were starting to move randomly. Endi stepped over a completely naked one with a tiara covering his eyes. He kicked the body twice. It stirred. Endi said, "For Christ sake, put some panties on Doctor, there's church goers going by." He turned to Johnny Walker and said, "That's Dr. Jack Slack, our dentist. And coroner. And magistrate. Need anything signed?"

Jack Slack pulled the tiara off one eye, opened it a crack and said, "It might look like I'm doing nothing, but at the cellular level I'm really quite busy. I don't sit the bench until tomorrow. Come back then." The eye closed slowly.

Endi said to Johnny, "If reproduction is the ultimate biological goal of Mother Nature, then apples and potatoes are the worldwide true victors. And gay guys are the worldwide losers. So why are there so many gay guys?"

Johnny was trying to figure out what Endi had just said only then realizing that his friend was still drunk. He said, "Endi, I just want to unload the stuff I brought you and get the hell out of here. Where are we going?"

Endi didn't say anything as he turned the corner and entered the ice cream store.

Johnny whined, "I don't want any ice cream. What we doing here…?" his words trailed off as he saw blood streaked across the floor and all over an open deep freeze.

Endi looked into the empty freezer. Looked at Johnny. Looked back in the freezer and asked, "Where the hell did the colonel go?"

Johnny sighed, "I think he's island hopping."

Coleman walked into the ice cream shop just then. He introduced himself to Johnny. Everybody looked into the freezer.

They had a heated discussion.

"I didn't say it was your fault. I just said I was going to blame you," Endi said to Coleman. "What kind of damn murder investigation is this gonna be where we got to find the body again? You should have been watching it."

Coleman said to Endi. "You're the cop. I'm just a Secret Service guy. Not a cop. I didn't do one damn thing for twenty-five years except baby-sit. First ladies, at that. And their goddam mothers. From foreign countries. Where the hell would you have put the body if you wanted to move it out of the ice cream shop?"

Endi answered, "That wasn't the goddam question. Why did you let him get away? You should a *locked* him in that freezer. You're the native. You live here. I'm just a guest. And I'm getting ready to leave. Me and Johnny Walker and May. Well, I might leave May—she's getting pretty beat up looking. You're not going to tell me he got out himself?"

Coleman said, "I think it was Slack that got the colonel out. He thought the colonel should attend his inauguration."

Walker thought, *what the hell? They're both still drunk.*

Coleman said unenthusiastically, "I guess we better go get the body?"

Johnny said, "If I take you to the colonel, will you get your stuff off my boat so I can get out of here?" He added morosely, "You're gonna try to make me help you find the killer, aren't you? I'm gonna get in my boat and dump your shit in the ocean. This island is worse than Key West."

Slack said, "What you mean go get the colonel? Where is he? Isn't he at the Tasty Freeze? It's not like he can walk or drive?" Jack Slack had crawled out of the middle of the parking lot and was sitting in the shade on the steps to the marina office, holding his head in both hands. Coleman found a pair of women's panties on the grass and made Jack put them on. Slack had complained to Coleman that his balls were sun burned.

Endi said, "Let's go get him back. I guess it's important to have the body. Johnny you gotta take us. You know where he is."

Walker said, "If he isn't continuing his island hopping with the tides as we stand here. Why do *you* need to get this dead colonel back? Where's the law? EMTs? Dead body removal crew."

Coleman looked at Endi and they both raised their eyebrows and dropped the corners of their mouths in the maybe-he's-got-a-point look. Endi said, "He's right you know. We aren't the law anymore anywhere, much less here. Let Slack figure this out." They looked at Slack on his hands and knees now, his panties showing almost all of his butt crack, dry heaving on the grass. He had his tiara back on.

Walker said acerbically, "Right."

Walker said, "Let's get the stuff unloaded so I can get out of here. I'm taking a shower first. This a shower house?"

He pointed to a public bathroom sign on the wharf with his thumb over his shoulder.

Coleman pointed to a building next to them, "Yea, showers are in there. Bring your own towel." Johnny headed to the *Drama Queen* for soap and a towel.

Endi said to Coleman, "All we need is that equipment. We don't need to bring Walker in on this mess."

Coleman answered, "The thing I got to do is get sober. The colonel is Jack Slack's problem. He'll just have to sober up and step up to the plate. He knows everybody. He probably knows who The Elders are. Did you see Amanda's Flamingo dance?"

Endi said, "Well, we did find the colonel in your tool shed. We, or rather you, may have to prove your innocence. Does Amanda have different colored nipples? It that why everybody was calling her *Rainbow*?"

Coleman answered, "You're the one that saw the colonel alive last. What you mean prove my innocence? Yes, she has different color pubes too. Don't call her Rainbow to her face."

Endi said, "I think we should just leave until this blows over. I don't give a respectable healthy bowel movement about the silver. It's gonna be too hard to refine, and besides the damn government, or the Spaniards, will take it anyway."

Coleman said, "Leaving might be an admission of guilt. On the other hand, Walker could at least take us to Bimini; we can swim to Miami from there. It's only forty-nine miles."

They could hear an organ and a choir blasting out a hymn. The church was only a hundred yards away. All the doors and windows were open.

After scouting the grounds, Endi found May asleep in one of the women's bathroom stalls hugging the toilet. She was naked of course. She moaned on and off all the way up the bumpy Queen's Highway to Coleman's house. He had to hold her to keep her from falling out. Her head fell in his lap. She said she wasn't in the mood for giving him a blow job. He thought again about the exit strategy to Bimini... without her.

He hosed her off outside the house and put her to bed. After taking a shower himself, he lay down swearing abstinence from booze forever. He was wondering about his choice of women. Maybe he should look for one that was a little more traditional. He was thinking maybe a Methodist.

Coleman found Amanda in the next stall over. Somehow, she wasn't as alluring as she was last night, in the light of day, cuddling with a toilet. He carried her to a golf cart and took her home. She was awake and able to hang on, but not able to talk. She still had her cowboy boots on but nothing else. The different colored nipples reminded him that there was a weird Albright gene pool. He hoped he hadn't bred her last night. He didn't remember. She stumbled into her house on her own. Not a word. He headed back to the dock.

The wedding party left Sunday afternoon, as did the doctor and his bodyguard, and Mano's whore, all on the Albright Ferry, from which the colorful decorations had been removed. The ferry captain was an Albright. He was the only one on the ship without a terminal hangover. It was a quiet, appropriately clothed, group. They all needed shaves badly. There were complaints of painful sunburns in places not meant to ever see the sun. Many were sitting on multiple cushions, or just restlessly standing, obviously too painful to sit.

The doctor had to be loaded on the ferry. Someone found him a cervical collar as he couldn't hold his head up. They hosed him down and he was now wearing a brightly colored pink and blue Mumu. No one knew where his clothes and medical kit were. No passport. No nothing. The bodyguard had a broken arm. Someone had splinted it with a canoe paddle and duct tape which he dragged behind him. The whore wasn't walking well and was leaking. Her elbows and knees were scraped badly, as was her forehead. There were patches of hair missing here and there, the rest of her hair badly matted. In World War One they called it the "thousand-yard stare." She couldn't work her jaw without pain. It wouldn't close all the way.

The ferry captain had doubled as the wedding photographer. He made a deal on the ride back with members of the wedding party and went home with total tips of over two-thousand dollars, plus $750 for his $150 camera. He reluctantly submitted to a thorough search for memory chips and his camera was just thrown overboard.

Sunday was an early evening for everyone on the island. Johnny stayed on his boat. They had unloaded the guns, booze, and other supplies on his boat that were courtesy of the CIA and stashed everything at Coleman's house.

Around eleven o'clock Sunday evening Jack Slack lay motionless in his bed with a dental trocar in his left ear, and a periosteal elevator in his right ear. His heart had stopped pumping blood when the center of his brain was punctured by the first dental instrument. The right ear thing wasn't necessary—dead already. There were trickles of blood from his ears down his neck on each side. Jack had taken enough Demerol for a horse after the thirty-six-hour wedding extravaganza, so he mercifully hadn't noticed that someone was jamming a trocar and a periosteal elevator in his ears.

During the wedding reception Saturday night, Mano discovered that Jack Slack had been busy making pure silver diving weights out of melted big black rock. Slack used lead diving weights, like used on diving belts, to create molds in plaster then poured molten silver in the molds. After cooling, he spray-painted the solid silver "diving weights" flat black and threw them in with real lead dive weights to hide his activities.

Mano, wisely deciding to dispose of the body this time, took Dr. Jack for one last ride in Jack's customized golf cart and dumped him into the cistern under the colonel's house where Jack could bob around in the dark and not fret about his sunburned genitals anymore. Being *dead* in the pitch-black cistern was a "best-case-scenario" for Jack because that way he wasn't aware of what was moving around down there with him. Or feel them nibbling.

Mano took all the dive weights not taking the time to scratch the paint to discover which were silver.

He also took the marijuana and all sedatives he could find.

CHAPTER 26

Monday morning, after the weekend wedding.

Coleman and Endi headed to the settlement in the gold cart to get with Johnny on his sailboat.

They stopped at Jack Slack's dental office. No Dr. Slack. They went through the place quickly, worried that he was laying on the floor succumbed to the weekend's debauchery (Help I've fallen, and I can't get up). It was clear the office and living quarters had been searched; cabinets, drawers, and closet doors were open. A locked drawer in the dental office, where drugs were stored, had been jimmied and was empty. Clothes were strewn about. They discovered the hot water heater crucible and the propane and oxygen tanks. They put two and two together; Slack was refining silver.

They didn't find any silver, or Slack, but they found blood on a pillow.

Endi said, "A dead colonel. Doctor's office torn apart… and blood. Who knows where the doc is, or if he's even alive? This island is worse than south Chicago."

Coleman said, "If they killed Slack, they had the time to get rid of the body. Not like the colonel."

Endi said in a dry tone of voice, "Maybe he left on the fairy ferry."

"Very funny."

Endi said, "Maybe a debt collector finally showed up."

Coleman said, "We need a CSI team."

In town, it was situation normal. The Albright marina was pumping gas, the Albright Sail Shop was making canvas bags and totes, and the Albright grocery store had the usual three or four golf carts parked in front of it. Someone had cleaned up the empty cans and bottles, thongs, Speedos, tiaras, butt-plugs, cock-rings, condoms, vibrators, and dildos. (Items continued to wash up on shore for a week.)

Johnny was hanging under the mainsail boom in a hammock, drinking coffee and listening to weather on the boat's VHF radio. They filled him in on the ransacked dental office. Johnny said, "I wouldn't be surprised if he's in the hospital. Or he's dead from a drug and alcohol overdose."

Coleman said, "Slack's a pro. He did this once for an entire week. He's fine."

Johnny said, "You guys need to find out who killed the colonel and fast. Like yesterday. Or whoever it is will kill again. And find the colonel's body. I can't believe you village-idiots lost the body."

Coleman convinced Johnny to show him where he'd seen the body.

They took Coleman's fast outboard boat. The body wasn't there.

Johnny said, "Tide probably took him back out. Current's gonna take him to Bermuda, then on to Spain."

Coleman said, "That's too bad; he hates the Spaniards."

They searched around by boat for a while, trying to second guess the tides, and looking for a seagull swarm, but gave up, knowing there had been at least four tides since Johnny had seen the body.

Johnny, Coleman, and Endi sat at Coleman's kitchen table.

Johnny called Jim Rand, CIA, in the Florida Keys and Jud Justice, FBI, in Portland. They had run searches on the colonel and found nothing shady. He called his boss at the Portland Police Bureau.

Johnny said to Endi and Coleman, "Portland isn't expecting me anytime soon. My captain in Portland said I was liaison to the Feds as long as they need me. I guess you got me for a while. Neither has agents with boots on the ground in the Bahamas currently, so I'm it."

Coleman asked Johnny, "Is this you working for the Feds normal? Never heard of a city cop working for the Feds."

"When I have to chase a criminal across state lines, like my last case that ended up in Key West, the Feds let me continue the chase under their watch. They are actually trying to recruit me and want me to quit Portland and join one or the other of them. I like Portland. Have a cat. Don't want to be on the road with the FBI, much less international with the CIA."

Coleman asked, "Key West?"

Johnny said, "I chased a cross-dresser-high-end-country-club-bartender-serial-killer specializing in single rich people, and their money, across the country to Key West. Finally took him out with a paint-ball gun in a gay bar on Duval Street."

Endi asked, "A paint ball gun? You gotta be kidding."

"Hostages. Non-lethal. You had to be there."

Coleman said, "We need to finish searching the colonel's house. We didn't get the rest of the place searched before the parade." He told Johnny about the colonel's silver-smelting, the booby traps, and the parade.

They heard a golf cart coming up the driveway.

Amanda wheeled up to Coleman's front door. She had gotten the school day started and left the class to her aid. She walked in the open door. They introduced Johnny Walker. He stood. They shook hands. Amanda held on a little too long checking him out with a dazzling smile. He sat back down at the table.

Amanda took a stool at the bar facing the others who were sitting around the breakfast table. They caught her up. Johnny asked her if the islanders would talk to outsiders about anything, much less the secret life of Colonel Albright. She answered batting her eyelashes, "No, they wouldn't talk to you guys. But they might talk to me. Or Andy. Andy's my brother."

Coleman asked her, "Have you seen Jack Slack?"

Amanda was distracted. She loved Johnny's blue eyes, slightly reddish hair, and faded red baseball cap. The five o'clock shadow, open shirt, torn baggy cutoffs. Broad shoulders. *He's actually using a rope as a belt. Now that is adorable.* He was being evaluated as a ticket out of Conch Island like every man not-of-the-island she saw.

She answered, "Haven't seen him since Saturday night at the wedding reception. But I haven't set foot out of the house until this morning when I went to the school."

Johnny asked, "Amanda, who do you suspect killed the colonel?"

She answered, "No Albrights. An outsider for sure killed him. Don't trust any of my family—they are all gossips and thieves. Can't trust them with a secret and stealing from the Americans is normal for them. But they don't murder. Ten commandments and all that. Besides they are happy with what they got and covet nothing—they have all they need. The Haitians? Doubt it. Docile and high all the time; don't worry, be happy. Gotta be a third demographic, which is anybody on the planet that can come and go by boat to the island without ever being seen."

She crossed her legs flashing Johnny.

She went on, "The only ones we can really trust are the five of us original partners." She counted with her fingers: "Me, Endi, Coleman, May, and Andy. And of course, now you, Johnny Walker." She nodded Johnny's way with her best night-club-eye-contact smile. "We five were together, in a boat, far away from the colonel, and the ball peen hammer. At least we have that. And you weren't here, Johnny." She smiled and made eye-contact with Johnny again.

May asked, "Amanda, you left out Jack Slack?"

She answered, "Slack? I don't trust him. Period. By the

way, I'd still like to get some silver out of this deal. I really want to get off this island."

Coleman said, "Right now Amanda, you can have all the silver for all I care. It has caused a murder. If idiot Endi hadn't drug that big black rock out of the ocean, the colonel might still be alive. And frankly, I'm worried about Jack Slack. He would be in the middle of this conversation right now knowing him. If my office had been ransacked, hangover or not, I would be running to my ex-cop buddies for sanctuary and for help. He clearly doesn't know it was ransacked, made it look that way himself, or isn't even on the island, or he would be here. Hell, he could be dead, and in the Blue Hole. Maybe he left with the wedding party. Who knows?"

Amanda said, "Office ransacked?" They filled her in. They told her about Slack's smelting operation.

She said, "Told ya—I don't trust Slack. And you're right, he would be here without a doubt."

May said, "I think the perv is probably with Touch Me Not on his way to Key West."

Endi said, "With his newly smelted silver. And maybe the colonel's silver too. He may have killed the colonel. The whole wedding thing would have made a perfect cover for a disappearance act."

Amanda said, "It is possible that creditors finally caught up with him. Or some drug related enemy he has that we don't know of. Or he doesn't want to be here when the law comes snooping around the colonel's death."

Johnny asked, "Who can tell us if any boats are missing?"

Coleman said, "Boats come and go with impunity. No harbor tax. They can just drop anchor. Second-home ex-pat owner's come and go too."

May said, "He's probably on the mainland getting his newly acquired STD's treated."

Amanda said, "I don't care what happened to the asshole. I don't want to sound too calloused here, but again, I emphasize…I want something out of this at the end of the day. If he has gone to Key West with some pervert fine, more for me. I could use the money. A schoolteacher on a desert island doesn't make much. I want off this island and to change my name to Smith, or Jones, before my Albright ass starts to grow."

Coleman said grinning, "You could always take up exotic dancing, Rainbow. I was thinking about getting a brass pole for the living room."

Amanda stood up, and slowly walked over to Coleman, who was scooting his chair back anticipating a blow, smiling broadly. She leaned over, her hair hanging down covering both their heads and kissed him on top of the forehead, then punched him viciously twice in the stomach. "We will not talk of Saturday night ever again, thank you."

Coleman doubled over in mock pain, laughing.

Amanda said, "Let's find Jack Slack. I don't trust him. If he's dead, he'll start stinking soon. So much the better."

May said, "Maybe we better check the freezer at the ice cream shop? Maybe Slack's in there."

Endi said, "Let's head for the colonel's house first. Who knows? Slack may be there right now stealing the silver."

Amanda said, "I need a bucket of chicken. Fast food every meal for a week. God, I hate this island. I hope the colonel's silver is still there somewhere."

CHAPTER 27

Monday, late morning.

Coleman, Endi, Amanda, May, and Johnny, headed up the Queen's Highway to the colonel's house.

Johnny said he'd take the grounds. The two couples split up into pairs to check the house: boy-girl, boy-girl. They all had weapons now, and walkie-talkies. They showed Johnny where the colonel had been processing the silver blocks, and his notebook. Amanda said she would work on the notebook later.

Johnny found a trail going through the jungle that went south through an acre of jungle and into Coleman's property next door. He followed it right to Coleman's house noticing footprints from what appeared to be deeply treaded sandals all along the way, like sandals made from old tire treads. Offshoots from the trail ended in little clearings just big enough for one person to hide in and hear what was going on in the rooms. Someone was eves-dropping, and window peeping at least, and stalking at worst. He doubted Coleman knew about these little clearings. Why would he? The thick jungle provided privacy from the neighbors and the Queen's Highway. It was literally impenetrable without saws and machetes. Brush, sticker bushes, roots as big as an arm, branches of squat trees from knee level up to forehead level and beyond, vines, leaves the sized of tennis rackets and just as tough; all intertwined with each other like a massive three-dimensional spider web. Johnny could not stick his arm into the jungle straight in any direction. Who knew what else was in there? It occurred to him if the murderer had dragged the colonel even five feet into the thick vegetation, they would never have found him.

Working backwards on the trail from Coleman's and past the colonel's house, he found another path paralleling the Queen's Highway. And more tire-treads sandal impressions.

Suddenly feeling spooked, he looked around him. He realized someone could ambush him very easily. Someone could certainly be watching him. He thought about booby traps. He felt for the gun.

He keyed the microphone on the walkie-talkie and got Coleman. He told Coleman if he didn't come back soon, send a search party, and that he'd found a trail in the underbrush paralleling the Queen's Highway with tire tread sandal prints on it.

Coleman said "Come back in. We shouldn't split up. I'll go back out with you."

Johnny heard the surf pounding on the ocean side to his right to the east through the jungle. As he walked, he couldn't hear his own footsteps in the soft sandy jungle floor, much less anyone else's over the surf. He couldn't help looking around again. He suddenly had an awed appreciation for jungle fighters.

Instead of going back he decided to go just a little farther on the obviously recently used trail.

He avoided stepping in the footprints as much as he could. After another fifty yards he literally ran into a wall. It was six feet high and made of concrete blocks. There was a hole in it big enough for a person to crawl through. The hole was at the base of the wall and was hidden by dead and freshly cut palm branches. Kneeling he spread the palm branches aside, so that he could see through the hole, but dense vegetation on the other side completely blocked his view beyond that.

He heard a steady rhythmic thumping noise that changed its beat every few seconds. He climbed a tree and was just able to see over the wall and through the deep vegetation behind it. Someone was thumping a speed bag suspended from a trellis over the deck around a pool. Whoever it was had boxing gloves on. His hands were a blur. Jack thought the guy was good. But small.

He wondered *is that our killer.* He carefully piled up the dried palm branches on the hole in the wall, making a pattern, figuring if he found them moved later, the punching bag guy, or someone with him at the house, was using the hole in the wall to get to the trail. Someone with tire-tread sandals. He knew he had stumbled on something important. Maybe dangerous too.

Johnny tried to follow the wall to the east toward the ocean side but was stopped by thick, overgrown jungle; same going west toward the Queen's Highway. As he worked his way back to the colonel's house he wondered if the man he just saw working out was the one using the trail. It probably was, he decided. Those tracks were fresh. It hadn't rained since he had arrived. These tracks looked like they would be obliterated by a decent rain. If he could find out when it rained last that would give him a time frame.

He told the others about the trail and the neighbor using a punching bag. Amanda said she had no idea anyone was occupying the old Jefferson place. Mr. Jefferson had died years ago. They all agreed they needed to find out who it was and that this was an example of the problem with the island: there is no way to know who's here. People can come and leave, with no one ever knowing they were here, much less, who they are.

Endi reminded the group about the tire track prints around the Coleman's tool shed where the colonel was killed and said they needed to photograph the one's Johnny just spotted. They agreed it had been a couple of days since it rained.

The colonel retired from the Royal Marines Reserve twenty-five years prior and had a current United Kingdom passport. He was an Albright, but not a Bahamas citizen, which they all agreed said a lot. There was a box of awards, decorations, and medals. He belonged to several retired military organizations. There were old Wall Street Journal's, National Geographic's, Smithsonian's, Discovery's, and lots of books and other magazines everywhere.

He was apparently writing a history of his unit's efforts in several theaters. He had an ancient typewriter. There were books from England on the duties of a Magistrate, Justice of the Peace, etc. There were documents that appeared to be copies of requests to the British Parliament to absorb Conch Island into their protectorate. The replies were all negative. Amanda explained to the group that even though Conch Island considered itself independent, the government of the Bahamas didn't. The land that foreigners owned on the island was deeded by Bahamas real estate laws and titles. They paid taxes to the Bahamas; but the Albrights were exempt from paying taxes via some grandfather clause.

There were books on the history of the silver-years of Spain's involvement in the New World; books on ships, and wrecks of the Spanish treasure fleets; the Potosí silver mine in Peru; and a couple books on salvage, mostly about efforts off the Florida coasts. There were copious notes about different types of silver that were transported by freighter back to Spain in the 1700's.

There were pictures of a handsome young couple with the man in uniform. The colonel and his wife, Amanda assumed. And more typical pictures of both of them aging as time went by. Amanda knew his wife had left him, but couldn't find any documents or letters indicating when, or why. She wondered where his wife was and if she was even alive. Did she need to be notified? Maybe Luna Albright would know.

There were a couple of books about wildlife in the ocean, and one on snakes.

"Pretty much a dud," Coleman said to the group.

Endi said, "One place left to look folks."

Johnny Walker asked, "Where? Don't forget, I want you guys to check out this trail I found outside too."

Endi answered, "The cistern under the house. Maybe he's hidden the silver down there like we did at Coleman's."

Coleman said, "Let's find the trap door. The pump should be in a utility area. Follow me." It began raining.

Johnny Walker said, "Quick, let's get some photos of the tracks on the jungle trail before they are obliterated by this rain. Come on." The three guys headed out into the light rain while the girls stayed under the cover of the veranda that surrounded the house. Endi snapped multiple pictures of the sandal prints.

Even before they got back, their own tracks in the sand were beginning to disappear as the rain became a tropical deluge.

They found the trap door to the cistern easily, next to the washer and dryer. Endi hung down into it, his hips resting on the edge and his torso suspended in midair, head just inches above the water. He didn't have to lean in far. The water was almost to the underside of the floor above the cistern. He panned a flashlight around. Water was flooding into the cistern as it was raining. The guttering system was directing the roof runoff into down spouts. The noise made it hard to hear. The smell didn't smell like fresh water. It smelled fishy.

Suddenly, Endi thought he saw a dark movement beneath him, inches from his face. He boiled up out of the opening, panting, unexpectedly scared, knowing he saw something, but not knowing what. The others all asked him what was wrong.

Breathlessly, partly because he hadn't been able to fill his lungs while hanging partly upside down compressing his abdomen and diaphragm, and partly from hyperventilating, he said, "I thought I saw something shoot by under me."

Coleman said, "Nothing lives in these cisterns. There is no food. No light. Let me have a look." Endi gladly slid out of the way. Coleman went on explaining, "These cisterns are excavated out of the old reef, and then lined with concrete. Nothing gets in or out except rain. There are usually steel beams that are embedded in the cistern's concrete that also supports the house. The weight of the water trapped in the cistern acts as ballast during hurricanes."

Coleman poked his head down the trapdoor, admitting to himself he was a little spooked thanks to Endi, but rejected his apprehension knowing nothing could possibly be down there. Not even a drowned mouse. There were no mice, or rats, on the island. About that time Amanda said, "What's this switch for?" She threw a switch she found on the wall next to the trap door and the cavernous cistern lit up. The entire space was illuminated by a series of lights that appeared to be full spectrum fluorescent lights; banks of them fixed to the bottom of the floor they were on a foot above the water.

Coleman said hanging over the edge, "Holy shit. No one lights up their damn cistern. This is amazing down here."

Then he saw it swim by. Yellow, long, a black stripe down its back, and black polka dots on its fan-like tail. He pulled his head out fast thinking *whatever the hell that is, it's got to be ten feet long.* He slammed the trap door down and then sat on it, panting and shaking. "Jesus. There's something freaking big down there. And long. A snake for God's sake. Shit, there are not supposed to be snakes in the Bahamas."

Endi said frowning and not happy about being proven right, "I told you I saw something."

Coleman looked at Endi and Johnny with wide disbelieving eyes. "If there's silver down there, I don't want it. What the hell is a snake doing in a cistern? There are no snakes in the Bahamas. What the hell was the colonel up to?"

Endi said, "Booby traps, snakes…shit, what, zombies, next?"

They heard and felt a bump on the floor beneath them punctuating the zombie comment. They all stopped talking as if on cue, with heads cocked, ears toward the floor in unison. Listening. They looked at each other with wide eyes. Amanda said in a whisper, "Did you hear what I just heard?" They all nodded. Coleman put a finger to his lips and whispered, "Shhhh." Then they heard it and felt it again. Not under them. Away from the trap door. Like from under the next room.

Johnny said, "The snake wants out."

Amanda screamed all the way out of the house, got in her golf cart and fired it up yelling, "Come on, let's get the hell out of here. Bus is leaving, now!"

Endi and Coleman boiled out of the house right after May, who was screaming too. Johnny Walker backed out of the house, his gun drawn, and just as he was about to sit on the backward facing seat of Amanda's golf cart, she floored it. He didn't make it. She raced the cart down the graveled path toward the Queen's Highway, Endi riding shotgun, May in the middle. Johnny was "waterskiing" behind it hanging on with one hand, running, and his gun still in the other. He gave up and hopped on Coleman's cart that was catching up with Amanda.

As they came around the corner and turned onto the Queen's Highway, another golf cart was heading right at them.

Amanda slammed the brakes with both feet. She skidded ten feet in the crushed coral and sand before the impact.

Neither cart driver had seen the other coming because of the rain. There were no windshield wipers on either cart, and even if there had been, they couldn't have seen each other around the bend.

Coleman slammed into Amanda's rear end pushing her further into the oncoming cart.

How much damage can golf carts do to each other when one is pretty much stopped and the other is doing maybe about five miles-an-hour in its first and only gear? Not much. But some.

Endi went through Amanda's Plexiglas golf cart window, and the other cart's window as well, and onto the lap of Justice of the Peace, Luna Nausea Henry VIII Albright. May hung on to Amanda who was stopped from forward motion by the steering wheel.

Chance was driving Luna Albright's golf cart with Luna riding shotgun. He screamed like a little girl way before the impact with Amanda's cart, let go of the steering wheel, and raised his legs into the fetal position just before impact. If he'd applied the brakes, and steered a little, there never would have been a wreck. He ended up under the steering wheel grabbing Luna's legs and then pawed his way onto her lap like a lab puppy.

That put Endi on top of Chance. He had been on top of Luna, but Chance had squirmed himself between him and Luna, so Endi was perched on her sizable breasts, his crotch in her face.

Turns out Chance had never been in a wreck before. This was as bad as it gets for him. He'd never driven anything but a golf cart in his life.

Luna, all two hundred pounds of her no-neck, no-waist, no-shoulders, pear-shaped five-foot-four frame, had two men on her for the first time in her life. Endi and Chance flew in two directions simultaneously with one heave from her sumo-wrestler sized arms. (More blood.)

The rain stopped as quickly as it had started. There was no real damage to the carts, other than both the plastic windshields that Endi had gone through. Apologies were made, and since there was no doctor or hospital on the island, no one even considered calling an ambulance since there wasn't one of those either, much less a cop, not to mention there was no insurance to deal with, and although hard to even imagine, there wasn't a lawyer, or tow truck, on the scene, and it had already been three minutes since the head-on.

Back in the colonel's house, Luna and Chance explained that the colonel had things of theirs and that's why they were here and thought they might just get them back since the colonel was not going to need them much anymore.

Walker thought, *they're just everyday looters.*

They all went back inside the colonel's house.

Amanda asked Luna and Chance if they had seen Jack Slack. Luna Albright, still a little shaky, said, "Eh dinna say ocdor ack a eh ohvice o inna tone ni er nn."

Amanda was pretty sure she said I didn't see Dr. Jack in the office or in town either one.

Endi hadn't understood one word of anything an Albright had said the whole time he had been on the island. He thought they pretty much just spoke vowels and phlegm with an English accent.

Coleman asked Chance, "You know if the colonel has had his cistern cleaned out recently?" He knew that was side business for Chance and his crew—cleaning and maintaining cisterns. Chance answered that he had never cleaned out the colonel's cistern. He added that the colonel didn't use the water for drinking and used it just to flush toilets and take showers, and washing sand off feet, stuff like that. According to the colonel it was contaminated with ocean water, so he used bottled water for drinking and cooking.

Amanda said, "I gotta go to the bathroom."

Luna said, "Yu tnk e hid smtng inna c s trn?"

Endi tugged at Coleman's T-shirt like a little kid and whispered, "What'd she say?" Johnny said to Endi, "I think she said she thinks he is hiding something in the cistern."

Coleman said, "If the cistern has some salt water in it that explains how something from the ocean is living down there."

Chance asked, "Why you say something live down there, mon. Noting lives in cistern on de' island."

Endi tugged on Coleman's shirt again. Coleman elbowed him harder and answered Chance. "Because we opened the trap door to the cistern, found that it was wired for lights, and thought we saw something down there."

Johnny said, "A big-ass snake."

Luna said, "Lots of people keep things in their cisterns on the island. Valuables. Things they don't want anyone to find. But not live stuff."

Endi tugged on Coleman's shirt again and asked what did she say?

Elbowing Endi again, Coleman addressed Chance. "Go look in the cistern. You know these systems better than anyone. By the way we all heard a bumping sound under the floor after we closed the trap door. I'll admit, it was spooky." He didn't elaborate about all of them running out of the house in terror.

Luna said to Coleman, "Everybody wants to go to the colonel's funeral. What did you do with the colonel? Preacher says the colonel is losing the window to enter heaven. Anyone know where Slack is? He's supposed to be in charge of digging the hole."

Coleman asked, "You haven't seen Sack?"

Luna said, "You kill him too?"

Coleman: Eye roll, slight head shake (I don't believe this), sigh.

Endi asked, "What did the colonel do as a magistrate?"

Luna answered, "He didn't do much. That's why I told Jack Slack he could be the replacement magistrate. The Elders actually take care of everything. There are six of them that decide stuff like who gets to ride bicycles, no skateboards, and all that. Where is Jack Slack anyway? What'd you idiots do with him? You lose him too? Morons!"

Endi looked at Coleman exasperated and mouthed, "What the fuck did she just say?"

Coleman answered wearily, "Luna, you want to look down in the cistern. Maybe that's Jack Slack bumping around down there wanting out." Coleman visualized Luna swimming for her life in the dark. He whispered to Endi, "Luna had a charm-bypass."

Endi whispered back, "No shit. She needs speech therapy too."

Luna said to Coleman in rebuttal, "I'm easy to get along with once you people learn to worship me. Oh, come on Coleman, I'll look in the bloody cistern with you cowardly assholes. What am I? Flypaper for freaks!?"

Endi pulled Coleman's sleeve again. "Who's she calling a freak?"

Amanda came into the room and said, "I choked up. Couldn't sit on the toilet. Afraid a damn snake would come up and bite me. I still gotta go. I'm gonna go pee off the dock."

Endi had a beer craving. He hadn't understood much of the conversation except for Coleman's part. He grabbed Coleman's sleeve and wouldn't let go and said, "All this stress; I'm telling you, we ought to let this silver bull-shit go. Let's get a drink."

Luna and Chance each said at the same time, in perfect-to-understand English, with no accent whatsoever, "*Silver?* You said silver? What silver?"

"That's what I saw. That's it," Coleman said to the group, pointing with his index finger. Coleman was pointing to a picture of a yellow-bellied sea snake, *Pelamis platurus.* "OK, maybe it wasn't ten feet long. But it could have been five feet long. That what it says, they can grow to five feet." He read:

- ***Sea Snakes*** *are some of the most potent venomous elapid snakes, evolved from terrestrial roots, adapted to a fully aquatic life being unable to even move on land due to the lack of ventral scales. The Yellow-Bellied Sea Snake is the most widely distributed snake of any kind, land snakes included. Most species grow to between 3.9—4.9 ft. in length. All have paddle-like tails and laterally compressed eel-like bodies, no gills. They have to surface to breathe. They have gentle dispositions and only bite when provoked, while others can be much more aggressive.*

Coleman said, "That's just great. What a stupid sentence. That last one: '*Others can be much more aggressive.*' That means any sea snake you happen to come across can be gentle or aggressive. Like you're supposed to know how this particular sea snake feels about life in general today?"

Amanda had found the book about snakes prominently displayed on the colonel's desk. The page they were looking at was marked.

She read on with all of them looking over her shoulder again, including Luna and Chance:

- *Their lungs extend the entire length of their body, the rear part being not as oxygen rich, and probably for buoyancy. They also may be able to respire through their skin absorbing oxygen from the sea like fish.*

- *When mating, the male lies over the female and contracts from tail to head causing the oxygen-depleted air from the back part of her lung to move forward so she is temporarily oxygen-deprived. Her natural response is a gaping of the cloaca, releasing musk and giving the male an opening.*

May said, "He essentially chokes her. Like they have kinky sex!" No one laughed. It was a tough crowd. Amanda continued reading,

- *can handle lots of salt…secretes it if there is too much in its system…from some glands under their tongue…can't excrete excess salt in urine like most…*

- *Sea snakes do not occur in the Atlantic Ocean. Global warming may eventually cause aforementioned cold currents to become warm enough, however.*

- *Sea snakes prefer shallow waters not far from land, around islands, especially waters that are somewhat sheltered. Some sea snakes inhabit mangrove swamps and similar brackish water habitats and can become land locked.*

- *Out of the water their movements become very erratic. They crawl awkwardly and can become quite aggressive, striking wildly at anything that moves, but can't coil and strike like land snakes. They are active both day and night. They bask in the sun. There are sometimes huge aggregations of sea snakes. One such aggregation formed a line of snakes ten feet wide and sixty-two miles long. The cause of the phenomenon is unknown.*

- *When bites occur, it is rare for venom to be injected when handled. The venom kills fish quickly. A thrashing fish needs to die fast, or its sharp spines might poke a hole in the snake's stomach. The venom is about 25 times as toxic as a king cobra's. One drop can kill a man. Paralysis, vomiting, sweating, no swallow and respiratory reflexes…*

Amanda said, "Who wants to check out the colonel's cistern?"

Luna Albright asked in perfect English, "What I want to know is what is all this talk about silver?"

Amanda said to Coleman and Endi and May, "This is such a cluster. We might as well tell them what's going on. How many partners do we have now? I can't even count. Vote? I'll vote in Andy's abstention."

Coleman said, "Jack Slack isn't here."

Amanda ignoring him said, "All in favor say, aye." There were three aye's and a bump from the cistern on the floor beneath them. Chance screamed like a little girl. Amanda stomped an abbreviated Flamenco.

Coleman said, "Like I said, who wants to check out the cistern. Chance, that's your specialty."

Chance's reply was unintelligible.

They told Luna and Chance about the silver they had found. Luna's comment was, "Oh the colonel's been screwing with those big black rocks for years. Gets off on them, he does. Claims he's gonna…was claiming I guess I should say… gonna be rich someday. He was always talking about that. You mean it's true or are you idiots just so dense, light bends around your heads." She was talking in her island accent again.

Endi asked staring at Luna with a frown and sneer, "What she say? Something about us being idiots?" He was beginning to really dislike the woman.

Coleman said to Endi, "For God's sake would you quit asking me what the hell Luna is saying?" Then he addressed Luna, "This is common knowledge? You all know about the big rocks?"

Luna said, "We all know about the big black rocks. No one can figure out how to process them. The colonel said he did figure it out, but I haven't seen him running around the island in a Porsche. Hell, that's why his wife left him, I think. Him thinking he was an alchemist or something. Making silver from rock." She added, "His wife was a crazy bitch. Worse than him any day. I think he killed her."

Coleman said, "Well he had a smelting operation going on in his little outbuilding, and booby traps all over the house. He was hiding something."

Luna said, "Look, I'll be honest. The man was a spook. I wouldn't be surprised if you told me he danced in panties and bra wearing a top hat and high heels, beating his shoulders with a riding crop, in front of a mirror."

Endi wandered away and into the kitchen, giving up on understanding Luna. He produced a bottle of Mount Gay rum. (He muttered to himself, *Gay… figures.*) He poured three inches and looked in the refrigerator for anything to mix it with, found some orange juice and ice. "I got hit by a coffee can full of concrete," he said to himself. "I deserve a drink." He sipped the drink and said to no one, "Hey, this is good."

Endi heard Chance say from the other room, now in clear English, "Why don't we get Andy Albright to dive it?"

Coleman said to the group, "Well people, the issue now is what's in the colonel's cistern, isn't it? That is the next order of business." He looked at Chance and said, "Good call. Someone go get Andy."

Endi said loudly from the kitchen, "I wonder if we can just drain it?"

There was a bump, and only a half-hearted scream now from Amanda; but Chance did his golf cart little girl scream.

CHAPTER 29

Monday. Early afternoon.

Amanda went to town to get Andy.

Chance found the cistern's plumbing system outside the main house in the auxiliary generator shed. There was a six-inch PVC pipe routed through a pump that apparently pumped sea water into the cistern from the bay side of the island. Twice a day, timed with the tide as far as Chance could tell, set by hand a week at a time, the pump removed one-quarter of the entire volume of water daily, and then refilled the tank again with fresh sea water. Rainwater mixed in randomly from roof run-off, and the whole thing overflowed out to sea when the cistern was getting too full.

Basically, they determined that the colonel had a salt-water aquarium forty feet long, twenty-five feet wide, and six feet deep. And he kept it fresh by exchanging ocean water frequently. The group had to hand it to him, it was ingenious, not to mention useful if you wanted to keep ocean wildlife under you house for some reason.

They discovered the lights were on a timer as well. Providing full spectrum daylight on a twenty-four-hour schedule, keeping whatever was living in the aquarium sunny and happy.

They found invoices and paid receipts for bizarre deliveries from Marsh Harbor. He had live frogs flown in from South America, and goldfish from a producer in Florida, both delivered weekly directly to his dock, and apparently pumped off the delivery boat into the cistern intake pipe. His dock was in a small cove that had been cut out of the dead coral, like a miniature secret submarine base. Once in there, a boat was essentially invisible from any side.

Amanda told Andy at his shop about the cistern and asked if he would dive it, snakes and all. He gathered air tanks, spear guns and knives, regulators, masks, fins, etc. He decided he didn't need a buoyancy compensator, or weights. He and Amanda headed back to the colonel's house.

When Andy and Amanda got back to the colonel's house the crew was still trying to figure out how to drain the cistern.

Andy told the group he wasn't particularly afraid of yellow-bellied sea snakes, from what he'd heard, but hadn't ever seen one in the Caribbean. He brought up the good point that there may be other things down there, "Like a hammerhead!" he pronounced to the group in the same tone he might have chosen if he'd said, "Duh!"

Endi suggested again that they just drain the cistern; screw the snakes (toasting the air with his second Gay and O.J.) and whatever the hell else is down there. Let 'em die.

They had gotten used to the bumping noise from the cistern. They of course had no idea it was Jack Slack doing the thumping as the snakes playfully pulled him down and then let go, so he bobbed back up the surface, causing the thumps under the floor. (Snakes get bored too.)

Andy said it could take a day or more to drain it. It may have to be pumped. He thought they ought to just dive it and have a quick look around. He would dive it tomorrow, with another diver, but needed more equipment such as shark repellant and contact guns, as well as compressed air spear guns. Endi would provide surface support and backup for the dive with an M-16 assault rifle from the trap door. Andy said he was going to throw a dead chicken in first and see if anything "took the bait." Endi would try to shoot whatever grabbed the chicken.

Johnny said he would get on the satellite phone again and see if Rand had discovered anything about murderers hiding on Conch Island or surrounding islands. He asked Luna and Chance if they knew anything about the person, or persons, living next door to the colonel to the north. They both were surprised that someone was there next door to the colonel. They both said they thought it was empty. Coleman said he wanted a judge, a warrant, and a SWAT team.

Johnny said, "A murder, a snake, a silver smelter, a stranger next door no one knows about, a dentist missing, a magistrate dead, and his body missing…and no one doing anything about it, much less knocking on the next-door neighbor's door and asking if they know anything?"

Luna said, "We don't need any cops, including you dick-heads. Why don't you people just leave? None of us give a shit about whether the colonel or Slack ever shows up again. Why you making a federal case out of this. Tomorrow will be here, same as today—don't make any difference who did in who for what reason yesterday. You're the idiots making something out of something we just gonna forget. Go away if you don't like it here."

Johnny Walker said, "She does have a point. If no one cares, why should we. I say let's light the drinking lamp until we feel like napping. Hey, it's the islands."

Endi asked Coleman, "What the hell did Luna say?"

Mano slipped out of his compound when he had heard the screaming from the colonel's house. Listening from a little clearing, he freaked when he learned they had discovered his secret path, and that they were going to dive the cistern looking for silver, and that there were things living in the cistern. He'd watched them take pictures of his sandal prints. He watched the guy that had come in the sailboat with all the weapons and radios come back into the jungle and block his path using branches and vegetation. He had to think…which was difficult.

He had been perfectly happy to deal with the two retired idiot cops, and the one cop's retarded girlfriend. But now, there were people from all over the island chasing after *his* silver. Now he had to deal with the fact that he'd thrown the stupid dentist into the colonel's cistern, and now the ass holes were talking about draining it, or diving it, and of course they would run into a dead dentist. He thought maybe they wouldn't recognize him if whatever was down there had eaten on him. He was agonizing over what he might have left in the cistern…trace evidence. Not to mention a bowling ball with his prints on it that he had tossed out in the sand through a window; he'd been nailed by it during his first break-in into the colonel's house.

Mano was addicted to the TV show C.S.I. and figured the floating body and bowling ball would tell the stupid cops everything about him including the brand of toilet paper he used.

He hadn't had to worry about so many things at once in his life. It wasn't going well in his dented brain. Fifty wins, three losses, two draws. Who knows how many blows to the head? His thought-processor was sluggish, too many reboots. His lawyer said he was too dumb to teach to peel a banana.

One good thing he thought, feeling a little boost of optimism, was that there weren't any real cops showing up. His lawyer told him there wasn't any law on the island but that was not an invitation to commit lawless acts. Mano had said to himself *bullshit*. For him that had been a green light for another layer of freedom.

That evening, Johnny Walker had Coleman, Endi, Amanda, May, and Andy, to his boat for dinner. He had brought a frozen beef tenderloin with him from the mainland, and it had thawed and needed to be eaten. He had a propane grill mounted on the railing on the stern of his sailboat. He served up thick tenderloins, baked potatoes, and a couple nice bottles of merlot.

They watched the sun go down and stars begin to twinkle on a moonless night. They had a rum tasting, trying three different bottles, and listened to light blues from Johnny's sound system in the boat. The smoked Cubans, even the girls.

Endi told Johnny he should change the name of his boat from *Drama Queen* to *A Rum with a View.*

CHAPTER 30

Monday. Evening. While the "crew" went to Johnny's boat for dinner.

Mano watched the sun go down. He was watching his dream crumble. He had Jack Slack's silver dive weights hidden in a suitcase in his closet. But that wasn't enough.

Mano knew there were some "ingots" of silver in Coleman's cistern. It was time to get them. All he had to do was lift the hatch to the cistern and fish them out with a fish net.

As soon it was dark, he drank three fingers of rum; took a couple of deep hits of Slack's marijuana; swallowed two sertraline's and one prazosin and injected one cc of Winstrol-V into each bicep. Dressed in black fighting shorts, his tire tread sandals, and a black wife-beater, he crawled through the hole in the wall, and headed towards the colonel's house.

But Walker had put up a barricade on the trail hoping it might stop whoever it was from using it. In the dark Mano got diverted off the main trail at the barricade.

Trying to be quiet, he stifled a scream in pain as he

slogged through a bush with burrs. When he tried to pick them off, they pricked his fingers mercilessly. He lost his balance trying to get them off his toes and ankles and fell over a root. He fell on more burrs. The bad rib screamed again. He couldn't reach the burrs on his back. He took his shirt off and flung it into the dark. They left their spines in his back.

He'd dropped the fishnet and his flashlight. Feeling around only covered his hands with more burrs.

He headed toward the sound of the surf. The jungle gave way to the beach finally and he sat down and worked on burrs some more, his anger fiery. He knew time was limited. He stumbled along the beach back toward his compound trying to avoid outcroppings of old coral. He'd lost one sandal. Back at his house he picked off more burrs, slathered himself where he could reach with cortisone cream, put on a pair of loafers, then headed back to Coleman's house this time using the Queen's Highway. He was running out of time.

Coleman's place was pitch black. He figured he would hear them coming up the Queen's Highway, and up Coleman's driveway, in time to get out. He knew where Coleman kept a flashlight.

He shined the light through the trap door opening into the black water of Coleman's cistern and saw the silver bars. There were two pillowcases near them. He thought that must be some silver coins. There was no way he could reach them. Every sound he thought was Coleman and the others returning. Excitement and fear; he felt his bowels gurgling.

He remembered a large potbellied stove with a fireplace tong in the living room. He grabbed it and went back to the cistern's trap door and hung into Coleman's cistern, both hands and arms trying to manipulate the tongs to grab a silver bar, flashlight in his mouth. He heard voices. Half of his body was hanging into the cistern. He tried to back out. He dropped the tongs into the water, made a grab for them, lost his balance, and toppled headfirst into the cistern. The flashlight went out as it sank.

Lights came on and the voices moved into the house. He couldn't think of anything to do but close the trap door. He pulled a rope until the heavy hatch door pointed straight up over dead center and let gravity drop it. He tried to catch it so it wouldn't make noise slamming shut, but it closed on his fingers. He dropped under water and screamed. He popped his head up trying not to scream again but coughed and sneezed from the water gurgling in his mouth and nose. *I fucking crapped myself.*

The cold dark water was to his chin, and the underside of the cabin floor was still a foot above his head. He thought he felt something bump him. He remembered hearing that sharks bump you, then bite. Slivers of light seeped through cracks in the floor. He could hear people laughing and talking above him. Panic was replacing excitement and fear.

Most of the lights went out one by one not too much later, plunging him into a dark world of fear and dread. He tried to lift the trap door several times but just barely got it open a crack because he was so short.

He resigned himself to a long night of self-flagellation and bitter anger. Nothing had bit him. He was over the terror. He bobbed around on his toes, which he was good at, having practiced that lot in the ring.

He stood on the silver bars, and that gave him a few inches.

At least the thistles didn't sting as much. His rib throbbed fiercely though, made worse by the slide of his body over the edge of the trap door as he fell into the cistern.

Endi stayed up loading pictures from his camera onto his laptop. He flashed through the pictures absentmindedly. He finally turned off the light and climbed into bed with May. He held her, her back nestled against his chest. He cupped one of her breasts and tweaked the nipple with his thumb a couple of times. She mumbled, "Start without me."

But then the nipple got hard and so did he. She moaned a tiny sound and licked her lips.

Endi rolled her over and kissed her hard on the mouth forgetting May's still tender nose and dentistry. May screamed. Mano let out a startled yelp below. They didn't hear it because May shouted, "Watch the nose asshole."

Mano realized that they were going to have sex right above him. He had never felt sorrier for himself than at that very moment. But Endi shot up in bed in the sitting position and turned on the light and turned the computer back on.

May said, "Yea, watch some porn. Leave me alone."

Endi found the pictures of the tire tread sandal prints outside Coleman's tool shed and compared them to the ones from the trail into the jungle leaving the colonel's house. Then he compared those with the tracks just outside the wall at the old Peterson's place. He stood up and did a soft shoe tap dance, and then the Twist.

Mano got dust from the bouncing floorboards above him in his eyes and nose. He pinched his nose feeling a sneeze coming on.

The dancing and singing got worse. He heard May yell, "Jesus that was fast." The dancing stopped and he heard talking. A new sneeze wouldn't go away. It tingled and burned unmercifully.

Mano mouthed a silent fuck and ducked his head under water just as the sneeze screamed its freedom. Gagging and spitting, the lining in his nose stinging from the water forced into it, he thought, *I just water-boarded my dumb-ass self.* He had to go under again for the next sneeze.

Endi got back in bed. The lights went out again and he started tweaking nipples again. May was responding. "Go to sleep shit-head." "You need a wax job honey." "Fuck you." "Promise?" Giggling. Panting. Moaning, "Watch the nose and caps ass-wipe."

Mano listened to their grunts and groans. He had a hard on. He was shivering. He mouthed, "Why me?" He had bobbed to the area right under their bed so he could hear better.

Climax over, Mano heard Endi say, "May, I got a break. The sandal prints are the same on the trail leading from the colonel's house to Coleman's cabin as the ones we found outside the tool shed the day the colonel got murdered. And by the Peterson place, outside the wall. All I gotta do is look at every pair of tire-tread sandals on the island. They even make those things anymore?"

Mano farted a fear fart. (Actually, he *sharted*—his shit/fart-separator failing.) He heard the bubbles popping behind him. He tried reassuring himself that sandals made out of old tire treads were numbering in the quadruple millions and that there must be hundreds of them on this island alone. He was wondering whether he was wearing Dunlop's or Firestones. One was lost in the jungle. He made a mental to get rid of the one back at his compound.

He guffawed out loud covering his mouth with a hand. He realized he had just pissed and crapped in their drinking water.

He bounced over to under the trap door and felt around for the silver bricks with his feet, then stood on them again. His brain wouldn't turn off. He lamented that once again, his cursed lack of height was part of the whole world being against him—if he was normal sized, he could breathe, and probably get out. He suddenly realized he still didn't have a way out. What if he had to stay down there for another whole day? His anus spasmed out another shart.

Mano nodded off and of course woke up coughing and gagging after sinking. He put a hand over his mouth and gasped as quietly as he could. He knew he must have woken somebody. He had. Somebody got out of bed. He could hear boards creaking over him as whoever it was walked into the bathroom. He heard the toilet seat drop and a long multi-octave fart reverberate around the porcelain bowl, then giggling, and then urination noises.

Manu heard a flush, right above his head. His brain was mildly interested in what a toilet sounds like from below. "I am losing my mind."

It started to rain. Mano heard water start to pour into the cistern from the gutters on the roof. "Oh shit," he mouthed. He could hardly breathe now with the water almost up to his mouth. More rainwater was coming.

CHAPTER 31

Tuesday. First light.

Mano was shivering so hard he was making waves in the cistern. As the sun came up, its faint glow shimmered through cracks in the floor onto the dark water he had spent the night in. The grey-purple light, just barely there, did nothing to warm him, but he could begin to see shapes. Pissing in Coleman's water supply had long since lost its hilarity.

Mano whispered to himself, "I probably have moss on my back." He had passed much of his solitary suffering trying to figure out where the colonel's silver was. He just knew it was in the colonel's cistern. And he was never going back into a cistern, or a swimming pool, or even a bathtub, the rest of his life. He still had no idea how he was going to get out of the cistern. Any drugs he'd had on board jumped ship halfway through the night. He didn't know whether he was shaking from the cold or from drug withdrawal. He'd give his left testicle for a Percodan he mumbled to himself.

He pushed on the trap door with his wrinkled fingertip while standing on his toes. It only went up an inch. He decided to take a bounce-on-his-toes tour of his underworld prison and look for something to stand on.

He bobbed first to one corner then to the next trolling with his feet, hoping to stumble on something. He found two cinder blocks. He dove down and did the eyes closed Braille thing picking one up and hopped with it slung between his hands holding his breath with each dunk until he was back under the trap door, and then repeated the undertaking stacking one on top of the other.

Standing on them, he easily opened the trap door all the way. Right in front of him was a case of wine. He silently cursed.

He bounced up the hole like vaulting a fence, palms on the edge of the floor above him. He launched himself up in a fluid motion, pirouetting his butt a hundred and eighty degrees to the sitting position on the edge of the opening, feet still dangling in the water. He pinched a testicle on a backed-out nail. It took everything he had to stifle the scream. Dripping he grabbed the case of wine and sloshed out the front door, leaving a trail like a wet dog escaping midway through a bath. He didn't care. He just wanted out. He decided that he was just going to walk up the Queen's Highway to his compound, drink a bottle of wine, and go to bed, after a hot shower. Or maybe lay in the sun all day.

"Shit." He stashed the case of wine in the jungle a few off the Queen's Highway and snuck back into Coleman's house. He opened the trap door again, reluctantly slipped down inside the cistern again, carefully put all the silver ingots, and bags of coins, on the edge of the trap door, and vaulted himself out again, sitting on the nail again pinching his other testicle. He was getting used to stifling screams. He put the one-pound silver bars in a pillowcase he found next to the washing machine.

It had begun raining again, the timing nice for Mano; no footprints.

Mano was feeling good about himself after half a bottle of wine and a hot shower. He had Coleman's silver, a bag of silver coins, and Jack Slack's silver. He had a nice mixed case of wine. If he could get ahold of some of the Colonel's silver, steal a valuable boat he could sell, he might just be able to start a new life.

By the time Endi, May, and Coleman got up and made it into the living room the tracks of water Mano had left were long gone. It wasn't until later that they missed the wine and the silver.

CHAPTER 32

Tuesday morning.

Jim Rand, in Florida called Johnny Walker waking him out of a sound sleep in his hammock on the deck of the *Drama Queen.* The satellite phone was right next to his head. The 38 Smith and Wesson was on the other side of his head. He put the J-frame snubby to his head, the hand grip in his ear and the barrel on his lips. The satellite phone kept ringing. He figured it out. "Walker here."

He hustled below to the little galley with the phone held by his shoulder next to his ear, put the gun under a pillow, and turned on the small stove under a coffee pot.

Rand said, "Well, first of all, the big news; a body washed up on a beach at a Walt Disney cruise ship stop, on some deserted island there in the Bahamas, north of Nassau where Disney cruise ships anchor for one last night of debauchery on their way back to Fort Ladeda and this body has no eyes or lips by this time, or genitals I might add, so says my contact in the Bahamas and…where was I…so anyway, and there's a hole in the back of the head. So, could that be your missing colonel?"

Johnny answered, "I didn't lose a damn colonel. A Disney cruise found him? That's actually hilarious."

Rand said, "I haven't told anyone that it was probably the body you neglected to call in a few days ago."

Johnny answered, "I hate it when a day starts out this way. I quit."

"You'll be considered a deserter and prosecuted as such. Anyway, so now the Bahamas federales are pinging and freaking that the Disney Cruise Line stumbled onto a body on their island paradise turf. They made the cruise line police it up, and put it in their cooler, accusing Disney of losing a guest unless they could prove it wasn't a guest. I told them I thought I had an ident for them. You should have heard the guy cussing on the other end of the phone when I mentioned Conch Island."

Walker said, "The Island seems to have a reputation."

Rand said, "The guy I talked to said he was going to send a cop and maybe some troops to your island. And restore order. That he was sick of those pompous self-governing English dick-suckers."

Johnny said, "It's not my island. But that would be really good. About damn time. We need a real cop, real bad. Troops? They're really sending troops?"

Rand answered, "Maybe you should leave while the getting is good. You'll be the first one they cuff, knowing your luck. You know anything yet. Suspects? Crime scene stuff?"

Johnny said, "We got some guy running around in tire tread sandals killing people. I haven't seen tire tread sandals since the seventies. That's the only clue we got. We also have a missing dentist."

Rand said, "Who the hell would ever miss a dentist for crissake?" Rand laughed and added, "Kids on the cruise found the colonel. Disney's gonna have to pony up for some therapy for them I bet."

Johnny said, "That's all your news, I hope?"

Rand said, "Hardly. Got some gossip for you. There's a high-profile fugitive the FBI is after that is running around loose somewhere in the Bermuda Triangle; they lost track of him in Ft Lauderdale. Witnesses say he was last seen heading east as a passenger in a cigarette boat. The guy is a well-known professional boxer from Hawaii. Killed his wife. No one knows where he is. Maybe he's holed up on your island, but that would be a lofty long shot."

Johnny interrupted Rand and said, "What'd you say about a boxer?" The vision of a man working out on the speed bag by the pool flashed through his mind. He told Rand what he had seen.

Rand said, "Be careful. The guy I'm talking about has million-dollar hands. Fifty-five fights, thirty knock-outs. If it's him, he killed his wife. An O.J. thing. His handlers supposedly parked him on a desert island out there somewhere your way partner. No one can find him. No one is looking anymore. Figure he'll show up in good time. Maybe this is the good time." Rand described him, and Johnny's heart jumped.

Johnny said, "It could be the same guy. I only saw him for a second, but the size of the guy fits. And he was practicing on a punching bag."

Rand gave more details. "This guy's last name is Kamea. Means shark, or passionate-lover, or the-one-and-only. In

Hawaiian. First name is Mano. He is absolutely adored by his fans in Hawaii. He's had bit parts in movies, was thinking about running for some political seat, people literally lived and died with his every move. Some 82-year old farmer collapsed dead in his neighbor's house at precisely the same time this sucker knocked out some big deal opponent. You getting this Johnny?"

Johnny poured coffee. The sun beamed its first rays across the water and turned the white *Drama Queen* sailboat pink. The water was the blue of a robin's egg. He said dejectedly, "Yea, I'm here."

Rand said, "The guy made 12.5 million at his last fight before he disappeared. Reportedly, all his money is tied up due to asset-seizure warrants, litigation, and all that. But he's supposed to be living high on the hog down your way somewhere."

Johnny said, "How am I supposed to play this? The CIA, which is you, doesn't want him? Me, Portland Police Bureau, with no authority anywhere but in Portland, Oregon, can't possibly think of any reason why I would want him, or be able to arrest him, or know what to do with him if I did, even if this is him, which I seriously doubt..." His words trailed off, he caught his train of thought and continued, "It's just too big a Bermuda Triangle for him and me to be on one stupid island together. I'm pretty damn unlucky, but I can't be that damn unlucky. Like I said, I quit."

Rand went on. "I just woke your boss Captain Kellerman up. I forgot about the time zones, he was pissed as it was four in the morning on the west coast, but he cheered right up when I told him you weren't coming back. So, you are still on the clock with the Central Intelligence Agency. Congrats Special Agent Walker. Besides, I'll tell Langley you stole the sailboat if you don't cooperate."

Johnny mumbled a blasphemy.

Rand laughed on the other end and said, "The Bahamas cop headed your way is named Jergins Albright. Big girl I'm told. Too-tight skirts. Wears a tie. Sensible heels. Good news is they don't carry guns down there. Well maybe they do now. Since the English have finally gone. She's apparently quite black with an attitude about it. Also, not happy being a woman in a man's world. They call her 'Tiger Balm.' You might not want to call her that. She'll be coming on the Albright Water Taxi sometime this afternoon. And she's bringing a picture of that boxer from Hawaii. Hey, gotta go. Keep your head low."

Johnny got dressed, which amounted to putting his shoulder holster on under a faded work shirt he had cut the sleeves off at the shoulders. He had slept in his cargo pants cut-offs.

"Jim Rand can blow me. I don't have a dog in this fight." He thought he better call Portland and talk to the captain himself. He wasn't sure if he was getting paid anymore.

Johnny looked at his watch. It was almost 7:30 a.m. local time. It was still the middle of the night on the West Coast. Even if Rand had awakened the captain already, he decided he'd wait a while.

He took a shower. He walked to Amanda's. She gave him a ride to Coleman's.

Johnny filled them all in about the colonel's Disney cruise. And Rand's information on Mano. No news on Jack Slack.

CHAPTER 33

Tuesday. Late morning.

Andy Albright showed up. He had not been able to get his diving buddy to come with him, so the group volunteered Walker who confessed to being a certified diver.

Andy threw a dead chicken into the colonel's brightly lit cistern, and nothing happened. No swirl of intense activity like as in a thousand Piranhas stripping it to the bone. No bloody feeding frenzy by alligators. No giant serpent. Nothing. The chicken just floated there.

Andy turned off the breaker to the lights in the cistern. They were afraid a cord might be dangling in the water, and they might be electrocuted. Better to use high powered underwater flashlights instead.

They considered again just draining the huge underground reservoir. Chance had said it would take probably two days. He had calculated that there was probably six to eight-thousand cubic feet of water in the cistern. At seven and a half gallons per cubic feet they were looking at between 40 to 50 thousand gallons down there. Another problem: Chance said once the first rain started filling it who knows how many years ago it has had water in it. Empty, the concrete lining might float like a boat. Or the house may implode into it. Never empty them completely without shoring them up to prevent the walls of the cistern from collapsing bringing the whole house down.

So, Andy, donned with a tank, mask, and regulator, jumped in. He had his one million candle power underwater spotlight turned on. Immediately spinning in a 360-degree circle he swept the entire cistern with the lamp. At that moment the snake clamped onto his fin and shook it like a dog with a toy, pulling it off Andy's foot. Andy involuntarily screamed spitting out the respirator that was clamped between his teeth, it streaming forth a magnificent quantity of bubbles. He swung the flashlight wildly around looking for whatever attacked him while simultaneously trying to recover his regulator. A hand pushed a buddy breather into his mouth, and Andy instinctively cleared it and sucked in a deep breath of air.

Johnny jumped in when he saw Andy panicking from the snake attack. He was ready, mask on, regulator in his mouth, tank on his back, buddy breather in hand. He had seen the sea snake come from nowhere. After a few breaths Andy replaced Johnny's spare buddy breather with his own.

Johnny reached up and grabbed one of the spear guns from Endi. Endi passed down another flashlight. After another three-sixty scan Andy shined the flashlight on his foot. There was no blood. He felt no pain. He took the other fin off and threw it up to waiting hands.

Johnny saw the snake coming right toward him, swimming without effort. He thought venom stronger than any other venomous snake in the world. Just as he was about to use the explosive capture stick the snake went on by him without missing a beat of its tail and disappeared into a dark corner of the cistern.

Johnny saw a shape in a corner. Hand signaling each other, he and Andy slowly swam/walked toward the shape. Andy, knees bent slightly, walked backward covering them from behind, as Johnny walked forward. Both had explosive capture sticks in one hand, compressed air spear guns slung over their shoulders, and the flashlights in the other.

Johnny saw it was a human. He tapped Andy who turned around. They recognized Jack Slack. They towed him to the trap door hole. Andy surfaced, spit out the regulator, and rested his mask on his forehead. He told them they found Slack. Johnny kept panning the flashlight as hands reached down to pull Jack Slack's body up through the trap door.

The cool water and darkness had preserved the chalky white body well. But it was bloating, and the skin was doughy and waterlogged. The teeth were bizarrely perfect behind the macabre grin only corpses can have.

Andy and Johnny slipped below the surface again, capture sticks and spear guns at the ready. They found silver ingots, each the size of two hot dog buns, in a pile not far from the trap door. The colonel had apparently thrown them as far as he could into the cistern. There were literally hundreds.

He and Andy started passing some out like a bucket brigade.

Amanda calculated as she stacked them that if they were three pounds each, times sixteen ounces, they weighed somewhere around 40 to 50 ounces a piece. The price of silver was between 15 and 20 dollars an ounce. At 40 ounces an ingot, each would be worth around six hundred dollars. At 50 ounces a bar they could be worth a thousand each.

Andy and Johnny explored the rest of the cistern. The sea snake was nowhere to be seen, staying out of their way. They discovered more silver ingots stacked three feet high. The ingots on the bottom were turning black. Andy took his regulator out of his mouth and mouthed with a grin, "Fuck me."

They saw animal bones all over the floor of the cistern. As he waved the flashlight into the corner, he saw movement and suddenly there was a thick swirl of creatures coming right toward them. They instinctively ducked as the objects raced by them.

They recognized Lionfish. There must have been thirty or forty of them that flitted by. Andy also recognized some other types of fish. At the same time, they turned their flashlights on what looked like a huge beach ball spinning in place. As they inched closer, they realized it was a mass of sea snakes coiled around the chicken they had forgotten about. There was chicken skin and feathers suspended in the clear clean water of the cistern.

They backed away from the snakes toward the trap door as fast as they could. Johnny helped Andy out first, and Andy and Endi each grabbed Johnny's arms and pulled him out, Coleman grabbing the scuba tank, making sure it didn't get caught on the edge of the trap door.

Before Johnny had seen the sea snakes, he had picked up something he knew didn't come from the ocean.

He'd thrown it out as he reached for the edge. It was a human femur.

Johnny said, "That makes at least two dead humans in one dead colonel's flooded basement. We know the colonel didn't put Jack Slack down here, but he sure as hell could have put whoever this belonged to down there, and who knows how long ago."

Andy said, "That's not all we found down there."

Johnny and Andy took turns describing the huge stack of silver bullion.

The group just looked at each other. They were speechless.

Coleman picked up the femur, "I wonder who's this is?"

Endi asked, "The colonel's wife?"

Johnny said, "What I wouldn't give for a criminalist right now. I hope the cop from RBPF (Royal Bahamian Police Force) can hustle up a forensic unit."

Amanda said impatiently, "We need to get that silver out of this cistern." she pointed down and continued, "The cops are going to figure out the silver came from the *El Cangrejo* and confiscate it all, plus what we already have. I don't know diddly about salvage rights in the Bahamas, but you can bet my sweet growing Albright ass they will figure it their way, one way or the other."

Coleman said, "Let's drain this sucker."

CHAPTER 34

Tuesday afternoon.

Endi asked Coleman. "What we gonna do with Slack? We should have just left him down there."

Coleman said, "If the cops don't get here soon, we'll have to take him to the ice cream shop. Only problem is bodies get out of the freezer there."

Endi was looking at the body's hands. He lifted one up and looked under the fingernails. "No broken nails. No bloody fingers." He opened the slack jaw and looked in the mouth. "No petechial hemorrhage…" He looked at the others and saw their blank stares and added, "Like we see with strangulations."

Johnny said, "Wish we could get a postmortem. And a toxicology report."

Amanda said, "He was probably shit-faced and just died. It was a hard wedding."

Johnny said, "We may not be able to solve the case, but we may be able to prevent another murder. No one should be alone until we figure this out."

Coleman said, "True. I got an idea on how to empty that cistern quicker."

May said, "Make the hole bigger?"

Coleman answered, "Exactly. We punch a hole in her."

Endi asked, "With what? We don't exactly have a backhoe."

Coleman answered, "There is a forklift in town. Remember we were going to steal it."

"But it won't even make it down the road," Amanda said.

Coleman said, "To my tool shed then. Picks and shovels."

Johnny said, "You guys have this really well under control. I don't want your silver. I brought you your toys." He nodded to Andy and went on, "Andy isn't going to need a diving partner anymore, besides I ain't going down there again. Not for all the silver in the Caribbean. I need to make a few calls, and get back to Portland, and my job."

As if on cue, behind them his satellite phone rang. He walked over to the pile of clothes he had taken off before the dive and answered the phone that was resting on top of the heap.

"Hello… Yo, Captain Kellerman." He put his hand over the mouthpiece, and said to the group, "It's my boss." He took his hand off the mouthpiece and walked out of the room talking, "Great minds think alike. I was just reaching for the phone to call you. Weather's fine…huh-huh…raining and cold in Oregon? Well, there's a surprise…What?…

After a few minutes he came back in with a dejected look and announced, "That was my boss. He said I don't work for him anymore. I'm a special agent with the CIA, still, and I'm supposed to stay here and help you because my ass-hole buddy Jim Rand in Florida put in for me, and Portland is getting along fine without me. Rand apparently believes the boxer-wife-killer is on Conch Island. Not only is he apparently skipping court dates for his murder trial, but they want him because of illegal drug use and his testimony in parallel illicit drug use investigations. They want to strip him of all his belts and fine him a billion, or two. And the IRS wants him of course. I miss my cat."

Coleman said to Johnny, "Time for you to retire like me."

Endi said, "Yea, look how good retirement's working out for both of us." He nodded toward Coleman.

May said, "Cat?"

Amanda said, "Cat?"

Johnny said, "Name's Ruggles. Maine Coon… and weighs twenty-four pounds.

"Awwww…"

"Awwww…"

Endi said, "You are now the official authority here. Me and Coleman got no badge, no nothing. You're in charge. Go, Central Intelligence Agency!"

There was stony silence. Johnny said, "If I'm in charge, let's get a drink. I just about got killed down there by sea snakes and lionfish. And I really hate snakes. By the way if I'm in charge here, the silver becomes evidence and therefore police property."

Amanda said, "You're not in charge of anything Yank. You're so far out of your jurisdiction your next step will be falling into a Tasty Freeze freezer. I am an Albright and I claim salvage rights. Formally. At this moment. You are all witnesses."

Andy said, "We don't have the silver yet."

Coleman said, "Let's see if we can open this swimming pool up. Let's go outside and see if there is a low spot that isn't just concrete set-in excavated reef. I think I remember a low spot where the pipe goes in. I'm thinking if we can break a **V** above the drain tube, water could gush out four or five times faster than it can run out the drainpipe."

Amanda said, "Find two or three hoses and we can get a siphon going too maybe. Maybe there's a pump we don't know about too. Anyone got any dynamite?"

Andy said, "I think we ought to burn the house down."

Coleman said, "Maybe I can get the pump that pumps the cistern water into the house to pump water outside."

Andy said, "Pick and shovel? There's going to be reinforcement bar in that concrete. I'll head for my shop and get a cutting torch. I have some heavy chain. Maybe we can hook it to a golf cart and pull the concrete apart."

Coleman groaned. Endi said, "Golf carts don't work too well for that."

Chance said, "Maybe I can use the dive boat and a long cable. It was a net fisher. Geared to drag nets."

Johnny said, "Before we all split up, remember there is a killer out there. We should stay in pairs. At least one of the pair should be packing a gun. If whoever is killing off citizens finds out about this monstrous cache the colonel has, then all bets are off as to the odds of us making it out of this alive. Especially if there is more than one perpetrator. If you think it's been violent so far, get ready for a blood bath. That's why I say leave it where it is; snakes and all. Don't drain the cistern."

Amanda said, "For me it's worth fighting for. Gimme a gun." No one offered. She stamped her foot and said, "I'm serious. I need a good singles bar and a Wendy's hamburger. I'm sick of this island. This is my ticket out of here. I said, Gimme a gun."

May said, "Ka-Ching. Same here. I'm tired of living off husbands and boyfriends."

Coleman and Endi looked at each other and shrugged. Coleman looked at Amanda and said, "So much for romance."

Amanda looked at Coleman with her head tilted smiling sweetly and said, "I detect a sad little boy. Well, I'll tell you what, you help me get my share of that silver and I'll give you a blow job you'll never forget. How's that for sincerity, and incentive."

Looking at May, Endi said, "How about me?"

May said, "Same. Done deal."

"Underwater?"

"You got it big boy."

Endi said, "Let's get some dynamite."

Johnny Walker said, "I fail to see one damn thing in this for me."

Amanda said grinning, "Johnny, you can have Luna Albright. I believe she is available. I understand she is beyond pale with her teeth out. Or maybe Detective Jergins Batista George IV Albright, might be able to service you after she solves the crime of the century here on Conch Island. She was voted most likely to contract a STD in high school."

Coleman said with a huge smile, "Come on guys. Amanda needs her silver. Let Johnny lead the charge. He is legal with the CIA. That's all I need to hand the keys to him."

Andy said to Johnny, "I'll take you to town. I have a shotgun on the boat. I'll get my cutting torch. I volunteer us to take Slack to the ice cream cooler."

Coleman said, "I'll go get pics and shovels."

Amanda said to Coleman, "I'll follow you."

Johnny said, "Let's get a move on."

They found large plastic trash bags and managed to get Jack Slack's remains tucked in four layers of plastic. Covered with an old blanket, he made it to the internment facilities (ice cream freezer) without incident. No Haitians were harmed this time.

CHAPTER 35

They came back with picks, shovels, crowbars, and sledgehammers.

They ran into re-bar quickly. Andy fired up the cutting torch. As soon as the re-bar was cut, it only took a few good whacks by Jack and Endi, and two feet of concrete came off in one chunk and water cascaded out of the cistern so hard that it knocked the two workers off their feet. They scrambled thinking sea snakes would be caught in the vortex. Everyone remembered the caveat in the article about the sea snakes, that if caught out of water they panic and became unpredictably violent and aggressive.

The torrent of water raced through the loose sand and down the colonel's golf-cart wide driveway. After emptying to a certain level, the six worked the hole in the cistern wall another six inches and so on, until they could not get the concrete any lower. It was easier than they thought it was going to be. There was just a foot of water left in the cistern.

Amanda said, "You know what; screw the fish and

snakes. I want the silver. Let's Taser the bastards. I got an idea. Follow me."

They went into the colonel's house and found the main breaker-box. Amanda suggested they chop holes in a few places near the ceiling fixtures in the cistern, loosen a few and let them drop in the water, then throw the switch and see if they could electrocute everything in the tank.

They dropped the light fixtures into the remaining one foot of water in the cistern.

Johnny suggested bypassing the breaker that handled the now soaking lights in the cistern, because it would trip instantly as soon as the switch was thrown. He shut the main switch cutting the power to the whole house. He then wired around the cistern lights' breaker. He diverted other circuits around their breakers and dangled loose wires in the water.

Outside the house there was a lightning rod cable that came from the roof and ended up attached to a steel rod driven into the ground. He left the rod in the ground and threw the cable into the water through the drain hole they had made. His theory was that the power would go through the water and down the lightning rod's ground rod. He turned off every other breaker in the house taking every circuit out of action except the ones in cistern.

He said, "Ready?" Everyone nodded their heads. He threw the switch and left it on for five seconds. There were sparks and the smell of ozone. He pulled the power and let the wiring cool. He assumed some wires could get hot enough to melt their insulation and cause a short anywhere in the house if he wasn't careful. He zapped them again for ten seconds.

Looking into the cistern with flashlights Coleman said, "There's some floaters."

Johnny threw the switch again for another ten seconds. They saw some snakes on the surface now. And lionfish, and others.

Coleman said, "Forgot to tell you. When we went back to my place for tools somebody stole that whole case of wine that was in my laundry room by the trap door into my cistern. Guess what else they stole? The silver we put in my cistern; it's gone."

Mano watched and listened as best he could from a small clearing near the colonel's house. He caught snippets of the conversations. He saw them load Jack Slack. He watched them hacking away at the foundation. He assumed they were draining the cistern, but he had no idea why since Jack Slack was already out of there. He knew they were trying to figure out where the tire-tread sandals came from. Lots of worries for his addled brain.

He was a mass of sores. He itched mercilessly. The hours in the water had caused his skin to lose all its civility. As it lost its health, bacteria and fungi bloomed in each nettle hole. His one tube of anti-biotic ointment hadn't even been enough to treat his private places. Ironically, the only time he felt even half OK was when he was soaking in his pool.

He slipped back into his compound, grabbed a bottle of wine, took some more pills and capsules, and eased back into the pool. He absentmindedly massaged the damaged testicles he had sat on. He thought one felt bigger than the other. With the itch dulled, and his head on his arms on the side of the pool, he fell asleep. He slipped off the edge and woke up choking and gagging. He was getting tired of falling asleep in the water, but he couldn't stand to lay in bed.

He lamented to himself, "Used to be someone says fuck you, I knock their brains out." He scratched furiously at one knee; then rubbed his back on the side of the pool. "I want to go to the casinos again. Get free lobster and drinks everywhere like in the old days. I wanted something, I endorsed it, and I got it—car, gold watch, pallet of basketball shoes to give away. God, I loved those days."

Mano rubbed his nose and it brought tears to his eyes. It wasn't in the greatest shape from the poundings through the years, but now with the multiple near "drownings," it burned and stung too.

"So far, they got zero evidence. No one's got nothing on this backwater island to do any police work. Jesus, this is the gold standard for looser islands of the planet. I could kill assholes all day long and no one could prove it." He was trying to cheer himself up a little. He picked at another nettle under his arm pit. "They got no fingerprint stuff. They got no cool ass forensic experts or labs or blood splatter types or special lights or nothing. What am I worried about?"

He felt better. "They can't prove this is anybody's wine either."

He made a decision.

"I'm gonna steal me a big ass cabin cruiser and blow.

The dumb shit owners all keep their cruisers' keys in them. Boats are worth a million apiece, or more. I'm gonna grab what silver I got and get the hell out of here tonight, sell the boat somewhere in the Caribbean and that's where I'll stay. Buy a little place. A bar and a liquor store. Fuck you lawyers. See if you can find me on the high seas. Trinidad, Antigua, St. Lucia, Saint something."

He thought he heard something to his right. He looked at the wall surrounding the compound, and gave the finger to whatever it was, shaking his hand up and down and sneering "Fucking island. Lizard. Cat. Whatever? Fuck you."

CHAPTER 36

Wednesday, late morning.

Endi almost fell off the ladder. "He just gave me the finger. I think I been spotted."

Coleman said, "You're one foot from me and I can't spot you through this overgrown vegetable stew." He shook a sea-grape bush for punctuation. "I can't even hardly hear you over the ocean."

Still perched on the ladder Endi raised his head carefully and peeked over the edge of the wall again. Coleman followed him. Their two heads were ear to ear balanced on the step ladder. Endi whispered, "Next time we get two ladders."

Endi snapped the shutter again, just as Mano tipped the wine bottle to his lips.

"That's my wine," Coleman whispered.

Endi had the telephoto lens on his Nikon. The stepladder was against the compound's wall. They could both see the man hanging on the side of the pool. He took a few more shots and they climbed down and carefully pulled the ladder away.

They didn't say anything until they were fifty feet down the path. They were carrying the ladder. Coleman said. "Whoever he is, we know he's moving around the island. And raiding pantries. He probably took the silver too."

Endi said, "Gotta be that boxer from Hawaii. How the hell did he even know about the silver in my cistern?"

Coleman answered, "I think we found our killer."

Amanda, Andy, and May, heavily armed, were sitting on Coleman's back steps as the two guys stepped out of the jungle with their ladder.

Amanda said, "Colon…?"

Endi said, "Clogging."

Amanda said, "You may pass."

May frowned at Endi and said, "Password?"

Endi said, "Sounds like the name of a town in Germany; Colonclogging." Amanda guffawed. Endi and Coleman too. May didn't get it: blank, frown, pissy, defensive…

Coleman, smiling ear to ear, sing-song-ed, "Endi was a dumb man and a fool…who discovered red spots on his tool… said the doctor a cynic, get out of my clinic…just wipe the lipstick off, you tool."

Johnny came out of the house with a shotgun in his hand. "Just got off the phone with Rand. He said he talked again to the Marsh Harbor police and they said they still haven't got anybody scheduled to come over and investigate. You guys want silver; you better get it out of here? Snakes are dead by the way. Did you get pictures of the guy?"

Coleman said, "Yep." He took the memory card out of the camera and handed it to Johnny. "Pretty sure he's the boxer from Hawaii. Couldn't tell much. He was in the pool. And I think he was drinking a bottle of my wine. Wouldn't be surprised if he was the one who stole the case of wine in my pantry, and the silver in my cistern. Scary. When was he there? That's what's scary."

Johnny said, "Amanda, can you e-mail the pictures to my CIA guy in Florida?"

Amanda said, "I'll go right now. You think the island is safer since we know who and where our bad guy is?"

Johnny said, "Unless he has a gang of accomplices. He may not even be the gang leader."

Coleman said, "I'll ride shotgun Amanda. Let's go."

When Coleman and Amanda got back, the group talked about what to do next.

Amanda said, "I think we hide the silver, and fast. It's time for buried treasure and a map. We dump it in the ocean, whatever. Build a wall around it where it sits. The Marsh Harbor Police are gonna have enough to deal with chasing down Hawaiian fugitives, dead colonels, dentists, and somebody's bones in a cistern. She can confiscate the silver only if she finds it. She doesn't have to know about it."

Coleman said, "I like the build-a-wall-idea. I've got a pile of cinder blocks. We could just build a wall around the silver ingots where they sit now and hope everybody thinks the cinderblocks are just part of the foundation. We can tell them that we drained the cistern to get Slack out. We had to kill the snakes and lionfish, which are an ecological foreign species disaster anyway. They needed eradication."

Amanda said to no one in particular, "I'm a rich bitch. I been doing the math. We're sitting on seven million here. I'm thinking about ordering a couple of pizzas from Ft Lauderdale and having them helicoptered over."

Coleman said, "How about that blow job?"

Amanda pretended she didn't hear him.

Coleman said, "Anyone do the math on how much that shit weighs?"

Amanda said, "Seven tons give or take."

Endi said, "How many ingots?"

Amanda said, "Over five thousand."

Amanda did the math for the group out loud. "If each weigh three pounds we are dealing with approximately 15,000 pounds. Even if silver is worth only $15 an ounce, we are sitting on three million plus. A twenty-percent rise in the market adds another million."

Coleman whistled. "No way we can move that. We'd need a forklift and a barge. Let's hide it in plain sight. Wall them up until this blows over. Like wait until next year."

Johnny said to Coleman, "You got any mortar to go with those cinder blocks."

Coleman said, "Yep."

Andy said, "Mount up people."

Rand called Johnny from Florida. Rand said, "That's our man, Mano Kamea."

CHAPTER 37

Wednesday. Mid-afternoon.

Mano put on a floppy hat, bandanna, and large sunglasses, and headed into the jungle and toward the marina. He was going boat shopping. He was planning to get off the island tonight.

In Hawaii during his whirlwind boxing career, he'd owned several cabin cruisers and finally a seventy-nine-foot sport-fisherman. Twin diesel inboard-outboards, two state rooms, flying bridge, spotting tower and helm, twin fighting chairs, outriggers, bow and stern thrusters, the whole deal. He used to live for fishing. Took anybody that wanted to go. He had a lot of time on his hands. After all, sixty matches in the ring, averaging ten or twenty minutes apiece, only amounted to a thousand minutes tops. Most were shorter than that. That adds up to maybe a 170-hour career; three weeks and change, was all he worked in ten years. He had a lot of time for fishing.

A sixty-five-foot *Outer Reef* full-displacement trawler style cruiser had just come in, the *Petty Cash, Miami.* Mano watched an overweight cigar smoking man, probably in his sixties, hanging out with his girlfriend, in her thirties. She had dark glasses on as big as her face and long black hair down to her waist. Petite. Oriental. She looked like she had been passed around. He brightened; maybe she should come with me cruising. He liked them bigger than him, and blond—so they take a little punishment. But, some of these Orientals are a lot tougher than they looked. The boat was scarcely a couple of years old, he bet. Probably worth two-three million plus, retail. Maybe even more. Sell it for half and settle down and start over. Buy a little cash-cow business like a bar and a small hotel. Hell, maybe even in Cuba.

Mano boldly went up to a black man reading a bible at the gas dock and struck up a conversation. He asked about the *Outer Reef.* The dock attendant said the couple was staying the rest of the week, living on board. There was no crew on it right now. The attendant said he had pumped 600 gallons of diesel into the big twin engine boat. The attendant said he had pumped over 600 gallons of diesel into the big twin engine boat topping off both engine tanks and the generator's tank. Mano noticed a sign that said *Credit Cards Only.* He thought to himself he could run up some serious pocket money just with the guy's American Express card. At one time he had a 100k limit on his Am Ex card. The gas attendant said that the owners were supposed to be meeting up with friends coming in in a sailboat.

The gas attendant said there was a lady cook and a guy steward, a couple, but they had been given a week off, and were gone.

Mano figured: Full of fuel, provisioned, credit cards on board, dump the man in deep water. Dump the woman after I'm tired of her.

Mano had checked the tide tables and found that at 11:08 that night was a high tide, two feet over datum. Plenty of water to get out of town without scraping bottom on the way out.

He said to himself, *here I am worth millions, starting over again with nothing.*

CHAPTER 38

Wednesday. Midnight.

Mano simply drove a purloined golf cart he had "borrowed" down the Queen's Highway at mid-night straight into the settlement. He hid two suitcases with Slack's silver and drugs, and the silver he got from Coleman's cistern, in a thick fiscus hedge behind where he parked the stolen golf cart. He hadn't seen a soul.

He'd left a voice mail for his lawyer saying that he was feeling great. That he was off the drugs, and to cancel the doctor visits for now. He was doing alright without a woman too. He told them he was happy as far as that could go, but it beat prison, and he was writing a memoir. He was lonely, but finally adjusting. Just call when they knew something. He still had plenty of supplies. Thanks for all you do.

He went shopping. He broke into the Albright Grocery (no alarm). He put boxes and sacks of groceries in the back of the golf cart. He found a fat bank deposit bag at the store too.

He wondered why he hadn't thought of that sooner.

He stealthily climbed onto the boat. The sliding glass door to the salon was open. He quietly crept through the boat until he found the stateroom. It smelled of cigars and perfume. In the dimness, lit only by LED lights, he could see two figures in the full-sized bed. Without hesitation, he hit the sleeping man on the head with a baseball bat he had found at the stern that he assumed was used for stunning fish. The man didn't make a sound. The woman rolled over on her elbow.

Mano slipped in beside her and wrapped one arm around her neck from behind. With her throat in the crook of his elbow and the other hand over her mouth he squeezed. In a matter of seconds, she passed out from having her carotid arteries occluded. She was naked. He cupped a breast in one hand and evaluated size and shape. He smelled her scent. Her long hair was all over her face. She was breathing evenly. He got hard. Later, he thought.

He had duct tape in his pocket and covered both their mouths. The woman was quickly awake but still dazed. She didn't fight as he taped her hands behind her back and her ankles together.

He whispered in her ear, "Hello princess. If you don't just lie here, I will throw you overboard. Princesses that can't swim because their arms and legs are duct taped are not happy princesses. Nod if you get my drift." She nodded vigorously.

The man was still unconscious. Mano thought he might have over done it. He didn't care. He was going to kill them both anyway. Unless the woman was exceptional and ready for a lifetime of kinky sex and didn't mind going to

Cuba—and came with a dowry. Maybe she was the one with the money: *Crazy Rich Asians,* the movie, popped into his mind.

He used the duct tape to secure the man's arms and legs too.

He loaded his supplies, the suitcases of silver, and the partial case of the wine. He was looking forward to some cold beer and some whiskey. He was sure the boat was well stocked.

The boat started right up, burbling softly, its exhaust pipes partially underwater. He jumped off, and unhooked the power cable umbilicus, and the water hose, and undid the lines. The boat didn't move. Heavy he thought. He put one engine in reverse and quietly slipped out of the fifty-foot-deep slip. As soon as the bow cleared the slip, he put the starboard engine in forward leaving the port engine in reverse and the big ship pirouetted in place ninety degrees. He popped the port engine into forward too, and the ship eased out of the dock area into the harbor. He tapped the throttles and the big engines responded with another two hundred rpms and he smoothly and quietly slipped out of the harbor, the green harbor entrance light to his right, and the red to his left.

And he was free. After he was several miles from Conch Island, he turned on the helm lights. He moved the curser on the combination GPS, radar, weather, and depth finder, and highlighted a spot in the middle of nowhere thirty miles to the south. He punched the autopilot. The big vessel got up to seven knots. He kept the throttles there. He stowed all his groceries. He drank a couple cold Mexican beers, and then had two fingers of Chevas Regal Scotch on ice while the boat chugged along on autopilot.

He went below. He turned on the stateroom lights. The man was awake staring at him with fierce eyes showing no fear. Mano had seen that plenty of times from opponents. He would take that look out of this guy, like all the others.

At dawn, Mano set an anchor off the bow in a deserted cove and cooked a steak, had some more of the man's Scotch, and slept.

When Mano woke up around eleven a.m. after sleeping three or four hours, he got up and checked on his captives. They were gone.

He found them. They hadn't gotten too far just hopping. Only to the next stateroom. He left them there and slid the pocket door shut after he had tied them to each other back-to-back, leg to leg, neck to neck. They wouldn't be hopping around now he figured; if they did, so what. It might be amusing. Falling down steps, falling overboard, whatever.

He was on his way to somewhere south. He knew the ocean was big and even aircraft carriers were hard to find out there. He figured no one would be looking. The boat probably wouldn't be missed for who knows how long. He was having fun thinking about what he would do to the man and woman. He smiled as he thought about tying them to the anchor and tea bagging them in the ocean, leaving just their heads out. Maybe torturing them a little for being assholes. Maybe troll with them. Or use them for Marlin chum.

He figured he'd probably just shoot them when the time came if he could find a gun on board. He knew a boat this size cruising in the Bahamas would have an arsenal to protect the owner from pirates. Usually automatic assault rifles. He'd sell those too.

He found the man's wallet with lots of credit cards. He knew he could probably get away with using them for a week or longer. The wallet also had a couple of thousand in cash in it, U.S. and Bahamian. He found a safe that was hidden behind a picture of a schooner. The man wouldn't give him the combination. Maybe a teabag session might be necessary. He knew getting into the safe was just a matter of time. Maybe if he threatened to have sex with the princess in front of the man, he'd cave. He thought that was going to be on the agenda anyway. The more he looked at her, the more he thought philosophically *it's a crime to waste pussy.* The man's eyes had lost their anger already. The eyes were afraid now. Mano knew he would soon do anything, even if it was just for hope.

CHAPTER 39

Thursday. Morning.

Detective Jergins Albright was not happy. If she never went to Conch Cay again it would be too soon.

Her mom had been a black Haitian girl working as a maid on Conch Island. Mom got laid by an Albright, and Jergins was unwanted a minute after conception, and for the rest of her life. Mom started showing pregnancy and was banished from the island to the slums of the city. Jergins grew up, pissed-off from day one, in substandard housing with Albright's Pigeon Peas and conch for breakfast, lunch, and dinner. Her mother told everyone it was the Jergins Hand Lotion that got her pregnant, hence the name. She was Chance's half-sister—same father.

Jergins was the only Albright besides Amanda in the history of the island that had gotten a college degree. Police Science at Florida State. She'd been twelve years on the Police Force now. She got in college because she was female and black. And got into the police academy because she was female and black. If her mom had been white, she would have been stuck on Conch Cay the rest of her life. Her minority status paved the way. She turned out depressed, with a big head and a big butt (Albright, *and* black genes), diabetes, and a weight problem. She didn't get the Albright good teeth; she got Haitian terrible teeth. Her life was one great paradox.

She had a tooth ache right now. All she wanted to do all day long every day was pee. Her type-two diabetes wanted to be a type-one. She thought maybe she'd see Jack Slack while she was on the island and get her tooth looked at. She didn't know he was dead and frozen in an ice cream shop freezer. She hadn't read the memos; she thought there was only one murder to investigate.

She didn't fit in her uniform; a hot navy-blue two-piece suit, with a skirt too short and tight to even climb stairs or sit down in without showing everything. She wore regulation dark pantyhose, old lady high heels, and a heat producing police wool felt hat. *In the Bahamas? Really? Why didn't they just let her wear a track suit?* She kept her hair dyed a bright yellow blonde and wore it trimmed in a long crew cut which heightened the awareness of her oversized Albright head. The high humidity was not good for black peoples' hair. Hers looked like a rusty Brillo Pad.

And it was her period.

When she found that she was going to have to investigate a murder she begged her boss for a criminalist to take with her, but the experienced one was on vacation. She got a rookie named Thurman Winer who had just graduated from tech school the week before. He was the bottom of his class, hence the job in the armpit of the Bahamas.

She also got Corporal Constable Uriah Albright as her assistant. Everybody called him "Urine." (She and he were cousins of course.) He had been advanced to a level of complete incompetence where he stayed in arrested development.

She had to take the Albright Ferry, which she hated; she hated anything with the Albright name on it. They wouldn't take her in the police launch because the pilot of the police launch always ran aground in Conch Key.

She had called her brother Chance. He told her there was a serial killer loose on the island. He didn't know how many dead. She whined that there was supposed to be only one dead, the colonel. She asked who else? He wouldn't tell her any details and hung up. (Phone calls to other islands also cost 8 dollars a minute to both the caller… and the called.)

She had a fax from the U.S. with Mano's picture on it and an urgent request for help from the United States CIA. There was supposed to be a CIA agent in place on the island to help her. She thought *oh, that's just brilliant.*

So, she found herself riding on the very same ferry boat (the *Albright Conch Island VI*), that she had ridden on in her mother's womb thirty-seven years before, only now sweating in pantyhose, cursing a soggy maxi-pad, and having to pee. She was pissed and getting more pissed every nautical mile the boat traveled.

Thurman dropped the crime scene box in the water while boarding the ferry and it had to be fished out with a gaff. The other passengers laughed. They laughed again when Jergins' skirt rode up while climbing aboard and she did the splits on the transom. Thurman had to go back to the cab for his gun. Jergins had pointed out that his holster was empty. *They wouldn't even take me to the ferry in a squad car!*

The toolbox fell in the water at Conch Kay too. The tight skirt rode up, but everybody had turned away having seen all they could stand the first time.

Jergins hugged Chance her half-brother. Luna Albright, always there when the ferry arrived, to give people rides, didn't make eye contact with Jergins at all. The Albrights were practicing racists and still believed they were living in the slave era.

Johnny Walker looked arrestable to Jergins. He had a week's growth of facial hair, was wearing cut offs with a belt made from rope, and a work shirt with the sleeves cut off, and had a faded bleached out red ball cap on that looked like it had been through a hammer mill. He introduced himself as the CIA-man-on-the-scene. He flashed a badge that said *Portland Police Bureau.* WTF?! she thought.

Behind Johnny, were Coleman and Endi. They didn't say anything. Nobody introduced them. Jergins smelled booze. They all had guns under their shirts. She asked in a clear British accent, "So which one of you people thinks you're in charge?"

Luna, with an attitude, had inserted herself into the small group and said to Jergins, "Did you know Dr. Slack bit the bullet too? You're the one in charge, and you better hurry up because people are dying every time the fucking tides change." *Ugly black bitch.*

"Slack is dead?" Jergins asked visibly stunned; she needed that tooth looked at. "How many goddam murders I got to investigate on this dead reef?" Luna didn't like her tone and grunted an insult at Jergins in Albright that only an Albright would understand.

Walker interrupted, "Officer Albright, have you got a picture of Kamea?"

Jergins gave Johnny the look. She snapped her fingers next to her shoulder with a pouty chin jut, and the side-to-side head slide of black attitude. Thurman was looking at fish congregating beneath him that were hoping for a handout. She snapped her fingers again and said, "Thuuuur-maaan."

He produced the wanted poster. Johnny held it up for Coleman and Endi. The two nodded their heads and said, "Yep, that's your boy."

Jergins felt a few drops of liquid squirt out her anus. Her first homicidal maniac! She puckered her sphincter so hard nothing more would evacuate from there for three days (She finally had to drink some aloe and senna steeped in seawater to get blown out). She felt a drop of sweat run from her neck all the way down her back then trickle between her butt cheeks. It was getting pretty wet under the panty hose.

Jergins said, "You boys wanna draw me a picture."

Johnny answered, "Like in a briefing?"

"Absolutely."

Johnny instantly disliked this woman. He hated mean officious cops, and this one had gender and race chips on both her shoulders as well. He said, "Up front, officer, I want you to know the CIA doesn't give a conch's shit whether this dick-head Mano lives or dies. His lawyers do, however. Apparently, he is known as The Kamea which stands for 'The Shark,' or the 'One and Only' in Hawaiian. He is serious hot shit in the boxing world, and a Hawaii favorite son. His lawyers and fans will storm the beaches if we don't do this right. All your government must do is apprehend him and we will extradite him in about ten seconds. This will be international… AND… will be all over the papers."

Coleman said, "Me personally, I just want him off my island. We don't have to prove he killed anybody to make that happen. Besides he may not be the killer. But if we get him off the island and the killing stops, well… there you go."

Jergins asked Johnny in her condescending tone, "Who the hell are these guys?" She pointed to Coleman and Endi.

Amanda said, "Coleman owns a place here, and Endi is his buddy. Both are retired cops."

Jergins said to herself *oh, that's just brilliant.*

Johnny went on briefing Officer Jergins, "Two murder scenes; the colonel was found dead in a shed (he left out the part that the shed was Coleman's). Slack was under water in a cistern under the colonel's house, which by the way had a variety of non-indigenous poisonous sea life in it. We did drain the cistern and killed the aquatic wildlife for you, but so far all we found, in the now empty cistern, was Dr. Slack.

We don't think he was drowned. But at least we have Jack Slack's body for you to process. The colonel's body is, or was, on a Disney cruise; no idea where he is now. Dr. Slack is at the ice cream parlor. We should probably take him out and let him start to thaw if you want to examine him."

Jergins said morosely, "I already heard about the Disney cruise."

Johnny continued, "The best evidence I have to offer you concerning the colonel's demise is what Coleman and Endi have collected at the scene. They processed the murder scene as best they could, using what little they had. That includes some latent prints and some secondary fingerprints in blood and blood splatter from a ball peen hammer with bloody prints all over it, lots of pictures of everything, and pictures of some suspicious tire treads in the jungle, presumably from tire-tread sandals, presumably worn by the perp or perps. We have the ball peen hammer in evidence. The fingerprints are in talcum powder and scotch tape, as there was no crime scene equipment available." Johnny looked at the two cops with Jergins. Neither appeared to be listening. They both were looking at the panhandling school of fish under the dock.

Jergins snapped her fingers and said sharply, "Either one of you mental deficients making notes?" She gave her two assistants the look. They both scrambled to get out pen and pad.

Johnny continued, "I hope these gentlemen you brought with you are forensics types. There are no witnesses of course to either murder. Nor is there even any circumstantial evidence. All we have is rule-outs as far as who couldn't have done it. I can list those, and why, when you want. We think Dr. Slack was killed at his office and disposed of in the colonel's cistern."

Johnny decided to muddle the whole mess up even more than it was already just for fun. "It's possible that there are two different perps operating for two entirely different reasons. There is even the possibility that Dr. Slack's murder was a crime of passion or jealousy. Or, of course drugs, as he was a known dealer of pot, and other recreational drugs as well as keeping narcotics for medical reasons. He wore a Tierra and nothing else to the wedding for instance. Very provocative. The wedding party left him here when they went back to Key West. He apparently was newly gay and could have inserted himself (so to speak) into an already consummated relationship with jealousy-driven-homicide as the result. Gay guys are such drama majors."

Jergins forlornly asked, "Wedding?"

Luna said, "Wedding, as in…gay wedding. That's our specialty. Almost every weekend. The colonel and I firmly believe in diversity. Well, the colonel did. I still do. Except for Haitians, of course."

Jergins muttered in her most tortured Jamaican-English that no one could understand, except probably Luna, "Yea, right you white-supremacist big-head bitch." Luna stared at Jergins and mouthed, "fuck you whore-spawn."

Endi tugged Coleman's sleeve and asked, "What the hell these people talking about?" Coleman irritably brushed Endi's hand away.

Johnny continued, "We really don't have a motive for why the colonel was killed or why he decided to go on a cruise after his death. We do know that he got out of the freezer during the wedding somehow, even thought he had been pronounced dead by the Conch Island coroner. The now deceased Dr. Slack made that official determination while he was alive. I actually observed a corpse lying on a beach, that fits his description, some distance south. The colonel, if in fact that was him, then spent a night on a beach. Apparently, with the tides, he kept going from there. I would be happy to take you to that particular beach. Or show you on a chart perhaps?" Neutral, helpful, smile. "By the way, I found a human femur in the cistern too."

Jergins' mouth hung partly open, hostile tongue pushing out a cheek, and shaking her head almost imperceptivity, glowering. "Walker, I'm about to arrest you for making me angry. Let your CIA jump through hoops for a week or two making your bail. You don't even have any ID."

Johnny flashed her his Portland Police Bureau detective lieutenant homicide unit badge again. Jergins said, "What? You pick that up at a gun show or something? What the hell am I supposed to think with you flashing me that badge. You assholes trying to make fun of me?"

Johnny said sourly, "You can call my boss if you want."

Endi said to Jergins, "As a cop, and having been in your shoes more times than I'd like to remember, I suggest you summarily execute Mano as soon as you spot him. You'll be a hero and save two countries' taxpayers a lot of money."

Amanda said, "Or The Elders can do the Blue Hole thing."

Luna inserted herself in between Johnny and Jergens, pointing a finger from each hand inches from their faces, her face looking from one to the other like watching a tennis match, said, "You people are a bunch of idiots. You want me to get rid of the Hawaiian, I can. I say we smoke him out. Throw a bunch of burning, smoldering, dried palm branches over the compound wall. Maybe a little diesel. Maybe a flash-bang if the Miss Jergins can come up with one or two." She wagged the finger in Jergins' face. "It goes like this; we have the place surrounded. All you guys with weapons are at strategic spots. The rest of us are armed with shovels, picks, machetes, axes, whatever. The dick doesn't stand a chance. He comes out holding his nose and rubbing his eyes, we all testify that he was brandishing a weapon. Shots are fired. We beat him to death, or you guys (she pointed at Jergins) shoot the dildo. Do you even have guns? We plant a throwaway gun on him. End of story. All you cops leave my island, and I go back to my weddings."

Amazingly, that is exactly what they did. (They had to translate the "Luna Plan" for Endi.)

But Mano wasn't home. He was on a cruise.

Corporal Uriah Albright fell into Mano's pool because he couldn't see due to the smoke. He couldn't swim and made quite a fuss. Thurman jumped in to help. Thurman used the CSI toolbox sitting on the side of the pool as a hand hold and it went under water again, this time sinking. He left it there. Jergins was on the other side of the house and didn't see a thing.

There was no per-diem budgeted for spending the night on the island, (not to mention there was no hotel) so they went home on the afternoon ferry. They got halfway back and Jergins asked Thurman where the toolbox was. Her tooth was throbbing mercilessly.

Jergins Albright derisively said to Endi, Coleman, and Johnny, before she got on the ferry, "I know about the silver, and it belongs to the government of the Bahamas. I'm gonna send the coroner for Jack Slack's body. I'm sending a Navy gun boat to secure the island, with marines. No one leaves the island. As soon as I get cell phone reception on the way back, kaka is going to hit your fan. Expect air support. We will find this Mano dickwad if we have to burn the island down."

Luna said to the gang, waving at the departing ferry, "Don't worry about the gunboat thing, boys and girls. The last time they sent a gunboat here it ran aground, blocked our harbor for three weeks, and they had to wait for a king-tide before the garbage barge could pull it loose. Besides, I don't think they even have it anymore."

Johnny decided it was time to bail. He left the next morning, Friday, with the tide around 5:00 a.m. There was soft orange light to the east heralding the sun rising dutifully again for another day of energizing probably the silliest island on the most ludicrous planet in the most ridiculous solar system, the laughingstock of the galaxy.

CHAPTER 40

Thursday.

Mano was feeling a little nauseated. He was in the engine room of the yacht where he had hidden the silver. He wanted to look at it again, hold it, and give it some love. But the fumes turned on a sea-sick switch and he bolted for fresh air leaving the door to the engine room open.

Mano was steering while standing, his rump resting on the captain's chair. He had programmed the GPS and was just about to punch the *go-to* button.

Something grabbed the hamstring of his leg viciously at his ankle. He screamed and tried to shake whatever it was off. It was white and had long hair. That's all he could see in the blur of activity. He thought *rat*.

Hamstring firmly in mouth, teeth locked on, puncturing the skin, and growling ferociously, the white hairy thing was trying to shake Mano's foot like breaking the neck of prey. The foot wasn't moving much so the biter was doing most of the shaking. Its ten-pound body was in midair as Mano tried to shake it off, hopping about on one leg, and screaming.

Mano realized he was being attacked by a dog. A damn small one at that. It was so small it was hard to take it seriously, and yet this hurt like hell. He was afraid to grab it to pull it off because he figured it would grab his hand as soon as it let go of his ankle. (Instinctively he always saved his hands.) Then go for his throat if he had it in his hands. It was a Mexican Stand-off. Lot of growling and cursing, but so far, the only one hurting was Mano.

The little white poodle with apricot-colored ears finally let go and raced off the bridge and launched itself into space over the ladder-like stairs and disappeared. Mano was gushing blood from deep teeth punctures. He pulled the throttles back to idle.

"Jesus, now I'm gonna get rabies," he screamed as he leapt around on one leg, holding his knee up afraid to touch his throbbing ankle. He sat down and took inventory. "How long do I have to live?" he lamented, almost crying from the pain. He could take punches all day long, but he wasn't in condition for a dog fight. He heard growling below decks.

Holding a five battery Mag-Lite in one hand as a weapon, he tried to negotiate the stairs, but fell the last few steps and did a face plant on a thick woven wicker rug that ran down the center of the stateroom area. The flashlight spun on the rug. The dog came out of nowhere and attacked the flashlight, giving it a ferocious shake then came for Mano's face still planted on the floor.

Mano put his hands in front of his face just as the poodle launched from five feet away. Sharkey's vision of himself was a pit bull, hanging effortlessly onto a rope with locked jaws. He clamped onto Mano's little finger. The skin started to tear as Mano shook his hand with the dog holding on. Mano was up hopping and cursing again. He was afraid to grab the dog with his other hand. He didn't know how to get the damn thing off him. He was backing up, his panicky mind telling his body to flee. He ran into the stairs and fell on his rump in the sitting position. The growling dog let go and bit him on the nose. It took a little chunk off, and Sharkey raced down the hall and disappeared.

Mano searched the boat, leaving a trail of blood. (More blood dear reader—how many now?) He didn't know whether to hold his shredded little finger or his profusely bleeding nose. He limped, blood still dripping from his ankle. He grabbed the flashlight and vowed to beat the damn thing to a pulp.

Sharkey swallowed the tip of Mano's nose.

Sharkey had been locked in the engine room where he had hidden when Mano boarded. When Mano left the engine room open, Sharkey catapulted into action. For the first time in his short life (he was only two years old) he was being allowed to achieve his full potential. He was at the prime of his life. All that working out as a puppy on socks, and toys, and plastic, and dining room table legs, and oriental carpets, was finally paying off. As he had grown into an adult all his extensive training and conditioning had been leading to this moment in the ring. He could walk on his back legs, front legs, climb a ladder, and any toy his mistress gave him he could destroy as fast as he wanted to. He could get the thing that squeaked in the toy out in less than sixty seconds. No one could wear him out throwing a ball. There was no rawhide or rubber tough enough. He was Olympic quality material for hide-and-seek events. No one could find him on the huge boat if he didn't want to be found. His first order of business upon coming aboard was exploration, familiarization, and territory marking. He knew the boat better than the owner.

His ancient predator brain deep inside his skull relished the human nose tip he had swallowed, and he planned to vomit it back up when things calmed down so he could eat it again.

Mano slammed open the pocket door to the room he had his hostages in, raging and yelling at the two still bound people. "Call your fucking dog off!" All he heard was muffled shouting beneath the duct tape gags. The dog ran in the room and did a drive by; Sharkey bit Mano in the other hamstring tearing flesh in a split second and disappeared under the bed.

Mano growled and hit both the terrified screaming people on their kneecaps with the flashlight and was about to hit them in the head. The fierce growling under the bed in response to the woman's muffled scream, made Mano conclude that he best leave and lock them all in together. Sharkey nailed him again on an ankle. Mano fled, slamming home the sliding door and corralling the monster in the room with the hostages. Mano slid down the hall wall by his back abruptly sitting on the floor, and then rocked over on his side into the fetal position. And of course, he sharted again. He was too out of breath to curse.

Sharkey allowed himself to pant for a while. He gagged once or twice, then decided now was not the time for the piece of human nose to reappear. He eased out from under the bed, head on a swivel, ready to attack anything in his way. After clearing the room, he jumped up on the bed. He urinated on the man. Then he began to chew his mistress's hands free, after licking her eyes and ears and the duct tape covering her mouth. He decided the hands were the most important. She was making all kinds of noises like she and the man did when they rolled around panting and moaning in bed and he was banished from the bedroom.

Sharkey did not like this man, because this man was currently humping his mistress and excluding him from the festivities. Sharkey was good at timing a nip just as the man's verbalizations really got going. That was why he was so good at hiding because the man didn't like him either. As he tore at the duct tape around his mistress's wrists rage was boiling up again. He quit working on the woman long enough to take a quick bite at the man's ankles. The man kicked but Sharkey was too fast for him.

He got her loose. She ripped the duct tape from her ankles and mouth. Then she tore at the bindings that held her to the man. She was cursing the man like he'd shit in bed. Sharkey knew what that tone of voice was like. She left the man tied up.

Sharkey was a hero. The woman stood up holding Sharkey tightly in her arms. He was French kissing her. She held him and squeezed him and kissed him and called him Sharkey the Wonder Dog, and her mighty Parisian Pit bull, and her killer French Fighting Dog, and told him over and over he was the greatest and that she loved him more than anything. Sharkey loved lovefests with his mistress. She went to the head. Sharkey thought she would never stop pissing. Inspired, he pissed on the man again and on all four corners of the room. He reported back to duty after the quick patrol. He was ready to go after that man again.

He threw up the tip of Mano's nose at his mistress's feet as a token of his love and devotion. She was not impressed, so he ate it again.

CHAPTER 41

Still Thursday.

Mano looked at his face in the mirror of the bathroom. His worst fight, he never looked this bad. "The dog BIT the tip of my nose OFF!" He was looking for salve and antibiotics and bandages. He couldn't find a thing. He assumed correctly that all the first aid supplies were in the bathroom in the room with the damn dog.

Blood was all over his face, his hands, and his feet. It was matting in his chest hairs, having run from his severed nose down his mouth, chin, and neck and onto his chest. He was still bleeding from all the other Sharkey-bites too. He cleaned his face in cold water and put a Kotex over his nose and wrapped duct tape around his head to keep it in place. He put both feet in the sink and washed his torn-up ankles. He put female napkins on them too, also secured with duct tape. He wondered how long before the rabies sets in.

He wrapped his finger with toilet paper and duct tape. Then he found a tube of Neosporin. He used it all anointing his crotch which was still burning from his night in the cistern, and the nettles.

He took a half dozen ibuprofen downing them with a half a glass of scotch.

He banged on the door where his hostages were and Sharkey answered with a horrendous tirade at the top of his lungs that would translate, "I hate you bad man; I'm not scared of you; I am coming for your ass," over and over for ten minutes.

Mano hobbled up the stairs and sat heavily in the captain's chair trying to figure out what to do next. He engaged the transmissions, gave a little throttle, and the big vessel began moving south again.

In ten minutes, he was on the floor unconscious due to baseball bat. Sharkey got in a couple more bites before Mano was thrown overboard.

Three minutes after that the vessel ran aground.

Mano had been thrown overboard in four feet of water. The dunking restored his consciousness instantaneously. The nose maxi-pad slipped over his eyes though and he wailed in terror thinking he was blind. The salt water agonizingly stung every puncture, pustule, and thistle wound on his body. Especially between his legs.

He finally got the water-soaked Maxi pad off his eyes and back on his nose. It was bleeding again. He thought *blood; SHARKS!* He crawled about thirty yards onto shore and sat with his back to a dead pine tree. He watched the dog and woman get off the back of the cruiser and head to shore too, fifty yards away. The man was behind her moving much slower.

She had what looked like a bright orange handgun in her hand. She was heading his way. The dog was out pacing her probably doing twenty-five miles per hour. He climbed the dead pine tree just in time to escape Sharkey's mouth again.

Treed like a raccoon by a pack of hounds, Mano froze. The little oriental woman took her time getting to him. She was laughing hysterically. He recognized the flare gun just as the muzzle flashed and a flare hit him squarely in the chest knocking him out of the tree. He fell ten feet onto the sand and stood up shaking one leg with Sharkey on it again. Just then the flare that had ricocheted off his chest went off causing the dead pine tree above him to explode into flames. Suddenly there was a thirty-foot column of fire. The flare after starting the fire fell on Mano. Bathing suit on fire, dog on one leg, and maxi-pad over one eye, Mano raced back into the ocean but not before taking another flare to the back between his shoulder blades. As he went down the flare ignited and followed him to the bottom. Sharkey let go, bobbed to the surface and dog paddled at a comfortable pace back to the beach where his mistress was laughing so hard, she was writhing around in the sand. Sharkey writhed with her.

Mano started wading and swimming as the woman shot another flare at him; it went off harmlessly in the ocean twenty feet from him. The woman started trying to put the burning tree out with sand. The fire was spreading with the wind to other trees.

Mano howled as he stepped on a sea urchin.

She didn't realize what Mano was doing until it was too late. He beat her back to the beached and listing cruiser, and had the dinghy launched and motor running before she and Sharkey made it back. She jumped up and down and cursed a lot; Sharkey barked hysterically.

Boyfriend was sitting in the sand with a silly grin shaking his head.

Mano headed south the way the direction the cruiser had been going. The engine wasn't running all that smooth.

He'd putted along for about fifteen minutes when the engine died. The wind was from the north and pushed him south. He saw no land in any direction.

He figured this was it. Another poor soul lost in the mysterious Bermuda Triangle. Of course, he wasn't romanticizing the adventure at all. He was in fluent nonstop blasphemy mode cursing every god he could think of in between howls of agony from the sea urchin stings. His foot had purple holes all over. He plucked the stingers out mindlessly.

"If I had a gun."

CHAPTER 42

Friday morning.

Jergins Albright was standing face to face with her chief the next morning at ten. He had ignored her calls on her way back from Conch Key the day before. By the time she got back it was past four, quite past his quitting time. He was already half drunk and had no intention of dealing with Conch Kay, or this uppity officer, Ms-Diversity-Jergins. His day was ten to four; no weekends, unless for his real job of course, which was collecting bribes. He was so busy with the bribe business that he had no real time for police work, or the stomach for it anymore. Early on he'd discovered and followed, a time-honored universal truth found in all Bahamian bureaucracies: honor those that bribe you and they will do the police work for you. Add that to his general disdain for the Albrights (they didn't do bribes) and he was bound and determined to make this whole thing a "non-event."

That is until Jergins informed him of the black-market silver trade on Conch Kay.

They were on a Bahamas Coast Guard gunboat in thirty minutes, passing the Albright ferry by double their speed. Jergins lost her hat. But at least she wasn't sweating.

Jergins briefed the chief as they made the half hour trip. She told him everything she knew. The last time anyone from the government had tried to do something with the Albrights, and their attempted revolution, the coast guard boat (this one in fact) carrying the officials had run aground, they had to abandon ship, and by then, the so-called revolution was over, and they had to beg a ride on the Albright Ferry to get back home.

They practically swamped a thirty-three-foot sailboat named the *Drama Queen* as the as they cut across her bow. It was headed away from Conch Kay. Jergins recognized Johnny Walker. She had a mixed bag of thoughts: It's that raggedy-assed cop from Oregon, wherever the hell that is. I told everyone that no one could leave the island. Too bad we didn't swamp him. There goes a possible murderer. That badge—you gotta be kidding me. He's probably taking silver.

The raggedly looking guy sailing the *Drama Queen* jumped up and down and gave multiple universal one-fingered salutes after the gunboat had almost swamped him. Two sailors flipped him off laughing.

It was after five later in the afternoon when an island came into view. Johnny saw smoke. A small forest fire was in the process of dying as the wind was coming from inland and pushing the fire into the sea. He ignored it. He kept sailing.

He was thinking about anchoring in a protected cove and pouring himself a nice rum cocktail. He'd been trolling and had a fresh yellow-tail already fileted and ready for cooking. Rather than wait for anchoring, he popped a beer and downed it in about a minute. That's when he saw the dinghy.

Mano was drifting. Mano had no idea where he was, had no water, no signaling device. No compass. No food. No oars. No drugs, no booze, no hat, no sunglasses, and no clothes. He was frying in the sun, the dried salt eating at his various wounds, and now a sunburn.

The flare had burned the back of his pants off but not before it singed his ass. He had a huge purple and black bruise the size of a dinner plate on his chest where the first flare had hit him. He'd lost his flip-flops during the poodle wars. He had a goose egg the size of a papaya on the back of the head from the crazy oriental lady and the baseball bat. Add all the dog bites, infected sores, thistle wounds, the sea urchin—it all added up to pretty much the worst moment in the history of Mano the Magnificent. He figured it couldn't get any worse.

About that time, he saw the sailboat. He had just enough energy to jump up and down and scream for help. He was ecstatic until the man sailing the boat fired a shot over his head and announced over a bull horn for him to lie face down in the dingy or get summarily executed. Another shot went over his head and Mano planted his face on the bottom of the boat.

Johnny dropped his sails and turned on the sailboat's small engine. He maneuvered closer. He had identified Mano with binoculars from fifty yards, even with the maxi-pad/duct tape face mask. Mano had no idea who Johnny was yet.

Mano would have crapped his pants, if he had any crap left (or pants), when the first bullet went over his head. He had been desperately praying to all the saints he could think of to be rescued. *Why is the fucker shooting at me?* He lay there curled up like a baby, in the bottom of the dinghy, when a pair of handcuffs hit him on top of the head. Whoever it was, told him to put them on with his hands in front and to be ready to catch a rope; he was going to be towed. The voice also said keep down or get shot.

Mano snapped the cuffs on and yelled, "Do me the favor."

As he tied the dinghy to the twenty-foot rope he recognized Johnny Walker.

Johnny said, "The last place I want to see again is going to be the next place I see dammit. We're going back to Conch Island. I suggest not falling overboard as these waters are heavily infested with sea snakes and sharks, not to mention lionfish. I'd rather shoot you and probably should. But first tell me how you got in a dinghy in the middle of the Bermuda Triangle. I'll start shooting holes in your boat if I don't like your story."

Mano said, "Got any water or beer?"

Johnny threw him a Kalik Extra Strength. He figured getting the boxer drunk and passed out would be better than any other restraint method he could think of. He threw over an umbrella too. Mano opened it and for the first time that day was in the shade. He drank the Kalik and Johnny threw him another. The two started the six-hour journey back to the island of the big heads; the little diesel making about four knots. Neither one had their hearts in it.

Johnny finally threw him a bottle of rum. He decided this was the best prisoner transfer he had ever performed. The prisoner was as docile as a lamb. He cooked his yellow tail and threw some of that to Mano too. He threw him some bottled water and Solarcaine with aloe and bandages. Mano bitched a lot about his wounds. Johnny thought for a boxer he sure was a pussy.

Every third beer Johnny had a cold Starbucks Mocha Frappuccino for the caffeine to keep him awake.

They made it to Conch Kay Marina around midnight. He'd left at first light that morning for Florida. He saw the Bahamas Coast Guard fifty-footer aground in front of Don't Island. (Don't Island was only visible at low tide as it was under water during high tide.) It was listing badly. A pump was running and bailing water. It was the same one that had almost swamped the *Drama Queen* that morning. Johnny said to himself, "Man, they really must have been moving to get that boat that high on the beach."

Johnny said to the comatose unhearing snoring Mano, "Looks like everybody is getting back what they threw out there. What comes around, goes around."

Johnny used a second pair of handcuffs to cuff Mano to an oar lock of the dinghy. With a flashlight between his teeth, he was awed by the amount of damage there was to Mano's body.

He threw a blanket over him and said, "We'll inventory your injuries in the morning asshole. We'll start with your nose." Johnny cross tied the little seven-foot boat in the middle of a slip so Mano would have just that much more trouble escaping.

Johnny pushed the choke button in on the dinghy's little outboard motor. That had been the only problem with the motor. It started on the first pull. Mano slept through that. But he woke up suddenly when he heard a dog bark—PTSD.

Johnny turned on the generator and air-conditioning on in the sailboat and went below. He was soon asleep surrounded by cold dry air, the white noise hum of the AC and the generator, with enough ibuprofen in his system to dull most aches and pain.

CHAPTER 43

Friday. Late morning.

"Sharkey save our life you fat dicky-head." The little oriental girlfriend was responding to her sugar-daddy's suggestion that they kill the dog with the baseball bat or a golf club. The tide had lifted the cruiser and they had made it back to Conch Kay figuring they would go back to where they had come from that morning to meet their friends and get their cook and steward and to report the piracy to the authorities. The cruiser had made it back way before Johnny and Mano.

First, they found that there were no authorities. Second, when the authorities did arrive their Coast Guard boat ran aground. (They were pleased at the quick response, but a little puzzled as to how the Coast Guard found out about the piracy so fast.) An inflatable boat with an outboard brought a load of police from the grounded patrol boat, which they met and helped off their boat. The girlfriend introduced herself and the sugar-daddy as the victims of the piracy attempt and asked if they would like to come aboard their vessel and examine the baseball bat, duct tape, dust for fingerprints—all that.

Jergins just walked by saying nothing. She hadn't understood a word the little oriental had said.

"You fat-panty-hose-freaky-yellow-Velcro-haired-big-head-bitch-blackie no care about our piracy!" didn't faze Jergins. Jergins said, "Officer Urine, cuff her." The chief agreed, and seconded the motion. As far as he was concerned, throw the whole island in jail, cuffed, wrists and ankles. Chain them all up to each other and to the biggest banyan tree they had on the island.

The hand cuffs unleashed cursing non-stop in some far-east language which was unintelligible to the whole group, so her tirade didn't really bother anyone, other than it was squeaky and shrieky. They told her to sit down and shut up. She followed them instead down the Queens Highway. Finally, she got locked in a room in Coleman's house where she eventually ran out of steam.

The sugar-daddy had eased back to his boat without saying a word. He undid the lines, fired the twins up, backed out of the slip, and motored to sea, never looking back. He still had all his money, credit cards, and all that. All he was missing was the dinghy that Mano was hand-cuffed to, his oriental sugar-baby, and her dog. He'd go dingy and pussy shopping in a week or so. He realized he had been over his head with the crazy female he had just jettisoned. He headed for the liquor store island. He was hoping for a titty-bar where he could do some shopping. No more Orientals he vowed. Or redheads of course. Or any one named Tiffany.

Sharkey came out of hiding. His mistress was gone. Didn't know where. Didn't care. No problem. He knew he was cute. He knew tricks. He had been passed around a lot when he was little. He'd always landed on his feet.

Johnny woke up with the sun the next morning. A poodle was licking his face. The Coast Guard ship was anchored outside the harbor; they had gotten it off the sandbar with the incoming tide. He looked in the dinghy. Mano was gone.

He gave the poodle some leftover yellow tail and some water. He looked at the dog's rabies tag on a rhinestone pink collar. Engraved on the back of the tag was "Sharkey." Sharkey jumped off the sailboat, sniffed around, pissed and dumped, then hopped back on the boat. He knew how important a first impression was.

Johnny was impressed. The little dog got in his lap and put its head on Johnny's knee, let out a big sigh, and promptly went to sleep. Johnny went back to sleep too. There was a certain somnolent effect caused by a dog or cat sleeping in your lap. He thought about Ruggles his cat in Portland.

An hour later Coleman and Endi woke him up.

"You been gone less than a day and you have a poodle. It smells like dead fish and seaweed. Needs a bath. Both of you do," Endi said. Sharkey hopped onto Coleman's lap. Sharkey was working the crowd. He licked Coleman's face and did the chin on the knee routine with him too.

The three, including the poodle, enjoyed some Mt. Gay rum and orange juice for breakfast.

Coleman said, "I like this dog." He stroked the small head. Sharkey was fifty percent thinking he had it made. He liked these guys. The oriental bitch was just finishing school for his real gig—being a cop's dog. As soon as he had smelled the oil, metal, and gunpowder on the men he had decided this was *it!*

Johnny told them Mano was missing, but that he now had a nice new dinghy. (The one Mano had been chained in). And he had booze for seventy-two hours as long as it was just the three of them. With the two women…maybe forty-eight. No cocktail-gap problem. "I'd say let's mount up and cruise out of here. Now. Dog and all."

Endi said, "They haven't found the silver in the colonel's cistern that we cinder blocked up. Amanda is teaching school, and just quietly slipped herself off the police radar. May is still asleep in Coleman's snore box. The cops are running around talking to stonewalling Albrights and getting nothing. They told us we were to stay on the island as we were people of interest. Wonder where the hell Mano got away to and how?"

Coleman said, "Jack Slack is headed for a night or two in a real morgue. At least he'll be able to stretch out. The Elders sent Andy up there to Disney Land Island for the colonel. Word from Amanda is that Andy is to drop what's left of the colonel in the Blue Hole on his way back."

Johnny said, "Mano will show up. He always does, apparently."

CHAPTER 44

Friday. Early morning. 2 a.m.

Mano woke up with a start. He was still drunk. He was lying on the bottom of the dinghy. He saw two thumbs on one hand. He thought he was hallucinating. The hand was hacksawing the oarlock. He passed it off as just another footnote in the worst day of his life. He closed his eyes assuming it was a nightmare, poor lighting, or he was seeing double, and passed out again.

When he woke again, he was loose from the boat. The hacksaw wouldn't cut through the hardened stainless steel of the handcuffs, but it did cut through the dinghy's oarlock. Albright Albright was barefoot. In the well-lit marina Mano swore the man he was following had two feet that didn't match, or maybe they did match, and that was the problem. And six fingers on one hand. But it was the pink bra loincloth that took shook him. Too much for my brain he thought as he limped sunburned, barefoot, and naked behind the man that didn't talk. There wasn't a part of him that didn't hurt.

They stopped by Amanda's cottage; a sandwich and peas and rice were in a covered dish on a windowsill. (She often left food out for Albright Albright.) The two ate and drank from the same bottle of water without saying a word. Finished, Mano followed pith-helmet and bra up the Queen's Highway, his hands in front of him still handcuffed.

Albright Albright stopped at a house with clothes drying on the line. He picked out a Mumu for himself and a large T-shirt for Mano. He went into the shed next to the clothesline and came out with a roll of duct tape. He wrapped Mano's feet with duct tape. They resumed their trek until they came to a hole in a sea-grape hedge, where Albright Albright disappeared, and Mano followed. He cut a hole in the front of the T-shirt for Mano's hand-cuffed hands.

Mano and Albright Albright stole an even bigger cruiser the next day. Albright Albright had been on every permanently moored boat in the harbor many times. He happily showed Mano around the boat. A fifty-nine-foot Grand Banks. Keys in it. Doors open for ventilation. Owners in Boston. No live-aboard crew.

Mano calculated that it had a two-thousand-mile range. The diesel tanks were topped off. Albright Albright gave Mano the silver bar he was wearing around his neck, and the others he had gotten in Coleman's cistern, much to Mano's delight. Albright Albright also had twenty-two thousand and change in multiple currencies stashed in fourteen places on the island that he had purloined over the years.

The cruiser had a fully stocked bar and a full pantry. Both refrigerator/freezers were full. There were fifteen cases of wine and twenty cases of beer. And a stocked bar. There was a large first aid cabinet with cortisone ointments, sunburn cream, aloe ointments, etc. Mano slathered himself with everything. The fresh water had been topped off with 1400 gallons. It had a fifteen-foot dinghy on its roof with a crane and winch. He found a lady's colorful tie-died Mumu that fit. He cut a hole for his handcuffed hands that also ventilated his still screaming crotch.

As Mano and Albright Albright cruised out of Conch Island for the last time, the satellite phone rang at the compound. Mano's lawyer left a message. "Got the murder charge dropped completely. Incompetent police work and circumstantial evidence. They didn't have the guts to prosecute you on what they had. I had a little talk with the judge. You're missing fifty K, but the bribe helped. Hawaii rejoices and can't wait to take its favorite son back to her bosom again, you perverted little prick. Call me… dick-breath."

EPILOG

Mano sold the giant yacht and bought a bar and grill, with an eight-room hotel, he renamed the *Wet Spot,* on a beach in Antigua. He doubled the prices, doubled the salaries, matched retirement contributions, and provided the hooker's medical and dental. He also paid his employees for daily tanning time. (*You Can't Go Home Until You Have a Tan like a Stripper!*) Every employee learned the hula and wear grass skirts and is topless if female, or just skimpy tiger patterned loin cloths if male. One happy family. Better than Hooters.

Every Monday (normally "dead-business-night") Mano has a sold-out Hawaiian Luau on the beach with a bon fire, drums, torches, dancers, Kalua Pig, Huli Huli Chicken, Laulau, and fruity rum drinks served in souvenir hurricane glasses personalized with tiny umbrellas with the drinker's name on it. (Mano learned "presentation" early on in the boxing business.)

The chain between Mano's handcuffs had been split by Albright Albright at a hardware store, but Mano still had to wear the cuffs for months. He eventually acquired a key but likes to wear them as bracelets whenever behind the bar or schmoozing customers—a conversation starter. (Individual single real cuffs, with a key, and a piece of chain dangling, sell well in the gift shop.)

Albright Albright had multiple plastique surgeries in Costa Rica. He walks better which is ironic because he rarely walks anymore. He gained a hundred pounds by eating regularly and not moving (like Jabba the Hut in Star Wars). He wears bikini tops instead of bras, as a jock strap, under his Mumu. He doesn't roam the island stealing anymore because women throw their tops at him on stage. His lush hairy head, unibrow, and foot long braided (with bows) beard sets off his round ever smiling (Albright-perfect teeth) mouth from which comes a beautiful soft high soprano voice. With his extra fingers he plays the ukulele epically. The little bar is packed when he performs. The gift shop can't keep his embroidered Mumu nightgowns in stock with *WET SPOT* over the butt, and picture of a pair of handcuffs on the front, one around each boob, with the chain broken.

Jergins and the chief of police gave up looking for Mano, and ordered the case closed. They assumed Mano went back to Hawaii since he had been acquitted. They never investigated the other two deaths. Colonel Albright was considered just missing as there was no dead body (thanks again Blue Hole). The other death was just a felon German dentist (Nazi)—and nobody cares about a dead dentist.

Jergins put in for a transfer to another island which was endorsed instantly by the chief. Officer Thurman replaced her as detective and aided the chief in the bribe business, taking a load of work off his boss. Crime does pay.

The small oriental concubine was released and pretty much instantly found another fat rich American with a yacht. She trained another Parisian Pit Bull—a white poodle with apricot ears.

Johnny Walker, and his new dog Sharkey, sailed to Fort Lauderdale with the sailboat's three-thousand-pound ballast replaced with the first load of the colonel's silver. He changed her name to *Rum With A View*. He leaves the sailboat in Florida and vacations there regularly, getting away from rainy cold Oregon where he is still a cop. He figured he might as well stay in police work because police work will find him wherever he goes anyway, even though he was now rich.

He periodically takes "ballast" to Bimini, where it finds its way to France, where it turns into Euros, which finds its way into an account in Grand Cayman. He keeps *Rum With A View* docked in front of his second home, a condo in Fort Lauderdale.

Amanda gave Coleman that blow job. Coleman: "She has a tongue that could split wood!. Suck the chrome off a ball hitch!" She gave up teaching children and teaches Spanish dance in Palm Beach. She owns three Kentucky Fried Chicken franchises. She has gained weight and looks like an Albright.

Andy Albright bought the condo in Palm Beach next to Amanda's. He founded the Non-Indigenous Species Eradication (NICE) foundation (501-3C) and spends most of his time killing lionfish by organizing scuba spearfishing tournaments all over South Florida. He still hopes that some sea snakes survived electrocution so he would have a new cause. Lionfish are getting a little ho-hum.

Endi bought the place Mano was holed up in through a blind trust in Delaware from the Albright estate. Endi and May became international experts and consultants for bra-fitting and design and have published their third book on the subject. Their underwater photo artwork project died a natural death as May sort of let herself go. Endi doesn't complain. He just throws a boob over each shoulder and soldiers on.

Coleman and Endi are in partnership with The Elders for processing options for the rest of the big black rocks. The Elders wisely don't want to flood the island with wealth as all they worked hard for for the last several hundred years would be destroyed. Instead, they are negotiating buying a neighbor island whose population could be used as breeding stock to get some hybrid-vigor back into the Albright gene pool.

The whore, in partnership with the doctor, sued Mano's estate (Mano was presumed dead at sea) for permanent work-related jaw injuries that prevented her from practicing her trade. Mano never showed up for depositions or court concerning the jaw injury lawsuit, so a summary judgment was handed out. Mano's lawyer, always one to stand by his moral and fiduciary duty to the Mano estate, fought the jaw lawsuit long and hard (one million of fiduciary duty), but in the end endorsed a check from the estate (managed by the trust department of a small bank he founded on Maui) for one million to the wronged lady, and her attending doctor. (The jaw problem, fortunately for the lady, resolved itself during the drawn-out lawsuit.)

The sugar-daddy of Sharkey's oriental owner found Mano's stash of silver in the engine room of the first boat Mano stole. He replaced the dinghy and used the rest to pay back taxes. (So, after all these years, the silver was finally used for taxes. Talk about irony.)

Sadly, shortly after that, the sugar-daddy had a stroke during a three way in Freeport with Jamaican twins. He didn't make it. The twins left fast after seeing what they had done. They took his wallet of course. His ex-wife took the boat, and, with her twenty-five-year-old, bi-sexual bathtub toy (boy-toy) discovered Conch Key and bought a house there. But the heat and threat of hurricanes cause her to spend less and less time on the island.

And so, some things never change: Death and taxes. Tax evasion. Smuggling. Piracy. Corrupt police. And of course, prostitution. And everything belongs to the banks in the end.

A never-ending story.

The island to this day never has allowed a liquor store. There are always three or four golf carts parked in front of the Albright Grocery. The ladies at the Sail Shop sew canvas bags in the open air shop every day but Sunday. The Albright Boat Yard always has something out of the water refinishing the bottom. Flowers bloom, coconuts fall, Albrights sit in waist deep water during the hot days of summer, ex-pats stay away because of the heat, but send money, music stars discover it, then forget it.

Every day the sun rises on the bay side and sets on the ocean side. Church bells ring on Sunday morning. The Big Heads breed and take their Valium.

The occasional tropical storm tries unsuccessfully to pull the roof off an Albright built house, but only succeeds in pushing it down harder, so it takes its business to another island to try its luck there.

And every couple of years National Geographic attempts to discover the bottom of the Blue Hole…but never finds it.

THE END

I appreciate you reading my book!
Can you leave a comment and a star rating
on Amazon?

Sign up on my website to see my other books:
www.jarviswrites.page.
(We promise not to abuse your time and
will only notify you once or twice a month.)

Fiction books by the author:
Dirty Money

Non-fiction books by the author:
Feeding Your Dog and Cat, The Truth!
Prayer Lite

Join my launch team and get my books for free before
they are published!